The Seasons Of Giving

A Second Time Around Love Story

Minna Marsh

8/17/2010

To a tall man with soft blue eyes that I met at a computer show, I will always love you.

Book design by Nadine Frush, Photography by Computer Studios, Inc.

Most Spark books are available at special quantity discounts for bulk purchase for sales promotions, premiums, fund-raising and educational needs. Special books or book excerpts also can be created to fit specific needs. For details contact Spark Publishing at nadine@sparkvisuals.com. Web site:www.sparkvisuals.com

Chapter 1

"Mommy, can I have the bedroom at the end? Please", begged Gabrielle from the second floor. "I go get my babies and put them here."

My little munchkin has been playing musical bedrooms, changing her mind every few minutes as to which room she wanted. No sense in worrying about getting her to nap. She has been in heaven with this house, our first house, with a real front and back yard. Adding to the wonder, there was a genuine staircase and fireplace. She's been running from one room to another laughing, opening and closing new closets and doors, turning on and off lights.

"Okay, pumpkin. I'll help you move the boxes and your furniture. But first, Mommy has to find a special box," I replied. *Mommy is going to find some wine, indulge in a glass or two, and regroup*. I was surrounded by a city of unopened boxes. *Remember, Vivi. This doesn't all have to happen today. Just go look for the wine, a glass, and a bottle opener.*

All these damn boxes. I thought that I had gotten rid of most of our junk at our garage sale. I saved all of Gabrielle's stuff; furniture, books, clothes, toys and the battered dolls so she wouldn't have a hard time adjusting to our new life. But where did all this other stuff come from? It was baggage from my California past that I couldn't part with. *Tell the truth, Vivi. Some of these objects are old friends*.

Where did the movers hide the emergency box that holds the wine? Try the kitchen. Gingerly navigating through the box maze, I made my way to the large old-fashion and inefficient kitchen. An ancient refrigerator stood at one end of the room and the monster range way down at the other end.

Wine box, where are you? Aha, there it is. I thought I packed some plastic cups on the side and a bottle opener. *Got it*. Now, I carefully walked back to the cardboard living room to contemplate my recent set of actions that led me to this house.

The living room was white-bleak. There was not a stick of furniture and the cleaning crew had turned it into a spotless stage for our cardboard boxes. We were starting afresh.

Newly purchased house, no furniture, only it was the same old town that I ran away from fifteen years ago and vowed that I would never return. However it was safe and far away from my California past.

I uncorked the wine and poured it into the plastic cup. *Good choice, Vivi. Bordeaux.* Well, I was off to a fine start. At least I found an excellent wine and my daughter seemed happy here. This move was the best action I could have made under the current situation. It was not like facing a great unknown. I've loved this house and its property ever since I was a little girl. I've loved growing up in this old university town and Gabrielle would be happy here. She was near her grandparents and it was a safe town for her. Princeton was a town where she could be free to explore the sounds of the frogs on hot summer nights and the old Quaker cemetery where her ancestors rested. She could stage the Revolutionary War under the Mercer Tree. It would be a great place for her, just as it was when I was a child. Now for me, who knows, I just might have signed my death warrant.

I always liked Princeton in January. It was cold and bleak, and looked like a black and white photograph with its white clapboard houses with dark green shutters surrounded by snow. It was so quiet here. No sounds of highways or freeways, just the occasional brave car slowly edging its way down the icy roads.

Fire, I needed to start a fire in the fireplace. That would warm things up. *Okay, Vivi, think. Where did you put the fireplace stuff? We don't want to open up all these damn boxes tonight, do we?* I saw it, box number 156 in the corner. I tore off the packing tape, pulled out the fire tools and andirons, and set them in their appropriate places. Wood, I needed wood. It was on the side of the house. *I'll go out and take a look.*

"Gabrielle," I hollered through the railings up to the second floor. "I'm going out to get some wood. Mommy's making a fire."

"Okay, Mommy," a high pitched voice replied. Quickly, without a jacket, I ran to the side of the house, discovered the wood pile, grabbed two logs and some kindling, and dashed back to the front door. *Vivi, this is a real smart way to get pneumonia. Keep it up*. Inside the house, I removed my snow-covered sneakers, and slid over to the fireplace. No shortage of paper to start a fire here. The matches should be in the grocery bag that I dumped in the living room this morning.

Now for the job of opening the chimney flue. It made a nasty creaking sound. It must have been a long time since this place had a fire lit. I'd better get a chimney sweep to clean out this fireplace, the dining room's and the one in my bedroom. *Time to find the matches. Good girl. Looks like my first try will succeed.* I turned and looked back at the living room. The room was transformed. No longer dark and cold, it had changed into a kinetic painting of flames and lights from the fire and the rays of a setting sun.

"Pretty Mommy, pretty," exclaimed Gabrielle as she descended the staircase and settled next to me. "Here, Mom," and planted a big kiss on my cheek. She got up and started dancing in front of the fire. "Music, Mommy. Please," she begged as she fluttered her eyelashes coyly and gave me a smile that rendered me helpless.

I got up, walked to the immaculate and ancient kitchen, found the stereo along with the CD and DVD collection and ran back to the living room. *Where is an electric outlet? Ah, under the bay window. What would be appropriate for this setting? Excellent, Vivaldi's Four Seasons*. Quickly to capture my capricious mood, I plugged the system in to the wall, and skipped over the music selections until I found Winter. The beginning reminded me of hockey skaters taking to the ice before positioning themselves and beginning their violent ballet. I missed not having ice hockey in California and watching the beginners trying to achieve equilibrium with their skates and sticks. Gabrielle began dancing and added to the magic created by the flames and the dying sun.

One more thing and I would be ready. I needed a cushion to lean on. Somehow, hard wood floors and boxes weren't as comfortable as they were in my youth. Finding my old faithful pillow, the one that made the car trip from California to New Jersey and that had about three weeks of life left in it, I propped myself against the wall and watched my daughter. The pillow, like so many other friends in boxes, would never be discarded but relegated to a shelf in the closet, only to be used by the unsuspecting guest who dared not complain.

Back to my train of thought and to contemplate the cup of wine. After all these years away from Princeton, and my vow never to return, here we were. I was even the owner of a ramshackle barn of a house from my childhood. Life certainly took some strange turns. After graduating from college and spending several years working in New York City as a graphic design grunt, I left this town for California. I ran as fast as my car could carry me, feeling free and unburdened from the family obligations and from the restricted East Coast mentality. I was out to make my fortune, to be the hottest designer I could be. For a couple of years I was growing and living out the dream.

Then I met Leif, my really big mistake. The dreams changed, died and one day I woke up to a harsh nightmare.

Now I have Gabrielle, and a lot of money. I had heard that when a person was in a major life crisis the "fight or flight" syndrome would take over. And I flew, with my darling daughter. In ten days I sold most of our furniture, called the moving company, and got back on Route 78 heading east. I phoned an old schoolmate from my old high school years who was in real estate, found out that the Potackis' Cape Cod-style home was on the market, electronically transferred the cash and voila, I was back.

So what was different?

I was older. No wiser, only fatter with a bit of gray. I had my Gabrielle safe with me, busily picking out her bedroom, not understanding why we left California. *Oh, Vivi. Give your life a rest; you've always been your worst enemy.*

Through the bare window I could see stars and the crescent moon. It was a cold crisp night and the frost began its magical patterns on the panes. Gabrielle, delighted in this new attraction of living where there was a true winter, began to make drawings in the frost with her fingers.

Gold. The fire crackled and a spectrum of red, orange, gold and yellow appeared in front of me. I'll paint this living room the color of the fire, a golden yellow. After years of living in white walls and pale rooms, I thirsted for rich, intense, brave colors. I wanted to surround my new life with colors. I would get a bright red leather Italian sofa and two deep blue chairs.

I took another sip of the Bordeaux and began daydreaming of the new living room. *Here's to you, Vivi; artist, mom, woman. Here's to you, and to this day. Cheers.*

Today I was home.

Today I turned forty.

Chapter 2

"Mommy, hurry, I have to build my snowman," screamed Gabrielle from the first floor. Ever since we moved to this house she has gotten in the habit of shouting from one room to another, ever fascinated by the science of acoustics.

"At your service, pumpkin," I responded and almost took a flyer down the stairs. They had just been refinished, waxed, and smelled wonderful of lemon and pine. Additionally, they were quite slippery. I mentally made a note to start looking for some Oriental runners for the hallway and stairs.

"Zip me, zip me, zip me," demanded Gabrielle as she tried to wiggle into her snowsuit. Sometimes I worried about that kid; all the things she inherited from my side of the family. My mother would repeat all commands three times. Now that she was older, she repeated everything five times with five minute reminders. God knows how many times I repeated myself. I wondered if lawyers could develop a murder defense based on "repeat abuse".

Zip, buckle, and snap. I opened the door, Gabrielle squealed at the sight of the snow, and out she went looking like a mini-Michelin tire child. I remembered being her age and hitting that fresh snow. We lived in Washington DC where it seemed that the snow was always hip deep. For the first hour, the snow would keep me busy. Once I realized that my mittens were wet, and my feet were cold, and my nose didn't wiggle very well and would get stuck, I was ready to get back to the warmth. The best part: being greeted by a warm house and a cup of cocoa with large white marshmallows. *Stop the daydreams, Vivi. Get a pot of cocoa started on the stove.*

I walked through the hallway, getting a glimpse of the living room and headed into the kitchen. All the boxes were gone, the floors finished and the living room walls painted. The house was neglected for so many years that these few changes were uplifting. However the kitchen was a different issue. The floor was of a non-descript linoleum from the fifties. There once was a pattern, but it was mostly gone now. It was a huge cold kitchen with a monster stove that had become highly fashionable in the magazines. I would keep it for it had character, but we had not yet developed a relationship built on confidence and respect. It was a mean brute with little patience for my feeble attempts at gourmet cooking. The white cabinets were of solid wood but looked worn and scratched. In several areas, I spied hardened paint drippings on the cabinets.

I lit the stove, poured the milk in to the double boiler and sat down at the Formica table lent to me by my mother. The decorator magazines on the table awaited my attention. In desperation of the state of the kitchen I picked one up and started aimlessly flicking through the pages.

These magazines always amazed me. In them I would find all these people living in perfect homes. One would think that by now everyone in American had a perfect house that had been photographed in one magazine or another. These were perfect house where everything stayed immaculate and in perfect condition. And all that stuff tucked in nooks and crannies. It would never get dusted, polished, or washed in my house. Oh well, I turned the page, got bored with perfection and turned my head to my kitchen reality.

Taking a visual scan of the kitchen, I noticed that in one corner the linoleum was badly cracked but since the pattern was so worn down, it was scarcely visible. I went over to it, bent down, picked at it a little more, and more and more, to discover that beneath this vile flooring and black tar stuff, there lay pine, lovely wide pine planking. It could become a beautiful kitchen if the linoleum was removed and the old planks sanded and polished. With the reddish yellow color of a pine floor, the cabinets stripped of the many layers of old paint and stained white, adding a dark green wall paper with a small print, the kitchen would be lovely. Finding a pad of paper, I jotted down to get the old faucets re-chromed and the immense tea stained sink re-glazed. More and more, I fell under the spell of this old house.

Why would anyone want to cover up such nice planking? My guess was that it wasn't clean, practical, or modern. I thought about the Potacki family who used to live here. I bet that Mrs. Potacki decided that the floor needed to be covered. Mrs. Potacki was my piano teacher and she terrified me with her imperial gaze and her large aristocratic nose. The Potackis left Hungary during the communist regime and by their lifestyle; I assumed that she had sewn the family jewels into the lining of her coat. She was an immensely tall woman, with large capable hands that could easily reach any set of chords composed by Chopin. During the lesson, she would sit next to me with perfect posture and raise her eyebrow when my little clumsy fingers touched the keys. Each time I hit a wrong note, her cavernous nostrils would flare and a sigh would escape her lips. I thought that we both dreaded the lessons; to her they were an affront to her ears; to me, misery. I had no musical talent, no touch for the ivory keys and I hated to practice. Not that it was difficult, I just didn't enjoy practicing for hours pieces that I disliked, such as those awful Czerny piano studies. Many of the pieces I enjoyed required spans beyond my hands' capabilities. But for eight years I persevered, mostly due to my mother's vision that someday, the piano and I would join in musical matrimony. She loved the vision of a little girl with a long blond braid, sitting at the piano. Oh well, in that arena I was my mother's failure.

Mr. Potacki was a nondescript man who would disappear quickly if he heard one of us students. But he was a fairly well-known scientist at the University and had grey intelligent eyes. Somewhere there was a daughter and two sons. They must have been older and out of the house because we never saw them. They were just pictures on the mantel piece to us. At recitals, we students would try to piece together the family story based on clues, photos, and gossip gleaned from our mothers. We knew that one son was in disfavor because he became a minister, but that was as far as we got. Now, living in the house, I could find few clues about the Potackis.

When I was in California, I heard that the husband died, but what happened to my piano teacher, I had no idea. When I bought the house, there was a different seller's name, so the house might have been part of an inheritance, or the Potackis might have sold out years ago. I seem to remember so much baggage from the past.

Hey, Vivi, wake up. It's the doorbell. I raced to the living room and answered the front door. Finally, the men delivering the living room furniture have arrived. I was getting tired of living in my house like a gypsy. Gabrielle thought it was fun. After two weeks and many moves, she finally took the bedroom at the end of the hall.

I opened the door to allow the two men inside. For the next fifteen minutes, despite the usual line about delivery people, they carefully and patiently helped me arrange the furnishings. After we laid out the Turkish carpet and placed the new furniture, they brought in odd pieces from the dining room. I gave them a generous tip for all their help, escorted them to the door, and turned around to absorb the new look.

The room was transformed. Treasured books and items that I collected on my travels lined the bookcases that surrounded the fireplace. The Turkish rug with its soft colors of blues, yellows and warm tomato orange that was too big to fit in the townhouse in California, looked as if it had been designed for this room, this wonderful, bright golden room. Oh, a warm red leather sofa and the bright blue chairs that fit so perfectly in this room were a recent purchase at a furniture wholesaler. The coffee table and assorted small pieces I found at the local antique store balanced well the room. It was all coming together the way that I envisioned, not some unlivable room from a decor magazine, but a room that reflected Gabrielle's and my personalities.

But something was still lacking. I was not able to put my finger on what was needed.

A blast of cold air entered the house. Gabrielle came in from the cold. Her eyes were a clear blue from the air, and her checks were glowing. I gave her a big kiss and helped her strip off all the snow clothes. A puddle began to form near her boots.

“Mommy, I love snow. It tastes good. I want to go out tomorrow and play again,” she said as she gave me an icy cold kiss on the checks.

"I’ve got some cocoa on the stove. You’ll like it. It’s nice and hot and you can put marshmallows in it.”

We went to the kitchen counter and I got out two mugs, the pot of cocoa, marshmallows, and placed them on a tray. We ambled to the kitchen table. Actually I walked to the table and sat down. Gabrielle danced her way to her chair.

“Good, Mom,” said Gabrielle as she sipped her cocoa. “I like hot chocolate with marshmallows. See, I can poke them with my fingers.”

As I looked at this scene, Gabrielle with her rosy skin sipping her cocoa surrounded by the horrid but efficient linoleum floor and thought about the Potackis with my mother and her dreams, dreams of a little girl playing on a baby grand piano, I realized what was missing from the living room. How stupid of me. How did I ever believe that I could get away from my past? The remedy was simple.

"After you’ve finished with your cocoa would you like to go shopping with Mommy?”

“Shopping? Where are we going, Mommy? What are we going to buy?” replied Gabrielle with a slight chocolate mustache.

“A piano, pumpkin. A big, black, grand piano.”

Chapter 3:

Crazy spring. Sometimes it snowed, sometimes it was foggy and sometimes it was that wonderful warm day when the crocuses started showing their tips. Today was a marvel. A bit of green grass was beginning to poke up from the brown front lawn. Buds were forming on the forsythia. When I was a child, I thought it was an untrainable bush that looked like a messy group of sticks in the winter and a fuzzy green mop in the summer. But my mother would go out in the early spring, cut branches and place them over the mantel to bloom in an immense crystal vase. In several days, a jumble of yellow would appear. Mom would always get excited and say, "See, it is spring. I think the forsythia will be more beautiful this year than ever." They were truly beautiful and I cannot remember a year in which spring, whenever it came, was not an extravaganza of yellows, baby pinks and blues.

Where Gabrielle and I lived in California, there were two seasons: Dry, hot, and brown or wet, cool and green. I knew that winter was over when my car would finally dry out under the hood. Spring was when it would rain once every two weeks instead of raining for two weeks straight. No seasons, no forsythia. My mother thought I was crazy to move to a land without real seasonal changes.

Every year in Princeton, Mom would get gardener's itch around mid-February and the seed catalogues would emerge from their hiding places. We would sit together at the kitchen table, open the catalogues, eyeing the melons (we never had success with them), sighing over cherry trees (only the birds got to enjoy them) and writing down our choices on the order form. Finally out of the dozen or so catalogues that we had completed the forms, Mom would randomly choose one of the forms and send in the order. We didn't have enough money for all the wonderful things we wanted, but getting a box sent back to us six weeks later with fat bulbs full of future promise made us giddy. Eventually after many years of using this system, we bought every plant we dreamed for.

True to form, on this early day in March, I started leafing through the plant catalogs.

"What are you doing, Mommy? I want to help." Gabrielle came in from the hall, pulling on one of her long fat braids. She wiped her drippy nose on her sleeve, hoisted herself up on to the table, and smiled.

"I would like it if you would use tissue paper in the future for your nose. It's much nicer."

"Oh Mommy, this is better. And it's much better for the Earth. No waste."She blew me a kiss and gave me another of her killer smiles. Her evil mother was vaporized. "Look, look at these Mommy, these are beautiful. Can we have these?' asked Gabrielle.

"Come sit beside me and help pick out our flowers for next year. We'll need lots since we have much more room than in California. You tell me what you want to grow, I'll see if it is a good plant for us, and we'll fill out the order. Okay?"

"Okay, Mommy," said Gabrielle as she jiggled her chair closer to mine. *Well, Vivi. Aren't we having an expensive morning?* True, but due to the wonderful weather, I was in a magnanimous mood, willing to spend a small fortune on the concept of a magnificent garden. This garden would take years to mature, but the rewards will begin in a few months.

My tiny beloved and I launched a most ambitious plan for garden ecstasy. Oohs and aahs escape our lips over each page, making selections, deciding where they would go in the garden, and calculating the required quantity. It was a fine insanity of German, Dutch, and Japanese iris, anemones, Canterbury bells, foxglove and snapdragons, blue and white lilacs, all varieties of lavender, day lilies, Asiatic lilies and Madonna lilies, carnations, peonies and the list kept growing and growing. This time all the order forms would be sent out and I knew that in return, we would be on everyone's mail order list. But I was not through with ordering. There were still the roses.

Roses. My mother was born in the month of June and always filled the house with her birth flower. I continued my mother's madness and my passion for these prickly, fussy plants had no bounds. So I went insane and ordered the full gamut from the charming and delicate pink Cecile Brunner to the elegant and sensual dark red Mr. Lincoln. I signed up Mme. Isaac Perriere with its rich raspberry scent, La Heine Victoria, Gertrude Jekyll, Ballerina, Gruss an Aachen, Nymphenburg, Penelope and Constance Spry. With another catalogue I added Souvenir de Malmaison, Madame Hardy and Zephirine Drouhin for the rose arbors that were forming in my head. I ordered like a crazed woman, and then completed the paperwork with rose arbors and accessories.

We probably spent a good two hours picking out the plants and filling out the forms. It was the largest order that I had ever made with a fairly amazing total cost. So what, the garden hadn't been touched for years and needed some new life. The Potackis were probably scorch gardeners — they would stick a plant in the dirt and if it made it through a dry summer, it was an acceptable plant. And if it died, it was an inferior mutant.

"Hey Mom, aren't you going overboard`?" Gabrielle woke me up from my little fantasy. "'This is like California."

In California we lived in a townhouse with a tiny patch of dirt at the entrance. I had it crammed with favorite flowers and roses — climbers, bush rose, teas, Bourbons and Albas. To be blunt, it was glorious, riotous, and was one of the few things I missed about that home.

"No, I promise, it will be under semi-control, Gabrielle. But can you picture it, off in the sunny corner, a rose arbor under which we can sit and smell the flowers? Just think about it, I can read to you your favorite books under the arbor."

Gabrielle just rolled her eyes. She slid off of the chair, ran over to me and gave me a big hug. "I love you, Mommy, call Grandmère for help." Then she skipped out of the kitchen, through the hallway, up the stairs and into her bedroom.

Grandmère was my mother, a diminutive commanding woman originally from Brittany, but whose parents moved to Paris after WWII, when she was a toddler. She met my father in Paris and had been in this country since my birth. With the illness of my father, my mother had evolved into one of the most competent women I knew. And to everyone who knew me, I was the disorganized, disoriented type only willing to rise when desperate conditions occurred. Even Gabrielle knew our strengths and weaknesses. So I made another of my famous notes in my head to give my mother a call and ask about gardening help. Maybe she knew of a high school student interested in weekend work.

The door bell rang and I ran to the front door. No need to call Mom, she was at my door with my stepdad, Richard. I would do well to hide the order forms since Mom believed that I was an idiot with money. In spite of my ability to acquire this house, my mother believed that no one with an art background could have money, and that at any moment, I would be destitute. She was so curious about my financial status and stock portfolio that it showed all over her face. I knew that she was dying to snoop and see the statements. She could not figure out my current situation for anything. I loved seeing her in such torment.

"Hi Mom. Hi, Richard, so nice of you to come. Come in. I was just working in the kitchen."

“I came for Gabrielle. They are having a children’s play at McCarter Theater this afternoon and we just heard about it. I thought that she may like to come. We can feed her lunch and let her have a short nap at the house. Can I take her or do you have plans?” commanded my mother.

“No, that’s fine. I’ll call her down. Why don’t you come in? Would you like some coffee?”

“Gabrielle, honey. It’s your Grandmère. Come down, please,” I shouted up to the second floor. A small voice replied, “In a minute, I’m doing something important.”

"Coffee would be nice, Vivi. Is it fresh? I'll have milk in mine, and Richard likes his black." Mom and Richard were in the living room, where Mom was impatiently waiting for me to go on with my hostess duties so that she could begin snooping, turning over some of my bibelots to see if they were authentic. Her behavior was confirmed by the time I was in the hallway for I could hear her "tut-tut" and "tiens-tiens" sounds.

I went into the kitchen giggling. Mom was so funny. The tut-tut sounds were her totaling up the worth of the items that she held in her hands, and the tiens-tiens means that I actually owned something of noticeable value. The sounds were getting stronger. Mom probably had included the cost of the piano and the leather sofa. I knew that the interrogation would shortly begin. *Well, just concentrate on getting the coffee made, and placing some little cakes on a plate.*

Carrying out the tray with the coffee and cake, I heard Mom and Richard quickly sitting down. I placed the tray on the coffee table and waited for the games begin.

"Vivi, cherie, the room looks gorgeous, gorgeous, gorgeous. Richard, don't you think that it looks gorgeous. I really think it looks gorgeous. Did you find the piano at an estate sale? How did you get it in the house? Wasn't it terribly expensive? I like the colors in the room. I first thought it would be too strong and make the room smaller but I was wrong. You are so creative. And where did you get the sofa? It is not my type, too hard to get out of. They don't make good sofas the way they use to. I hope you didn't buy it new, you know those furniture people can take you to the wallet. And you are such an easy person, always letting people walk over you. Look what happened with Leif. I know, I know, you don't want to talk about it. But it is a mother's right to protect her family from thieves. It must have cost you a fortune, the sofa. And the piano, can you afford it?"

I hesitated in correcting Mom's phase "take you to wallet" when she meant "take me to the cleaners", and instead focused on answering her questions in a way that would create a two-day conversation with Richard on my foolhardy spending and my need to cut coupons from the grocery store. Actually, I rarely heard Richard talk, he lets Mom take over for him, and so it would probably be a one-way conversation. Since I had just moved back, his entire days were most likely filled of details on my comings and goings. Poor man.

“Thanks, Mom. I found the sofa at the designer center in New York. You know I have a pass to get into those places. But it still was not your average garden variety sofa. And yes, doesn’t the piano add to the room. I found it in the classified ads in the paper. A divorce, their loss and my gain and I got the Aronson Company to move it. It was costly but worth it since there is not a nick on the piano.”

Now, to go for the kill, Vivi. “And Mom, after I got the floors done, I was thinking of painting this room yellow, but you know how sloppy I am. It seemed a shame for me to mess up my new floors, so I called in some painters just to do this room properly. I think it turned out quite well. Do you think I should get them to do the upstairs too?”

Bingo. Mom was tut-tutting away and rolling her eyes. She will have gobs of data to rehash for the next few days. Mom believed in never giving jobs to trade people when you can do it, no matter how badly, yourself. To her, it was just a waste of money. She would badger Richard for a couple of days to paint my upstairs. Richard was a very good painter and he would probably enjoy it the job if I got him a good bottle of scotch and a six pack of beer. And since I didn’t mention Leif, she’ll probably go on and on about how I was a pantoufle, a spineless bedroom slipper, and probably still waiting for him to come back.

“Hi, Grandmère, what are you talking about? Can I have a gateau?” I was saved by my little cherub.

"Viens, cocotte. Your grandfather and I are taking you to lunch and to McCarter Theater to see the marionettes. Hurry and bring me your good shoes and a dress.”

We sprang into action getting Gabrielle ready. Soon the party of three was out by the entrance door. Mom turned toward me and says, "We will bring her back around six tonight. You should get out on a day like today. Get some color back into your cheeks. And some exercise won't hurt you. You look like you have lost some weight, but don't stop. When I think how I sacrifice for you to have ballet lesson so that you would take good care of yourself —."

"'Thanks, Mom, for taking Gabrielle. I love you. Bye-bye."

And they were off and away.

Chapter 4

Vivi, it's time to move them bones. Get the bike out of the garage, snap on the helmet, grab a jacket, and push off. This was going to be funny since I was so out of shape. I planned on taking a bath tonight to recuperate. I had forgotten how wonderful these back streets were in Princeton. I could meander for hours, or minutes, in view of my physical condition. How could I let myself go? Easy. All I had to do was to look at the traffic and the size of the hills in the San Francisco area and I'd chicken out. What a wimp. *So, my dear, where to, today? Well, let's see if this creaking carcass of a woman can ride all the way to the Institute of Advanced Study.*

Nice day with a wonderful smell in the air. Soft and perfumed with the promises of spring. At no great speed, I passed Marquand Park and crossed Nassau Street. Slowing down, I rode through the great broad avenues, enjoying the passing of homes and the preserved beauty of the elms. I didn't realize how much I missed this freedom and tranquility. Finally I made my way to the Institute.

Queen of all she can see. When I was a kid, I first found the Institute and declared it mine; the library, the club room, the labs, and the land. All of it mine. It had a wonderful library with a ribbed ceiling, just like a scallop shell. I never walked through the library, but would peer in the window at the beautiful offices with their leather chairs and oriental rugs, full of books for the professors, dreaming of the day when I would work there.

Hey, Vivi. Remember when Max and you would come down during the summer to fish near the swinging bridge. You know, beyond the vast lawn, past the library and pond, and deep into the woods. We'd pack up a lunch, ride our bikes here and pretend to go fishing. It was usually after a hot game of tennis. Funny kids. We never bought a license for if we caught a fish, we would have to do something with it and we would rather not have to deal with that decision. So we would come down to the bridge, talk about life, and pretend to fish. It seemed that the older we got, the more time we spent talking on the bridge and less time looking for fish.

All right, Vivi. Let's dump the bike. Nothing had changed. Time had stood still in this place. Everything was as I remembered; the pond, the buildings, the woods.

Oh, the woods, memories of those woods. Memories came flooding back of a warm summer night in June when frogs were singing their funny love songs. A night of whispers hopes and dreams. A night of our fierce beauty. Memories of Robbie. How could have I forgotten that night, that boy?

It was so long ago. Senior year of high school. Exams were finished. There were decisions to be made about colleges and acceptance. Where would I be next year? Would I like it? Would I make it? All of us were asking the same questions with tensions and spirits running high. Girls becoming women, boys becoming men. Each torturing the other with newly gained sexual skills. We aimed for college men for they were much more mature. Now a Princeton man was a feather in any girl's cap. But after a while the new challenge began to fade. The Princeton men were too old, too drunk and too unpredictable for us. We had no control over them, and the high school boys were beginning to mature into a college mode, yet still controllable. No longer did we need to worry about sex and doing "it", we completely had the upper hand. Finally, after years of patiently waiting, the senior boys were able to realize their meager dreams and began dating the self-appointed "princesses".

Lena. Celina Daggett, my best friend. We looked like clone dolls. Same height, weight, build and same hair length. Two little blonds, one ash and one golden with big, thick, long hair. Two pretty moppets, testing out our female claws and feminine wiles on any unsuspecting male. Both of us were fluent in French, using it as our secret language. Lena proclaimed her superiority. I had better hair; however her chest was significantly larger by at least several centimeters. I had been humbled and allowed Lena to become top princess of the group.

Christmas vacation in our senior year. Lena was dating Robbie and I was dating Mark. I remembered that we were all sitting in Mark's car when Lena had her brainstorm.

"Okay, I'm bored. It's time to change. Robbie, now you'll start dating Vivi and I'll date Marky. Okay, let's change places," commanded Lena.

Musical chairs, musical dates. Why not switch? After all, the command came from the Princess, and we were bored with each other. We had been double dating for some time, and we needed some spice to our lives.

Lena slid into the front of the car and I went around to the back seat. Robbie put his arm around my shoulder, and gave me a lopsided grin that went from ear to ear. I immediately fell for him, smiled back and snuggled up to him. It would be a good spring.

What did he look like? Funny, how could I have forgotten? His face resembled a child-angel that had fallen off of a stone carving. He had soft brown hair with uncontrollable curls and tendrils. A beautiful mouth and a nose untouched by his beloved lacrosse. The softest blue eyes of a dreamer, eyes that would awake with his smile. Tall and thin, not yet reaching his promise of a man, and slowly losing his innocent beauty of a boy.

Talk about being smart, he was already slated for Massachusetts Institute of Technology and taking intermediate levels of math and physics at the university during his senior year. He had ability to whip out an English bullshit essay in a half hour. Thank heavens he was inept at foreign languages and worshiped artistic skills. There, at least, I could compete. And he was also the stupidest boy I had ever known, with an ability to infuriate me within seconds. My fourteen year old cousin, Max, was more emotionally developed. Poor Robbie.

He was mincemeat in the hands of a future vamp practicing her new feminine wiles and always in the dog house. There was no tranquility in our relationship. I had memories of a make-out party. Robbie, after completing a fairly successful pass under my shirt, stopped everything, took a look at me and said, "Got you horny, didn't I," and then gave me that sweet lopsided grin. That was it. No interest to progress to the next stage. He had achieved his goal and was satisfied. His curiosity had been fulfilled. I on the other hand, in the breath of passion, stared at this idiot savant that I had the stupidity to date and realized that Robbie had no clue as to my stirring emotions and was like a kid at an arcade game. Push the button and see what happens. He was never boring and sometimes sweet. He was always a challenge. Pity, we met too early in our lives. Wondering what he was doing now? Probably working for a computer company, spending hours surfing the Internet and living in some suburb.

Senior Prom Night, the most important thing on our minds. I was still dating Robbie especially since I needed a steady for the big night. Lena and I put twice the energy to get ready for the prom as we did to get into college. We went shopping for days. We finally found the dresses to die for at Betsy's Bridal and Formal Wear Shoppe. We consulted various magazines on hairstyles which were absolutely useless with our long heavy tresses. Most importantly, we worked on getting the perfect tan to set off our dresses to perfection. Not one part of our body was forgotten; toes, nails, eyebrows and skin. Even our blackheads were removed days before the great event. No red blotches would be found on our skins.

Seven-thirty, the witching hour. Robbie at my house, sweet and uncomfortable in a rented tuxedo and nervously awaiting a princess to descend from the small staircase. Shy and embarrassed about our new beauty, we looked down at our feet and murmured sounds of approval. Mom broke the spell and sent us off into the night.

"It is time to go, you both look lovely. Now drive carefully, no drinking, and bring my princess home safely."

I had vague memories about the prom which was held at a Holiday Inn on a hot, steamy night. The air conditioner was on the fritz causing wilting hair and damp tuxedos. A mediocre band cranking out Mitch Ryder tunes. A dangling silver ball, strobe lights, lukewarm punch and feeling bored and queasy from the heat.

Then Robbie leaned over towards me and said, "Let's get out of here."

Chapter 5

Silence: Not a word was spoken in the car. It was an old Volkswagen bug that made its own particular sound. We left the windows wide open while trying to cool off from the heat and humidity. Robbie drove until he came to the Institute, killed the engine and rolled into a parking space.

The Institute was closed. No one was allowed after hours. We didn't make a sound. Robbie reached into the back seat. A bottle of champagne and two glasses appeared in his large thin hands.

"Take off your shoes. They'll get wrecked in the dew," he whispered. Robbie carefully placed the glasses into his pockets of his tuxedo. °°I saw this in the movies," he murmured.

It was a clear night with a crescent moon. We walked hand in hand down the long damp green lawn with the sounds of my dress swishing in the damp grass and the beat of my heart pounding. We sat on a cement pad with our backs propped up against the Institute's library walls. Robbie popped the bottle's cork, poured the champagne, and for hours and hours we talked about our hopes and dreams. We talked about our goals in life. For the first time we were not at battle with one another.

"You know after tonight, it ends," whispered Robbie. "All of this. Princeton, high school, and the friends we have. We are going to leave it for new places. I'm going to Boston and you are going to Chicago. As of tonight our world as we know, ends."

I looked up at Robbie, this tall boy with his soft blue eyes and the face of a fallen angel. He was right. Our childhood was over. It was time for new beginnings. It was time for us to give each other a gift, one of love and trust.

We walked down to the right of the pond, surrounded by large trees where the moon could not give us away to strangers. My hair had fallen out of its intricate pins. Somewhere, Robbie had discarded his jacket.

"You know I'll miss you very much," I whispered afraid of being discovered, afraid of what we were going to do, afraid of the changing life.

A kiss. A magical kiss that blew away the fears. The tall thin boy leaned over and kissed me, a kiss that came from his heart and soul, a kiss that I wished would go on forever. When it ended we silently took off our finery and looked at each other naked, standing among the trees with the moonlight softly touching our faces and shoulders. We kissed and descended on the damp warm grass where we laid in each other's arms, staring into each other's eyes.

Slowly and deliberately we started making love. No urgency, no rush. Just two people learning about each other's body for the first time. Not embarrassed about being novices but asking each other for guidance and approval.

The night air was so sweet, so heavy, so quiet. Robbie and I merged into the surroundings of the pond, the trees and sounds of the animals. No fear of the future, no fear of losing control. We were free and open with thoughts and passions. It was the greatest gift that I could give Robbie.

Consummation, culmination, fulfillment. I looked into Robbie's eyes and said, "I love you." I knew that my gift was now complete. Robbie looked at me and whispered, "I love you too. Thank you," and held me tightly.

Later we quickly put back our clothes on, and exited the Institute in the same manner that we had entered. We dared not break the spell for it would always be magical to us.

An enchanted moment; a magic spell. A cold wind touched my shoulder, and I shivered. The spell was broken and the afternoon was coming to an end. It was time for me to get back on the bike and pedal home. Funny, after all those years recalling that night, and remembering a tall thin boy with the face of a fallen angel.

Chapter 6

Oh, Vivi. Looking good. From biking and gardening, my fat was quickly disappearing. *See, there are my shoulder bones.* And my tummy was getting smaller. Men, beware. A flower was beginning to return from a long and nasty winter. Maybe moving back home wasn't such a bad idea after all. I was still alive. In fact, I was flourishing. *Darling, you look marvelous.*

My bedroom had a large, obnoxious mirror that magnified fat-sucking parts of my body. But see, oh mirror, those areas were going away. Clothes were much looser. Actually I was starting to look like a saggy, baggy elephant when wearing my sweats. My face looked better, clearer and smoother. I'd lost the pockets under my eyes and the chubby-cheek, chipmunk face was thinning out. Soon, my mom will lose one of her favorite subjects to torment me.

My art business had been growing nicely. I spent four to eight hours a day in the makeshift studio with good results. My agent had been calling me to see how close I was to finishing the fairy book. Two more pages and I was done. All credits went to Gabrielle. When she was two years old she asked me to draw a lilac fairy. I exhibited prints of the fairy at an art show where it did well. Since then it developed in to a nice little business of stationary, books, limited editions, and original art. I had a small following who bought my work. The art actually made Gabrielle and me a cozy life style even though I never needed to work again if I was very careful.

My poor mother, all of her life fighting against me for being an artist and believing that I was incompetent at money matters. Here I was making a good living drawing, and making a better living with my investments. I was always amazed at the stories people tell themselves in order to justify their action and beliefs.

"Hey, Mommy, are we going uptown?" Gabrielle entered my room and ended my daydreaming.

It had been raining for three days, and today there were clear skies. Gabrielle had gone stir-crazy staying inside our house and Loretta's. Loretta was her day-care provider and a blessing from the Gods. Gabrielle, with her high energy level, would quickly try my limited patience, and was a happy birdie at Loretta's house, playing with Whitney, her best friend and Loretta's daughter. I thought Loretta had it made, getting paid while her daughter played with her best buddy.

"Why do you want to go uptown?" I answered back.

"I want to go shopping and see things. I want to see the puppies. And Grandmère is right. Your hair is messy. You should go fix it," replied my little bossy love.

I don't know who was more controlling, my mother or my four year old daughter. I thought that I was controlling, but I was just a mere novice compared to these two harden pros.

"What do you want me to do with my hair? Shave it off, like a mohawk? And what else do you and Grandmère want me to do?" I began drilling my miniature sergeant.

"I want you to look pretty again, like in the picture. And Grandmère says you need to get married again," replied the diminitive commander.

"What picture are you talking about?" This was beginning to get on dangerous ground and I wondered where it would lead us.

"The picture Grandmère gave me of you. Wait, I go get it." Gabrielle ran up to stairs to her bedroom. A minute later I heard her cautiously descending the steps.

"See Mommy, you're so pretty. Please be pretty again," pleaded Gabrielle. I looked down at the picture and sigh. It was of Lena and me, dressed in white summer dresses, hair tumbling down over our shoulders. We were sitting on the trunk of the old willow tree that fell over many years ago in a hurricane. It was the most beautiful tree, with a long horizontal trunk with branches heading up into the sky.

Sophomore year at Northwestern on my summer vacation. It was a lovely cameo, and it captured our incredible beauty of entering womanhood. It also was the last picture before the skies opened with a terrible storm that re-charted my life.

"Oh, look how young I was." The picture brought back a flood of memories that I didn't want to explore on this nice sunny day.

"But see, Mom. See how nice your hair is. Do it again. For me, pul—ease," begged Gabrielle.

"Okay, I'll call up Annalise and see if she is free." I looked up Annalise's phone number in the yellow pages and jotted it down. Gabrielle was staring fiercely at me to make sure that I didn't chicken out of the call. "Annalise, it's Vivianne Bergstrom, Ghislaine's daughter. I know it's been a long time. Yes, I'm permanently back and Gabrielle is now four years old. Yes, it's true, my hair is a mess so I need an appointment for a cut and color. Today? A cancellation? Three o'clock would be fine. Thank you. I'll see you later."

Gabrielle was beaming. I could just visualize it now, her reporting back to the Supreme Commander and the two of them sitting down to plot their next move.

"Okay, it's two now. By the time we dressed, get your things ready and get into the car, it will be two-thirty. We can spend a little time window shopping and then I will get my hair done. Take lots of books and toys because you'll have to wait a long while at Annalise's."

"Okay, Mommy. But what if I don't see everything uptown?" asked Gabrielle.

"Then we'll go "lecher les vitrines" afterward and I'll buy dinner at Chianti. Does that sound good? Now get going, we don't have much time," and Gabrielle shot out of my sight to get her things ready.

"Lecher les vitrines" means to lick the window, which is a phrase for window shopping. When my mother and I were in that depressingly poor period, we would go at night lecher les vitrines. All the stores would be closed but we would pretend that we would buy those beautiful things if by chance the stores had been open.

I was on target with our timing. Before going to Annalise, Gabrielle wanted to see her puppies. Actually it was a painting of puppies, mounted on a big gold frame that was hanging in the window of one of the art galleries down at Palmer Square.

"If I am really good, do you think Santa will bring me the puppies," asked Gabrielle, turning up her face to me after seeing her monstrosity in the window.

"We'll see," and I leaned down to kiss this wonder child of mine on the forehead. Since we were in the month of April I had eight months to figure out a way out of purchasing this artistic atrocity. Maybe she would forget about the painting.

"You know Mommy, every night I pray for the puppies." As they say, I was in the deep doggie pile and had better think up of something quickly to get her mind off of the painting.

"Look, there is Annalise's shop. Let's go in."

I was greeted at the door by Annalise who gave me a giant hug since we haven't seen each other for sixteen years. Annalise was one of the most striking women I had ever seen, tall of mannequin build, long legged, perfect features and with one of the most sexy Scandinavian accents. She must work on it. She was also plastic-surgery crazy, averaging three surgeries per husband. She was on husband number four. I sat down on one of the chairs. She placed a plastic drape around me and looked at my hair scornfully.

"Well, they don't have gut hairdressers in California? What did you do to yourself? Tank heavens you came before it is too late. You're not married anymore, are you? Well you are lucky; you still have time to get another husband. You know they are real pain in the ass, but you need them to keep your plumbing gut. Next time, look for one with nice fanny to keep you warm, a big wallet to pay the bills, and that his ting works," she said casually.

Gabrielle beamed hearing this conversation. I could see her reporting new entries to her Grandmère and their two heads nodding in agreement. I quickly ended Annalise's chain of thought by asking her about her new husband which of course would lead into a fine description of her three previous surgeries.

"... so I have decided next month to get a light blasting around my eyes". You are so lucky; your skin doesn't wrinkle like mine. Well here we are, how do you like it?" Annalise turned the chair around. I looked in the mirror and saw a familiar stranger, a girl that I once knew a long time ago. A strange feeling came over me.

"It looks lovely, Annalise, really lovely. You've done magic with the coloring bottle," I hoarsely replied.

"Oh Mommy, you look so pretty again. See, we have the same color hair," bubbled Gabrielle.

I quickly packed up Gabrielle's things, got our coats on and paid Annalise. We left her beaming at her handy work. I walked up the street and turned on to Nassau Street with Gabrielle holding my hand and dancing. As we strolled down to Chianti, I took one more look into a darken store window.

A beautiful woman looked back at me. The years and the troubles had been stripped away and it was as if the last sixteen years never took place.

I smiled at myself. Not bad for forty. Maybe moving back home was what I needed. Maybe coming back to my past would give me a future.

"Come on Gabrielle, race you to Chianti." Gabrielle placed her hand in mine and we started running down the street. If any stranger was watching, she'd see a small blond and her tiny friend dancing and laughing their way down Nassau Street, hair flying, without a care in the world.

Chapter 7

Rain, rain, go away. I guess that the old adage about April showers was true, but did it have to rain so much? My mother's house had flooded once. So far, I had been spared. Our house was set on a hill which in Princeton meant four feet above sea level. Many home around here were built on swampy land which was indiscriminate as to whose basement got flooded, rich or middle class. There were no poor in Princeton. Who would have ever thought that sea level was the Great Equalizer. It was always amusing to see huge mansions in Princeton with temporary piping off of the downspouts, exiting the house, going over the massive lawns, and flushing the intruding waters into swollen street gutters and sewers.

No one could tell, by looking at the house that a lot of work had taken place. It still looked like the same rundown Potacki home. It must be of great relief to the neighbors. There had been for the past five years so much rebuilding of the old homes that the town was beginning to lose its favor. Many houses resembled the nightmare from *Architectural Digest*. I might have the house repainted this summer but would restrain from applying intense wild colors that I bestowed on the interior walls. I would keep the house's prim and proper Cape Cod character, and then blind my guileless guest upon entering the house.

Renovations? A bit spotty at best. The living room, little bathroom, kitchen and pantry have been completed downstairs but I have yet to tackle the dining room or the downstairs bathroom. There was a large bedroom downstairs that someone once used as a sickroom and an adjoining bathroom. At the moment, that was my studio. The room would have to wait until I knew what I wanted to do. Nothing had been touched upstairs. Gabrielle's room had all of her things but I hadn't figured out what color to paint it. Since Gabrielle was such a particular creature it would make sense to consult her. Otherwise, the house wouldn't be big enough for us two. Then there was still the question of the two spare bedrooms, now wonderful rooms for Gabrielle to play with the moving boxes and build her cities, and my bedroom. *Oh, someone is at the door. Let me go see who it is. How nice, Richard.*

"Hello, Richard. Come in. Been raining enough? Let me take your coat." I grabbed his sodden raincoat and hung it in the empty entrance closet to dry off.

"Damn wet weather, Vivi. Listen, I've been sent on a mission. Your mom said that you need your room painted. Don't have too much to do with all this rain, so I thought I could come over and help. But if this is a bad time for you, I'll come back later."

Oh, what a wonderful person. Gabrielle was playing with Whitney, so we'd have the day to ourselves. I wondered why Mom had decided that my bedroom should be the next project. Between the two schemers, Gabrielle and my mother, I just didn't trust altruistic offers. But who cares? Like, had they already found my next husband-to-be?

"No, no Richard. That would be great. I've got some color samples in the kitchen and I have pretty well narrowed down the choices. It would be great to finally have a nice bedroom. Come in and I'll get us some coffee."

We made our way to the kitchen and Richard took a seat in one of the kitchen chairs. I scrounged up the coffee beans, ignited a gas burner, and placed the kettle on the stove top. While waiting for the water to boil, I took a last look at the color samples and decided. It was a heavenly color of plum and would look wonderful if we applied a cream color on the heavy woodwork trim and the mantelpiece. I had an Amish quilt made up of blues, purples and roses and in the back of my mind, there was a wonderful painted metal head board that I've been coveting at the consignment shop.

"Jesus, Vivi, purple. Your mother is going to have a French fit when she hears about this."

“Don’t tell her until it is done. If it really looks bad, we can always re-paint the room white. Anyway, remember the kitchen? And the fit she pitched when she heard that I was wallpapering it a dark green pattern.”

“Yeah, maybe it will be all right. She did like it once it was finished and admitted that she was wrong. Funny, your mother is never wrong. Well, I’ll go upstairs and figure on how much paint we will need. Oh and I brought Gabrielle a little present. I’ll just drop it on her bed.”

As Richard tramped up the stairs, I silently congratulated my mother in absentia for choosing such a nice sweet partner. While brewing the coffee, I heard some movement upstairs and several minutes later, Richard descended.

“Well, I’m going to the paint store. Want to come?”

“Sure, let’s put the coffee in two thermos cups, and I’ll grab some fresh muffins I made this morning”, I replied.

For a free paint job, I’d go anywhere. I grabbed the mugs, filled them with coffee and cream, stuffed two muffins in a bag and got my purse. We slid into our rubberized raincoats, closed up the house, and made a dash to the Caddy. Richard turned on the ignition, turned up the volume on the radio, and the monster car began the journey.

"You know, Vivi, if you need to borrow money, I’ve got some that your mother doesn’t know about. You really need a better car. How old is yours anyway? This Cadillac is wonderful. Nice acceleration, safe, moves really well. By the way, the coffee and muffins are great, especially on a day like today”, said Richard while trying to find a large muffin crumb in his lap.

"Oh thanks, Richard. You know I have been too busy with fixing the house to think about cars. Maybe you’re right. Maybe Old Faithful should retire,” I responded with a mouth full of muffin.

He was right about my car. Old Faithful, my beloved Volvo, was ancient and ugly. But I had this problem about cars. I hated to spend money on them as long as they were running properly. Old Faithful had been with me everywhere and knew all about me and my quirky driving habits. Richard, on the other hand, was of the old school of cars; replaced them every five years whether it was needed or not. And the cars he liked were of the cream puff variety, like driving cruiser boats. Me, in a Cadillac, wrong woman.

It was so cute about the borrowing of the money offer. I guessed Richard believed that I was on borderline poverty even though I have purchased a house that was worth more than the value of Mom's current house. Boy, had Mom been doing some great PR on her part. Wonder if her circle of friends believed that I was Tin Cup Mary of the Neighborhood. What I liked the most is that Richard had his own money stash hidden away from Mom, and Mom had the same. The trust that created true relationships slayed me. I should talk. If it hadn't been for my secret stash, I would never be at this level of comfort. Leif would have made sure that I begged for every dime.

The paint transaction went smoothly at the store, and since the walls were already prepared, the painting went quickly. Richard had his beer, and forbade me to paint any of the tricky areas of trim. I was merrily painting the flat walls with the roller, managing to speckle every unprotected place on my body. In a couple of days, the paint would wash out of my hair. In the meanwhile, I had a purplish tinge in areas that the shower cap missed. Gabrielle would get a real kick out of me.

"Well, that about does it, Vivi. I'll clean up these brushes and get back to the house. Oh, yeah, your mom wants you over for dinner. She picked up Gabrielle at Loretta's and is making spaghetti."

"Sounds good to me. The house stinks a bit from the paint. A couple hours and the smell should be gone. I'll pick up the newspapers and the drop cloths. Did we get all the trim tape off?"

We dragged all the clutter out of the room and Richard took the brushes, rollers and trays down to the basement to rinse. The room was empty and pristine. It looked lovely and was exactly what I had hoped for; the dark walls and cream trim looked lovely especially around the fireplace. The dormer windows were without curtains and the sliding door leading to the private balcony looked bleak. I would put inside shutters in the dormer windows and change the sliding door to a French door. It would be charming.

I sighed contentedly as I quickly closed the door of my private domain and went down the stairs to meet Richard, always the patient escort of capricious and incomprehensible women.

"I am ready, Richard. Shall we close?" And he whisked me out into the wet night in the trusted monster of a car to meet my mother and child.

Chapter 8

Good smells were escaping from the kitchen. After entering my mother's house, I left my dripping raincoat on the porch to dry off, and stepped in to the living room. My guess was that the commanders were in the kitchen, plotting and cooking.

Being at Mom's for dinner was an epicurean delight. She was the great French chef. Unless she was testing a new recipe, the meal was guaranteed to be superb and that there would be plenty of leftovers to take home. This arrangement suited me fine. I had never been a sponge to my mother except when it came to cooking; something I enjoyed but rarely had the time to indulge. I would get so caught up with my artwork, that by the time I thought about food, it was usually well into the dinner hours. Gabrielle was complaining more and more about the food quality since we left California. She had developed a refined palate chez Grandmère. The leftovers were our safety valve.

Gabrielle and her Grandmère had an incredible budding relationship. When we were living in California, Mom and Richard would visit as often as possible. Gabrielle loved it when her grandparents would come to visit, but these were far and few between for a close relationship to grow. Leif's mother could not accept the fact that she was a grandmother and took her son's position, never to acknowledge Gabrielle's existence. Now that we were back in Princeton, Gabrielle was able to visit her grandparents daily. Her grandfather doted on her and indulged in all of her whims and her Grandmère was her identical twin from a past life. They would cook together, they'd laugh together, they'd scheme together and they both would shake their index finger at me, together. Sometimes I found them unnerving.

"Hi, Mom. Hi, pumpkin. Smells good. Do you need help setting the table? Thanks for lending Richard to me. The bedroom looks gorgeous and I'll move my stuff back tonight. I can't believe that I put it off for so long."

Mom turned to look at me and with a wooden spoon and tasted the spaghetti sauce.

"Gabrielle and I made spaghetti and Gabrielle made the vinaigrette. I am glad Richard could help. He has been in my way with all of this rain. Maybe he could paint Gabrielle's room?" she inquired.

"No paint, Grandmère. No paint," said Gabrielle with a frown on her face.

"What do you want, pumpkin?" I asked with a slight hesitation in my voice. It had better not be something like those damn puppies. I was on the alert to hear her answer.

"I like flowers, Mommy, blue flowers. I want wallpaper. Like at Loretta's. Blue flowers, no paint."

Well, the kid had a mind of her own. Some day we would go uptown and look at the wallpaper books. I recalled some pattern of violets, or was it hydrangeas? Oh, whatever, we would give her an old-fashion bedroom. Obviously, Gabrielle wasn't ready for Matisse and fauvist design in her room.

Great dinner and good wine. Richard and I cleaned up the table and washed the dishes. Mom and Gabrielle were sitting in the living room and my moment to shine as the obnoxious ungrateful child began in the form of the top ten subjects that Vivianne hated to discuss. Here they were:

The Top Ten Subjects That Pushes Vivianne's Buttons

1. **Don't you think you are spending too much money?** It was not a bottomless pit.

2. **Have you done anything to get alimony from L-e-i-f?** (Mom would never bring up his name fearing to incur psychological damage to the poor fatherless Gabrielle). After all he is the father.

3. **How much weight have you lost this week? You shouldn't stop; you could use to lose ten more pounds.**

4. **Your house is a mess. You really need a maid.** Then the comparisons to other women in my age group whose houses had a sanitary shield wrapped around them.

5. **You've taken on to much with that big house. You could have had a nice condo.**

6. **Are you dating? Gabrielle needs a father. And you should have more children. It is never good to have only one. I know, see what happened to you** (Gabrielle solemnly shook her head on the dating question-I knew that the two of them were scheming on this issue).

7. **How is business? You know that Gabrielle needs you more often. It is not good for a child to have a working mother. If you were married.....**

8. **I am glad to see that you are grooming yourself better. But your clothes, really. You should get rid of those horrible leggings and buy some nice dresses** (that would be really useful when I am painting).

9. **You need help from some professional. Let me get you the name of my lawyer/ accountant/ some doctor. . .**

I0 **And the number ten subject that pushes Vivianne's button:** You're not getting any younger, ma chèrie.

Ra—tat—tat—tat. Bang, bang. The questions would hit me like a machine gun. Mom randomly picked one of the subjects as her starting point. By the end of the evening, she had managed to work all ten into the conversation. Ah, now time for the Grand Finale, the Coup de Grâce.

"But, chèrie. You know how much I love you. I am only saying this for your own good. I want the best for you." She flashed a beatific smile at me. Bang, bang. I was dead. I gathered my few remaining resources.

"Mom. I loved the spaghetti. Listen, it's time for Gabrielle to go home. We should leave now." Please, I needed asylum from the verbal attack.

"Oh yes, chèrie. I didn't realize it was so late. I am so happy that you came over. It's so nice having you close to home."

Swiftly, I grabbed Gabrielle, snapped her into her raincoat, and slipped her rubber boots over her shoes. Richard made haste getting on his rain apparel. We headed for the porch. I slipped into my somewhat dry raincoat. Kiss, kiss, and we were out.

Richard drove us home. I was still in shell-shock from Mom's attack. Gabrielle made up for my silence by singing all the songs of Snow White. Hi ho, hi ho, hi ho.

I gave Richard a hug, thanked him for his work and for the evening. He then pressed fifty dollars in my hand so that I could buy myself something nice. Gabrielle gave him a big hug and kiss.

Back in the house, I was almost back to being a conversant human being. Gabrielle and I went upstairs and she took a bubble bath while I got the small furniture, rugs, and paintings arranged in my bedroom. Gabrielle was now singing all the songs from Cinderella. Soon, she'd be ready for Broadway. My bedroom was looking better and better and was beginning to take on the glow of a warm and comfortable ally. But the paint odors made me decide to sleep on the living room couch tonight.

"Hey, Mommy. I want out," shouted Gabrielle from the tub.

"I'm coming, princess," and I walked to her bathroom. "How was your day?"

"Nice. Grandmère and I cooked and I told her about the puppies. I like your room. But I want flowers," said Gabrielle with a definite air. "Hey, Mom. Stop kissing me."

"Too bad. Mommy's prerogative," I replied as I dried her off. "Now, into your nightgown and into bed. You're up way past your bedtime."

Au natural, Gabrielle ran to her room. Nice little body. She slipped into a freshly cleaned nightgown. I lay down next to her, read her *The Twelve Dancing Princesses*, and kissed her goodnight. Quietly, I rose from her bed, closed her door, leaving a crack open so she could see the hall light. I quietly strolled over to my bedroom.

Oh, Vivi. What a mess. All those boxes you have been avoiding. I grabbed a pillow from the bed, placed it under my butt, and started opening the boxes. Many were filled with books for the bookcase next to the mantelpiece. There was the junk from the past that I still needed to file, old business cards of acquaintances that I couldn't toss out, health insurance forms, correspondences and funny cards. *Well, into the night table drawers you go.*

Last box, Vivi. Time to celebrate. I lit a fire in my freshly painted fireplace and started opening this box. Memories, many memories. Awards, certificates, licenses, and diplomas. Now for the pictures. Gabrielle at birth, Mom & Richard's wedding, more pictures of Gabrielle, faded pictures of my childhood. Finally I came to the last picture. It was of my dad, a photo of him taken on the last trip to France before the illness incapacitated him. My poor dad who died so young. Daddy, my dear darling daddy who I loved and lost. My Daddy with the blue eyes.

Chapter 9

Dad. He came from the deep woods of Oregon and blew his magic on everyone who knew him during his brief tenure on earth. He was the boy you wanted to adopt, the friend that you always needed yet never found, the man that you could depend on. To the few that knew and loved him, he was a giant.

He came from good stock, but his father had died from the flu, and all eight children supported their mother, who began her slide into mental illness. By the time he was thirteen, she was crazy. The children took it on themselves to provide food, clothing and shelter.

One day I had noticed that my father's little toes crossed over the adjacent toes. "Daddy what happened to your toes? They're funny."

"Well, Poupée, when I was a boy, we were very poor and got our clothes from the church boxes. The nice ladies would give you a bundle of clothes and some shoes. Seems that someone didn't check too hard, and I often got shoes for right feet only, and then shoes for left feet only. So my toes grew kind of funny."

Daddy never complained about growing up in total poverty, having a bi-polar mother, being shipped off to one relative or another. He just told me wonderful stories about growing up in the woods with his family. To this day I didn't think he remembered it being a bad or hard life, I knew that he was happy. Some people would look at their glass of life and see it as half-empty; Daddy would look at a glass mostly empty and see it as full.

He once told me about the cabin he lived in when he was a boy and how he and his brothers and sisters wallpapered it with the cartoons. I was envious. To have a house wallpapered with cartoons would have been so wonderful. Many years later, Daddy took me to see the land he still owned in Oregon and on it, the old log cabin built by Daddy and his brothers, was still standing. We went inside, and the wallpaper was as he described;

hundreds and hundreds of cartoons. It looked like the perfect home to me. Several years after Daddy's death, Mom and I were informed that vandals burned down the house. We soon sold the property.

Poupée. I was his little dolly that he took everywhere. I remember him taking me on his photo shoots sitting me on his knee as he adjusted the camera. My father knew the day he was born that he would be a photographer. Even during high school, he found ways to shoot photos by contracting with the local newspapers.

Daddy, to my eyes, was a large heavy set man that in years time would look like the perfect Santa Claus. But when he graduated from high school, he was a photographer from the sticks going to art school for real photography courses. A really skinny boy with blond hair and blue eyes that would be lost in daydreams. Then it happened. The world changed. The Vietnam conflict escalated. For Daddy, it was the opportunity he was waiting for and he enlisted as a photographer.

He had luck, charm, a wonderful spirit, and was adopted by people as he took their pictures. He was later promoted and assigned to Europe. He fell in love with France, finished his tour of duty and returned to the West Coast with a heavy heart. He was about to apply to art school in Oakland, California, took one look at the long registration line, sold some acreage, and was back on the first plane he could find to France. He swore that he would never leave. He was able to study photography and stay in school as long as possible, thanks to the GI bill. Life was good. And then he met Mom, Ghislaine Aumont, a tiny green-eye blond with an explosive temper. His French was terrible, he couldn't understand a word she was saying, especially when she was mad, but Lord, was she enchanting.

I would like to say that they lived happily ever after, and they did, for many years. Then, twenty years ago, in December I got a phone call at my dorm. It was the call that caused my whole world came to a crashing halt.

Chapter 10

"Vivi, it's your mother. Something has happen. Please, pack up everything and come home."

"But Mom, I'm going to be home for Christmas. Can't it wait?" I begged.

"No, I can't talk about. Please come home. Tell your professors and come home now." Mom's voice was thick as if she had been crying.

Two days later I was in our family's doctor office. Doc Mills was talking about something to do with nerves, muscles, and a deteriorating condition. I didn't quite get it.

Later, driving home with my mother, she turned to me and said, "So Vivi, did Doctor Mills explain it all to you? Do you understand about the illness? That he's going to die."

Die. No one spoke about death. No, there was no way he could die. He was just going to deteriorate until they found the problem. My mind blanked out for several moments.

"...and we won't say anything about dying to your father. The doctor and I decided in view of your father's mental attitude on life, it would serve no purpose; he would just fall into a deep depression for years. I need your father to have a positive attitude, I can't hold up if he is depressed. Of course there's no chance of you going back to school. We have no money. You could get a job here and help out. Please, please help me," she cried.

I don't remember it but we celebrated Christmas as if dad had contracted the flu instead of being diagnosed with Lou Gehrig's disease. Mom took Daddy to France for the last hurrah, so he could see the country he grew to love so much for the last time and that they could renew their vows of love. Then my parents came home.

I got a job, and to my surprise, I liked it. Without any experience I was hired as a cartographer for an oil company. Every day I would draw maps, and each night I would go home, help my mother, talk with my father, and cry myself to sleep. Cry out of love for my father, and out of the selfish whine "it's not fair." It wasn't fair that all my friends were going on with their life. It wasn't fair that my dad got ill, wrecking my life. It just wasn't fair.

There comes a time when a person hits rock bottom, and then must realize that any salvation comes out of one's own strength. One day I had it with myself, applied to night art school in Philadelphia and was accepted. Initially, I worked days, and commuted each night to school. When our family's financial picture stabilized, I transferred to the day school and worked stocking shelves in a grocery chain. To this day, I don't know how I made it, or found the time to work on art projects but one day in May; I graduated with honors from Art College and took a job at a top graphics studio in New York City. But every night I would come home to my parents' house, to be with my mother, to talk to my father, and to cry myself to sleep.

Over a five year period, I watched my strong father shrink more and more each day until one day in April, he was no longer with us. I woke up earlier than usual, went downstairs to his room, closed his beautiful blue eyes, and kissed him good-bye.

We buried Daddy on a cold, wet April morning in the old Quaker Cemetery. After the funeral and the reception there were only two tiny blonde women in the large house. My mother started a fire in the fireplace, sat down on the sofa and stared at the fire for several minutes. Then she turned around and said to me, "Cherie, this is no way to live. You must leave now. You must make a life for yourself. "

The following week I drove out to San Francisco in Old Faithful.

Chapter 11

"So Mommy, Mommy, Mommy, is this where my granddaddy sleeps? It's so old here. Is Granddaddy with really old people, like hundreds and hundreds of years old? Are there more of us here? Will you be here? Can I climb on the fence? I like it; it's nice and so old, so old."

Gabrielle was fascinated with the Quaker cemetery and was trying to climb the stone wall. The cemetery and Meeting House were built in pre-Revolutionary days and the old stone fence had withstood the test of time from the many little children climbing. The last thing I wanted was to be the mother of the kid who brought it down, so it was time to change her activity.

"Look, Gabrielle, here is your great-grandfather Jacob and his grandfather Nathaniel. And over here are their wives, Elizabeth and Susan." I pointed out the tiny worn markers that were nestled in the green grass.

"But Mommy, are you going to be here? Where will I find you?" she said with the beginnings of a sob in her throat.

"Well, Gabrielle, I could stay here. And then you could find me with all of the rest of the family. Would you like that?"

"It won't be for a long, long time. Like a million years, will it? I like it here. It has pretty little flowers and I like the funny house. I can come and see you," she said cheering up immensely.

"If we're lucky, it won't be for a long time. Now, leave the flowers for your grandfather. He always liked the spring flowers. I'll be in the little stone house, and you're going to playschool. I'll walk you there. See, there is a nice playground with a seesaw. Let's talk to your teacher," as I walked down the gravel path and entered the one-story school house.

Gabrielle met her teacher and settled down with the preschool activities. In several minutes she made two new friends and was happily chirping away. I thanked the preschool teacher, and briskly walked back to the stone meeting house, or as Gabrielle called it, the funny house.

Meeting was beginning and I quietly sat one of the back benches. Re-acquainting myself to the surroundings, I took a deep breath and scanned the balcony.

Same old musty smell, same old wonderful building. It had been years since I have attended a Meeting. I tried it in San Francisco without great success. The San Francisco group believed in politically correct shoes with knee socks and that deodorants and soaps were chemically poisonous to the body. I was the only woman there with stockings, heels, makeup and a haircut that had been refreshed in the last five years. I never returned. Leif always thought that my Quakerness was a joke, since in his eyes, it wasn't a real religion.

There were no hymns to be sung, no basket was passed and no minister shouting down from the pulpit. But sitting here on this beautiful early May morning, I congratulated myself on finally realizing how shallow and ridiculous were my former spouse's ideas.

Oh Leif. What joy you were initially and how much pain you caused me. I was so in love with you, I fail to think about the real man. You were the most beautiful man I ever saw, tall and charming, and in the eyes of my friends, a real catch. That was what I thought marriage was about; getting a real catch. I never considered the consequences. When I first met you I couldn't believe a man with your position and beauty would even look at a woman like me. Well, it was a too beautiful day and I had no intention to waste my hour of silent meditation on you, Leif Bergstrom.

My daddy and I would to come to this old building every Sunday. Dad was a pro at silent worship. He knew which seats were draft-free and where no one would catch him napping. My job was to hit him if he started to snore. Quakers are, on a whole, a noisy bunch. During a good silent worship you could hear the organ music of stomachs, the sonorous dirge of snores, occasionally punctuated by a fart or a sniffle. I, historically, had a hard time concentrating during Meetings. Today, as usual, my mind was wandering up the stairs and to the balcony.

I cannot recall once when the balcony was open. I thought it has something to do with its age and not having sufficient funds to restore the upstairs. But I would wonder what life was like as a Quaker girl living during the Revolution and coming here on Sundays. I didn't think that this train of thought was what the Quaker Elders had in mind for silent worship but at least it kept my concentration off of the symphony that surrounded me.

Worship was over. We all began shaking hands with one another. A few faces recognized me.

"Hello there, Vivianne. It's been a while since we have seen a Bartlett. Are you here visiting?" greeted Mr. Porter, one of the Elders.

I quickly explained to Mr. Porter that I recently moved back to Princeton. Gabrielle came running up the path; school was out. I introduced Gabrielle, whom to my surprise solemnly shook hands with everyone.

"Mom, it was fun. Do you know what they have here? They have a swinging bridge. And you know what, Mom. When you cross over the swinging bridge, there is a building with a big pond and a lawn. What is it, Mommy?" asked Gabrielle.

I had forgotten. It had been so many years ago. I thought for a second about Robbie and smiled.

"Why Gabrielle, that is the back way to the Institute of Advance Study," explained Mr. Potter.

"You know, Gabrielle, we could take the back way home. And I could show you all my favorite places to explore. I would go there all the time when I was a kid with my cousin, Max."

"Come on Mommy, let's go, now. And don't start daydreaming there like you've been doing. Grandmère is coming over for dinner. I have to talk to her and it's important. I want you to make us a nice dinner. I make the table. Hurry, Mommy," demanded Gabrielle while pulling at my clothes.

Somehow, we politely said our good-byes and departed. It was a lovely walk, just the kind meant for kids, with mud puddles to avoid and new life springing up all around us. We stopped at the bridge for several minutes and watched the fish.

"I'm glad we came back to your home, Mommy. I am very glad. I like having Grandmère and Richard and Loretta and Whitney. I like it better than our old place. You like it better? We won't go back, will we, Mommy? Please can we stay? please, Mommy, please," implored Gabrielle.

"I think we'll stay for a long, long time. Did you see that fish? I think that was the biggest. I've got more to show you. Did you know that the pond has the biggest sounding frogs in the world. And there is a library, and some nice buildings and a circle of fairy trees," I whispered while pointing out my favorite spots.

I paraded my poppet all around the Institute. She was enchanted with its beauty and grace. She loved the pond, the lawn and especially the ring of trees in the front entrance. We decide that there were little trolls that came alive at night and would dance with the fairy trees by the light of a full moon.

The walk back passed quickly. Gabrielle skipped and danced her way home. When we got to the house, we were ravenous and I made Gabrielle a peanut butter and jelly sandwich. After lunch Gabrielle volunteered (surprise) to take a nap. This was a first. We went upstairs to her room; I took off her shoes and tucked her in bed.

"Don't forget, Mommy, to start dinner. I love you. Don't close the door, okay, mom, okay, okay?" whispered Gabrielle with sleepy eyes. I kissed Gabrielle on the forehead and left her room.

Downstairs, I cleaned up the kitchen from lunch and made sure that I had all the ingredients for tonight's dinner. All set, and the meal took thirty minutes to prepare. Maybe I'll bake an apple pie.

I started peeling. Funny, I showed Gabrielle the Institute, and there was one area I avoided; a magical grove of trees where I lay down with Robbie. Oh well, she would find it when her time comes. Then one day she could show the Institute to her daughter and forget to point out her own special area with her guarded secret. What a laugh, we'll all end up in the Quaker cemetery, exchanging notes on who did what and where.

Life really was a funny circle. But it took me this long to laugh.

Chapter 12

"Gabrielle, please open the door for your grandparents," I shouted from the kitchen.

Gabrielle slid off of the piano bench. She had been taking lessons from a friendly, enthusiastic lady who lived in the neighborhood. Gabrielle had been a funny kid with the piano. She never banged on the keyboard; instead made little tinkle sounds and strange tunes that she tried to sing. Maybe my mother's dream of a pianist will finally come true.

"Hi, Grandmère, hi, Papi. Mom's cooking. Guess what we are having for dessert?" chirped Gabrielle wearing her favorite plastic tiara and rain boots.

"Cookies?" asked my mother.

"Cream Puffs?" said Richard.

"Gateau?" replied my mother.

"Pizza?" retorted Richard.

"Grandpa, you're silly. No one has pizza for dessert. It's apple pie and Mommy made it. I watched."

"Zat's sounds lovely, poupée. Now where do we put our coats? I have brought a few things. And may I see the new bedroom? I hear that it is purple," requested Ghislaine.

"Mom, is it okay that Grandmère sees your room?" shouted Gabrielle.

"Sure, why don't you take them up and show them around. By the time you're through, I will be finished with the dinner and can join you. Mom, by the way, what do you and Richard want to drink?"

"A sweet vermouth for me and Richard, une bière," shouted my mother on her way up the staircase.

They didn't take as long as I expected. I guessed that the bedroom was to my mother's satisfaction; that it didn't display any latent insanity on the part of her daughter. Several minutes later my mother entered the kitchen.

"You really have a good sense of color. Have you thought about being an interior decorator? Mrs. Caruso's daughter, you know the one that married the dentist from New Brunswick, is an interior decorator and makes a good living. Did the new door cost a lot? It is a very charming bedroom. Isn't Richard a dear to help you paint?" questioned my mother in her verbal machine gun style.

I never know which of my mother's questions to answer first and which ones I should avoid. It always seemed that I was picking the wrong ones. My mother not only kept tabs on all her friends' children but had a rating system for those who had made it and those who were still floundering failures.

"Wasn't Sylvia Caruso a Moonie or something? Didn't her parents drag her away from some cult and then had to lock her up? Remember, she insisted on being naked and her parents couldn't take her anywhere. Wasn't that the story?" I replied quickly. I always made sure that Mom's paragon daughters were destroyed. "I don't know about interior decorating as a profession, Mom. Remember your friend Marthe who tried it and almost bankrupted the family with sofa purchases. And yes, it was so nice of Richard to help out. He really has been a life-saver."

"I don't know, maybe you're right." Mom looked crestfallen as I vaporized yet another virtuous daughter. Maybe I should let her win the next round. She was getting older and needed to have some fantasies to hold on to.

"Grandmère, I need to talk to you. Up here. It's important," shouted Gabrielle from her room.

My mother looked relieved. She was now on her territory with her little colonel. "Je viens, poupée," and Mom headed up to Gabrielle's room. Richard and I looked at each other knowing that the two were plotting something on my behalf. Richard decided to sneak in another beer.

Everything on my part was ready. Since the dining room wasn't finished - I hadn't yet a vision of what I wanted - we were eating in the kitchen. I just needed to unload the three bags of food that my mother had brought; she never traveled without dinner for eight. When we were younger she would only travel with dinner for four. I think it had something to do with having too many brothers and sisters in her family. *Let me see, what have we here.*

Brie, a baguette of bread, pickles, pâté, a roasted chicken (nice, we'll eat that tomorrow) and three desserts. I didn't know who the desserts were for since Mom would not eat them, and as she reminded me, I needed to watch my waistline. I guessed that Gabrielle and Richard would just have to go through a total of four desserts tonight.

"Dinner is ready," I called out to the troops.

"Coming," shouted Gabrielle, Richard and my mother in unison.

We quickly settled in to our seats and began eating. Tonight I had prepared linguine with a great sauce from sun-dried tomatoes, pesto, pine nuts, chicken, mushrooms and gorgonzola. Salad was romaine and radicchio lettuce topped with a vinaigrette. We sliced Mom's bread and drank a nice, young Beaujolais. Once everyone had decided that I cooked a passable meal, the serious looks were abandoned and the conversation continued. Gabrielle was winking at her grandmother. I awaited the next bomb.

"Vivianne, Cherie, this meal is excellent. I must say that being in California developed your cooking skills. Was this hard to make? I would like the recipe. I was talking to Richard today and saying wasn't it nice to have you and Gabrielle back. I like having my family together," said my mother in her sweetest tone. Something major was up. Mom was being incredibly sweet. She should be going for the kill about now. Mom was still talking and I quickly re-entered her conversation.

". . .and so I was at bridge playing duplicate with Inez Carlsen and guess who showed up? It was Kiki Harrington, who by the way, looks terrible from all of that Florida sun. Anyway we were talking and I told her that you moved back in to town and that you were divorced with a daughter. It seems that her son Winston married one of the Dodd girls, I think it is his third or fourth wife and they are very, very rich. Living off of the Great Road in one of those mansions. It must be her money," said my mother with a knowing eye. She continued, "So I gave her your phone number because Winston is having a party in two weeks and Kiki says he'd love to have you. It should be fun and maybe you could meet someone nice. After all, I must say that you are still a pretty woman and you haven't wrinkled like some of the women in your age group."

Well my goose was cooked. Winston was one of the most good nature, good-looking, sweet idiots that I have ever met, and would probably love to invite me at his party. Knowing him, he'd do his best to introduce me to all the eligible (under seventy, not currently married, semi-certifiable alcoholic) males. Anyway, it was about time that I presented myself to the Princeton society.

"Oh, Mom, thanks. That's awfully nice of you. It should be fun seeing Winston and his new wife. He was such a sweetheart when we were kids," I smiled at her.

Silence. My mother was in shock. I had allowed her to win and she was missing the verbal argument that should occur. She smiled back at me.

Dinner continued without any new disruption. I served coffee in the living room and Gabrielle played her new piece on the piano. At nine, Mom and Richard bided their adieus, collected their coats and disappeared in the Cadillac. Gabrielle helped me clean up the table and placed the dishes in the dishwasher. I looked down on my poppet. She was concentrating on some thought and nodding her little head.

"Pumpkin, what did you and Grandmère talk about?" I asked Gabrielle.

"Oh, about things and Christmas," replied Gabrielle in a thoughtful manner.

"What about things and Christmas?" I replied wondering what really was on her mind.

"Well I told her what I wanted for Christmas. Grandmère said Santa will try to get it for me."

"What do you want for Christmas," I gently asked her. Once again this was sounding dangerous.

"I want a Daddy for Christmas, Mommy. I want a Daddy."

Chapter 13

For a moment I was taken aback by her request. “Wait a second young lady, what do you mean by that?”

“Can I have a cookie?" begged my little poppet.

“First explain to me why you want a daddy. You’ve never had one and most of your friends don’t have them either. So why this idea?” I asked totally confused where this latest out-of-the-blue idea was hatched.

“Mom, we need a daddy. Grandmère says that all women need a husband. It’s time for a baby. Grandmère says we should have one. She says I need a brother or sister. Grandmère says that you need a husband. Grandmère had a talk with me and said that life was too hard for you when I was a baby. She says a husband makes it much better. Everyone needs a daddy, and all the kids in the books have daddies, and we need one. So can I have a cookie?” demanded the mini-admiral of the house.

“Sure,” I mumbled, somewhat reeling from Gabrielle’s great plan for our future and amazed she could string so many sentences together. So that was what they were plotting. Maybe I should put an ad in the personal section of the paper. Forget it. If I even mention that crazed idea, the two schemers would pounce.

“Mommy, telephone.” Gabrielle tried to talk but was hampered by a mouth full of cookies.

Still numb, I picked up the receiver. “Hello, Vivianne speaking.”

“Vivi, it’s Winston. Long time, no see. Mother says that you are back in town. Seems that the old crowd is returning, everyone getting divorced elsewhere and coming home to settle down. So how are you getting along?” queried Winston, sounding still like the tennis pro I knew fifteen years ago.

"Fine, it's a little strange living in Princeton again, but I like it. Gabrielle, my four year old just loves the town and even the change of climate. The one who likes it the best is Mom. Gabrielle and Mom have a real tight relationship." I admitted to Winston on the phone.

"And what's his name, your ex, Brook?" asked Winston cautiously.

"Leif," I said with sigh.

"So he isn't having a fit that his daughter is three thousand miles away. Not screaming about custody rights of the father?" asked Winston.

"No, we split up before her birth. He wants nothing to do with her which suits me fine. I haven't heard from him for close to five years," I admitted.

"Well enough of the past. Your mom probably got you up to date on my activities. It's now the fourth wife, three kids, mucho kiddy cash, no alimony payments, and one loyal golden retriever. Anyway, we are throwing a party next Saturday and I would be greatly honored if my old childhood friend that I offered to seduce in her nubile teens, would bestow us mere mortals, the presence of her company," said Winston ending his invitation with a very false British accent.

"Oh Winston, you're always are a love. I would be most honored. So, what time, what place and most important to womankind, what to wear," I asked hoping that it was not some formal event.

"Party is at eight. We live off of the Great Road, do you remember the old Bennett estate? Good, we are on the left with all the cars in the driveway. And don't take out the tiara, we are celebrating Ginny's cousin's return to Princeton. She just got rid of husband Numero Cinco, a person with an uncanny resemblance to a halibut. Okay, got to go, the dog just got loose in the house and there will be hell to pay. Saturday at eight. Okay?" Winston said in his normal voice.

"See you then. Thanks, Winston. Bye. And thanks for the invite," I replied thinking that the event could be fun. After all, everyone seemed to be divorced at least three times, making my disaster positively tame.

"Who was that, Mom?" asked Gabrielle with cookie crumbs all over her mouth and a near-empty box in her hands.

"Winston Harrington, who, like a good little boy, invited me to his party in two weeks. Would you like to spend that night at your Grandmère's?" I asked knowing all well the answer.

"Yes, yes, yes. What are you going to wear, Mommy. Don't wear those leggings. Wear a dress. There is a pretty one in a store window in town. It's pink. Please let's go see it. Now, Mommy, now," begged Gabrielle with little suns in her eyes.

"Kiddo, it's late. Why don't you and I go shopping for my dress after Loretta's tomorrow and I promise, no leggings," I vowed.

"Why can't we do it tomorrow morning, Mommy," pouted Gabrielle.

"Because my agent is coming to see the new fairy alphabet book. It is going to be boring adult talk. So why don't you have a nice time with Whitney and then we can go shopping," I replied.

"All right Mom. But remember, you promised."

"I know. Now off you go to bed. Get your pajamas on and I will come up and read you a book."

"Rapunzel."

"Fine, now get going."

Gabrielle ran up the stairs and into her bedroom. I stared out of the kitchen into the backyard. It was a warm May evening, and the garden was in full bloom. I turned on the lights to gain new appreciation of our catalog-ordering folly and walked out into the garden. What a beautiful place this will be in five years. Although the plantings and the landscaping we worked on in early spring are new and will take several years to mature and blend, it will be beautiful for the summer. The wisteria arbor that took us hours to trim and clean up, had set out its bunches of flowers and will bloom in three weeks. There will be a soft purple snowfall of petals for days and the scent will waft in the breeze. The pink magnolia that needed a severe pruning, will soon show its tulip-like flowers. All of the roses that had been newly planted were sending strong shoots with buds. The irises, tulips and daffodils were popping up in elegant disarray, and best of all, the new grass was coming up thru the soil.

The night air smelled of spring and the fresh rains. Soon it would be summer bringing the muggy air and its sensual fragrance. No longer will my garden be shy with buds peeping up and delicate blooms of pastel colors. Summer would bring the hoyden spirit to the garden, the riot of color and fragrance, pastels and rain scent. I'd like a dress of my garden but they were usually frumpy and old-ladyish. Well, we would soon see what is in town. Princeton was never known for its fashion sense, more like a haven for Lilly Pulitzer dresses and Brooks Brothers shirts. Thank heavens or I'd really be in a pickle, the woman who lived in sweatshirts and leggings.

"Mommy, I'm ready. Read me my story, please?" begged Gabrielle from her bedroom window.

"Okay, sweetheart. I'm coming. Did you know that the Japanese irises that we planted are going to bloom soon?" I replied still under the spell of the flowers.

"Oh Mommy. Get out of the garden. I want my story, please, please, please." I quickly went inside and up the stairs to Gabrielle's room. Gabrielle was in bed with her book, sitting up and smiling.

"See, Mom. Tomorrow we'll get you a nice dress and stuff. Then you'll go to the party, look beautiful, and find me a daddy. It's easy, Mom. Now can you read me Rapunzel." Gabrielle was looking angelic but I wasn't fooled for a minute.

"You know to find a daddy, isn't that easy. There are lots of people in the world but to find a good daddy that we love takes a long time. Remember Beauty and the Beast? Remember how long it took for Belle to fall in love with the beast? Everything takes time, honey. We need to make sure that we get the best daddy in the world, so don't hold your hopes up too high that I'll find one at the party. Is that clear?"

"Yeah, but I'm going to be five soon, and I can't wait forever. I am getting old, you know. So work on it Mommy. Here's Rapunzel," and Gabrielle started wiggling to find a comfy spot in her bed.

I took the book from her. I must have read this story a hundred times, but she was still enchanted with "Rapunzel, Rapunzel, let down your golden hair." Ten minutes later, we finished the story and I kissed my wunderkid goodnight.

Quietly, I rose from her bed, turned out her light and left the door open. Tempted to go back outside and sit under the rose arbor, I walked out the kitchen door on to the terrace. It would be lovely to read out here in the night during the summer, if the mosquitoes could be controlled. Perhaps I could get a special light or high intensity candles. I stepped down from the terrace, on to the lawn and cross over to the wood chair in the arbor. Sitting down, I reviewed Gabrielle's request.

Such a mess I made out of my marriage, such a mess. How could I trust myself not to make the same mistake. I was very reluctant to find a new partner. Our life was settled here, I liked my work and myself. All I needed was another person intruding on my space, demanding time and devotion from me. I did that once, and it was misery.

It really wasn't all Leif's fault. He was only being true to himself. Only I was not able to get a clear read of his personality and thought him to be someone else. Only after a year into our marriage, could I see clearly that I had misread his character.

Was I too lazy to get a divorce or too proud, or did I think that the situation would improve? Maybe I thought that with patience and love, Leif would become that man that I had once seen for a brief period. Maybe having a family would straighten things out. I had a terrible strength and at the same times, it became a weakness. Loyalty and stubbornness. I didn't think that I had a good reason to let go of Leif, to let go of my wedding vows.

It really was funny in a way. All of this never would have happened if Lena hadn't come out to California. Lena, in her racquetball craze, making me go out to buy a racket and sign up for a court at the club. Oh Lena, sometimes I could kill you.

Chapter 14

"Hurry up, Vivi. We only have forty-five minutes to play," commanded Lena.

Lena decided to give me a racquetball lesson. Since I was a tennis player, the learning period should be short. The real reason for racquetball was that Lena said it was a great way to met eligible men and since I was living in San Francisco and working in an art environment, I needed to meet straight men with real professions.

Lena was always a scream. Not only had she picked out the proper racquetball club, but she had also orchestrated our apparel, so it appeared that we were born to the racquetball milieu. All I knew is that I hated indoor sports. It was always humid in the clubs and I would start to sweat the moment I opened the locker.

About a week ago, I picked up Lena at the airport. Since then, she had taken on the task of improving my social life, which although had been fun, was non-constructive in the aim of meeting Mr. Right. If she had her way, she'd get me out of the design field, too many gay men. Banking would be her top choice.

I liked my job. I worked for a top graphic design firm which provided me with stimulating challenges. The people treated each other as human beings, and the money was good. Every once in a while, when major projects approached deadline, the entire place went hyper-nuts, but otherwise it was great. Also, I was allowed to work at home. The creative mind was revered and management was sympathetic to our demanding and often childish needs.

Lena didn't care about these issues. She also didn't care for my apartment which was situated on Russian Hill. "Too many old people. You should find a better place in the Marina or Pacific Heights. Much better address," she informed me after surveying the area. I happened to love my place. It took me six months to find it and I had been living there for four years. It was a set of one-bedroom townhouses set away from the street. There was a lovely garden in front of my living room and the light streamed in all day long. To top it off, the rent was reasonable, no small feat in San Francisco.

So here we were, in another smelly locker room, changing our clothes. I slipped into a white Ralph Lauren polo shirt and a pair of shorts. Lena was already getting her white sneakers on.

“Now, don’t worry about looking stupid. Everyone has to learn sometime. Just don’t bash the racket on me. Also it’s better to lose the ball than to make an obscene lunge, missing it and falling. And most of all, don’t swear, like you do in tennis, Vivi. I heard you say “Shit” whenever Bobby Cairn would miss the ball,” reprimanded Lena.

At this point, if I was in my right mind, I’d leave. But I would lose all those years of teenage bonding, and the wrath of Princeton for being a bad hostess.

“All right Lena, I’ll be good. Really, I’ll try.” I finished tying my shoes, grabbed the racket, closed the locker door, and we were out into the new world of racquetball.

After the first five minutes of coaching, I got the hang of the game, and gave Lena, who was not a good tennis player, a strenuous aerobic work-out. In fact she was losing her temper and began, to herself, mumbling dire epitaphs.

"Vivi, it's only a game, take it easy. Hey, no fair placing the ball in the corner,” begged Lena. “You bitch, you know that I don’t like those drop shots.”

This game wasn’t bad after all and it was the first time that I've seen Lena break out in a sweat. Lena was trying not to look like a complete idiot on the court floor, since there were a few men looking down on us.

Time was up. Lena was looking relieved. We exited the court and two men rushed into our newly vacated space.

"I'm thirsty. Let's go to the water tank and get a glass," murmured Lena, totally red-faced. We walked over to the tank, grabbed some cups, and poured ourselves some water. Lena threw herself to the wall and sank down into the carpeting.

"Sorry for eavesdropping. You're a real good player for a new recruit," said a deep masculine voice.

I turned around. Standing in front of me was the most handsome man that I had ever seen. Tall, blond, green-eyed, chiseled face with the perfect California tan. I was awestruck but manage to reply. "Beginners luck. It will probably never happen again."

"Listen, my partner is late. You want to go hit some balls with me while your friend gets her breathe back?" Even his voice was beautiful. I looked at Lena, who gave me the big wink.

"Sure that will be great. I'm Vivi Bartlett, this is my friend Lena visiting from New York, and you are...?

"Leif. Leif Bergstrom At your service. We're at court fourteen. I'll bring her back in one piece, Lena. Thanks," and he threw Lena the perfect white tooth smile.

Funny, his name was Leif and I was trembling like a leaf. I couldn't even manage to string a sentence together. But at least my coordination was holding and I was not playing badly. Leif was being polite and placing well-behaved balls to me.

"You know Vivi, if you have evil thoughts while playing racquetball, the little blue ball hears them and will turn against you." Leif smiled at me and I was lost, like the moth to the light. We played a bit more, his partner appeared, introductions were made, and I began to exit the court.

“Vivi, if you and Lena are free, we invite you for dinner after our game. We are both single, unattached and will fax our resumes to your parents for approval,” said Leif and flashed again his killer smile.

Lord, we were free, since I couldn’t remember anything at all. “Great, we’ll meet you at the club’s bar in an hour. See you then.”

I found Lena, whose color had returned back to normal, and explained tonight’s plan. She grabbed my hand, dragged me to the lockers and threw us into the sauna.

“I want to know everything, everything. And what does his friend look like?” demanded Lena while dripping sweat from her nose

I went over my conversation with Leif and apologized for not noticing his friend since I was so blinded by Leif’s light. Lena hung on to every word and used her Gestapo-questioning technique when she was not adequately satisfied with my descriptions. Between the questioning and staying too long in the sauna, I was limp. We quickly took our showers. The questioning continued once we began to dry off and dress.

“Listen, Lena, you’ll meet them together in fifteen minutes. Then you can interrogate them to your heart’s content.” I was close to my interrogation threshold.

“Listen, my fine friend, if it wasn’t for me you probably wouldn’t have a date for six months. See what your old friend can do. And he is gorgeous. You need me and don’t forget it. Now remember to behave. And above all things, don’t drink too much. With all the exercise and sweating we’ve done, we’ll be drunk on the second glass of wine.”

"Maybe the guys are counting on that. You know, we go play racquetball to meet men, they go play racquetball to get easy and cheap maidens,” I retorted.

“Oh Vivi, you’re terrible, you’ll never change and I love you. Now don’t make me laugh at the dinner table. Either I’ll choke or the water will go up through my nose like the last time," she begged.

“Lena, it was so funny to watch. You with that pompous asshole. You should have seen his face,” I reminded her.

“Oh shut up, you nut. Now let’s go check out these guys. We’ve kept them waiting enough.”

Chapter 15

"Hi Vivi, hi Lena. This is Tom Gorman, my racquetball partner. Tom's from back east," said Mr. Perfect Dream Date.

We all politely made our introductions. This time I got a good look at Tom. Tall, dark hair, on the serious side. Nice looking. Lena seemed pleased.

"Hope no one minds but I took it upon myself to make reservations at Baytown Diner. It is only a few blocks over and by the time we walk over, they'll be ready to serve us. Is that okay?" Okay by me, Baytown Diner just happened to be the hot restaurant of the month. How on earth was Leif able to get reservations?

"...the chef there, Raoul, is a friend of mine so they can usually squeeze me in. By the way, if you like carpaccio, it's excellent," offered Mr. Incredibly Good Looking I Can't Believe My Luck.

Okay Vivi, stay alert. Lena was probably already calculating their gross value, or net worth, or some crazy financial analysis. The walk was brisk with little conversation. Baytown Diner already had a line of people standing around outside waiting for tables. Leif, the Sun God, made his way to the top of the line, gave his name and waved for us to follow. Lena and I were impressed and love being glared at by the unwashed hordes. We were quickly seated by a window and gave the waiter our order of alcoholic beverages.

"So Tom, are you visiting or here permanently?" Lena began the conversation in order to economize social interaction time. If she decided that the date was a loser she would shortly come down with the Lena Flu.

"I'm here for a couple weeks and then fly back to Boston. The bank that I work for is backing one of Leif's development projects. So I am here to check things out and make sure that the project is running smoothly," said Tom with a nice strong voice.

Lena's little brain started to whirl. "Oh really, I handle public relations for two banks in Boston, First Federal and Harbor Bank and Trust."

"I work for First Federal. The real estate section. So you're in PR. Do you know Adele Richardson at the Hancock Group ...... "

It seemed that Lena and Richard were chatting happily with each other, discovering mutual acquaintances and a few friends. In fact with all the people they had in common, they should have met each other years ago. I hadn't been mute during this period of time and had conducted my own investigation. Leif, who originally hailed from Chicago, was an architect with his own firm. He attended all the right schools, worked for several name architects, and after several requests, decided to settle down in the Bay area five years ago. He said that he was lucky, got some good breaks, and his firm was doing well. In turn he found out highlights of my life and seemed impressed that I was working for Walkins Associates. In fact everyone at our table was impressed and pleased with each other. What a splendid group we were and the wine was helping. I was able to converse and not drop my jaw staring at Leif, who got more gorgeous by the minute. I couldn't believe that this was real, and I kept pinching myself. I was a good-looking woman, but this guy was something else. Why me? *Oh Vivi, give it a rest, why not me?*

"There is a great little jazz quartet playing at the Fairmont. Is anyone interested'?" asked Tom.

"Oh Vivi and I love jazz," purred Lena already on her third glass of wine. "We're game." Lena hated jazz.

Tom and Leif handled the bill, which Lena, who flunked math for two years, had already calculated the tab plus tip. We piled into a cab and headed off to the Fairmont. I almost died from exquisite agony sitting next to Leif. Oh the Gods must have been pleased with some act from my past to allow me this evening. More conversation passed with deep meaningful eye contact. Bliss.

The jazz was great. Tom had great taste. In fact he was pretty great, Lena was great, Vivi was great and Leif was magnificent. A glass of Grand Marnier please.

"I hate to be the evening's wet blanket, but I need to get going soon. I've a corporate identity presentation for tomorrow morning with the client from hell." My mother always told me to leave some mystery for tomorrow and make a graceful exit before one turned into a pumpkin.

"Vivi is right, it is a bit after twelve. Listen why don't we drop you off at your place and then Tom and I can head to his hotel."

"Fine with me. Come Lena, time to get up." I received a big glare from Lena who didn't appreciate my graceful exit effort.

Once again, Tom and Leif took care of the tab and we piled into a cab similar to the first one, who knows maybe it was the same cab. I wasn't looking. And talk about looking, the eye contact became more meaningful and deeper. Finally, we arrived at my place.

"Listen Vivi, it has been a wonderful night. I can't believe our luck meeting at the club. I know you have a rough day tomorrow so I'll make this quick." Leif then kissed me and my insides exploded. The stars came out and some- where in the background, I heard the end of the 1812 Overture. Being hit like a ton of bricks is was understatement. I was enchanted, beguiled, bewildered, enraptured and totally in love with Leif. And like the poor moth, I was captured by his flame, mesmerized by his beauty, without a chance in the world of escaping without serious injury.

Good Lord. The human hurricane left and I was standing on the curb. I entered the apartment. Lena talked to me as we got ready for bed, but I had no idea what she was saying. I tried to go to sleep. The dreams were wonderful but strange.

The next morning, when I went out to get the morning paper, I found a delivery box of beautiful ice pink roses. The card read "Please say you are free tonight. Call 436-4839. Love - Leif B."

A magical time in my life. *All right Vivi, enough of this time-traveling.* At least there were some good memories. It was time to heal the wound in my life. Maybe Winston's party was happening at a perfect time. I could always use Max's advice to get over a man. Max would always say "Love the one you are with, you know, fuck someone new." Sounds a little drastic, but it was time for another man to enter my life.

I left the garden, entered the kitchen, and turned out the downstairs lights. Who knows what the great plan of life had in store for me. It certainly was a mystery to me. But what ever happened in the past, I had this wonderful child and home.

Sometimes I am the luckiest woman in the world.

Chapter 16

"Over here, Mommy. The store is over here. See the dress in the window. It's beautiful, really beautiful. Just like Cinderella," yelled Gabrielle down the street. Unfortunately Gabrielle had inherited from my mother a voice that carries. Today, it could be heard all over Nassau Street.

Much to Gabrielle's disgust, I was not scurrying over to the window. I walked pass the smoke shop, the gourmet store and the dry goods emporium. Gabrielle was impatiently waiting for me in front of the tasteful ladies shop.

The dress was ghastly, on the same scale as the damn puppy painting. I needed to humor her and let her see the error of bad taste. We entered the store and confronted an elegantly-dressed saleswoman.

"Excuse me, I need a dress to attend a garden party, and my daughter thought that I should try on the dress in the window," I said in a half-hearten tone.

"Certainly, I'll bring you one in your size. May I also suggest some alternative selections." The saleswoman was no fool and had recognized that the pink lace vision in the window would be a disaster on me. Gabrielle and I slipped into the dressing room. I began to strip off my leggings and caught a glance of myself in the mirror.

"Mom, you still have fat on your tummy." Gabrielle pointed at my pooch. Thanks kid, that really helped my wavering self-esteem. I was about ready to put my sweats back on when the saleswoman handed me the disaster through the dressing room curtain.

"Thank you, Gabrielle. Any more gracious comments on my physical being?" I unzipped the back and eased into the pink horror.

"No, you look better than before. Boy, Mommy. That dress looks ugly on you. Maybe you better try on the other dresses the lady brought," remarked Little Miss Tactful.

I looked at myself in the mirror. Ugly was not the word. It was truly hideous, a cupcake lace nightmare. The color had turned my skin sallow and the lace overcame my body and face. Immediately I took off the offensive number, and carefully placed it back on the hanger. Gabrielle stuck her tongue out at the dress. I scanned the saleswoman's choices. Excellent. One dress was white pique, fitted bodice, tight waist with a slightly gathered skirt. The second dress was a dream, my garden dress. I look at the prices and gulp. Lord, it has been a while since I went shopping in a real store. Well, I've earned the pleasure to splurge on a few nice frocks.

I tried on both dresses. Gabrielle gave me the okay on both. Actually she was making happy yippidy-yay sounds, which I presumed were a sign of approval. I slipped back into my old leggings and top, grabbed the two dresses and left the dressing room.

"How were the dresses?" asked the saleswoman.

"Excellent, you read my mind. We'll take both," I replied with a smile.

"Mommy looks really good in them. Really really good," chimed in Gabrielle.

"Is there anything else I can help you with, some shoes, stockings, a slip?"

"Actually, it seems that I've lost a lot of weight and none of my old stuff fits. And, I would like some nice sandals to go with the dresses," I said.

I liked making people happy. The saleswoman was happy with thoughts of a nice commission check. I was happy for the clothes looked great, and Gabrielle was happy that her mom would look nice. Why not make everyone a little happier.

"Listen, I'm an illustrator, and I work mostly in comfortable casual clothes. Most of them are ready for the rag box. Can you make any suggestions? I need about a seven day change of clothing and your taste has been on target," I said hoping that our sales woman understood the concept of casual.

"Oh great, Mommy, new clothes. Mom, I am going to look at the stuffed animals while you try on stuff. Okay?" chirped Gabrielle.

"Don't worry, she'll be fine. I'll have Maryanne come out from the back and watch her for you," said the saleswoman.

She went to the racks, pulled out some outfits and sent me into the dressing room with them. Then she disappeared off into the hinterland of a backroom. A few minutes later she returned with more clothes and hung them in my dressing room.

"After this we'll work on shoes, stockings and your jacket needs to be replaced," she said in a soft but firm voice. "By the way, I'm Sylvia Garth."

"Hi, I'm Vivianne Bergstrom. Thanks for doing such a great job. I always try to avoid shopping for myself. It's not one of my strengths." The clothes were a perfect fit and choice. The prices were somewhat imaginative for a woman who frequented consignment shops and flea markets.

"My pleasure. It's not often that I get to build a wardrobe for someone. It's a lot of fun for me. Well, let me take all these items, total your bill, and box everything. Why don't you join Gabrielle since it will take a bit of time. How would you like to pay?" she asked.

"I have regular local checks or charge. Which do you prefer?"

"Local checks are fine. I'll call you when we're ready."

Ten minutes later, Gabrielle and I walked out of the store. The bill was on the order of a mini-Pretty Woman scene. I loved every moment of shopping since Sylvia made the event pleasurable. It was the first time in years that I've spent a sizable amount of money on myself and thought it was about time. Gabrielle brought me back down from my euphoric cloud.

"Mom, can we see the puppies?" she asked using her "pretty, pretty, please" voice.

"Okay, pumpkin, but let's grab lunch first. I know, we'll have lunch outside on the terrace at the Nassau Inn. They use to make the best hot fudge sundaes," I answered.

"Okay Mommy, I'll race you."

Gabrielle ran down to the end of the sidewalk and waited for me. When I met her she was jumping up and down.

"I win, I win," she yelled.

"You are so fast, my racing champion. Now hold my hand and let's cross the street." We crossed the narrow little street, and strolled to the main entrance of the inn. Gabrielle had never been here, so I pointed out the highlights. She loved the enormity of the inn but was not keen on Norman Rockwell's painting of George Washington crossing the Delaware.

"Mommy, I am hungry. Can we eat, now?" asked Gabrielle using hushed tones.

"Can you tell the lady at the desk that we'd like a table for two on the terrace?" I replied.

Gabrielle handled herself very well, and we were immediately seated at a table with a green striped umbrella.

"What would you like to eat?" I asked taking a look at the pool area.

"French fries, chicken, French fries.

The waitress approached us. "Hi, what will it be today?"

"My daughter and I will split a chicken in a basket with an extra order of French fries, one lemonade, one ice tea, and for dessert we'd like to share a hot fudge sundae," I said to the assenting nods of Gabrielle.

"Great, that will be ready in a few minutes. Thank you."

Gabrielle chatted happily away about Whitney, Snow White, wicked stepmothers, and my new clothes. The hot fudge sundae was a big hit and of course, she got to eat the cherry. I cherished these moments since I knew that if she was a normal girl, she would hate me once she turned thirteen. I wondered what I would be doing then.

I paid the bill and we went to see the revolting puppies. We approached the art gallery. The puppies were gone from their spot in the window. Gabrielle was upset, her bottom lip was beginning to quiver. Oh please, oh please God, let them be sold.

"Pumpkin, let's go inside and ask someone about the puppies," I said using my most optimistic voice.

We entered the store and wandered through multitude of art and casually placed bibelots. I spied the owner in the back, grabbed Gabrielle by the hand, and marched over to him.

"Excuse me, but we were wondering if you still had the painting that had been hanging in the window. You know, the one with puppies playing in a basket." Gabrielle saddled up closer to me to hear the owner's response.

"I am sorry. They were sold yesterday. Weren't they lovely? Would you like to look at other puppies," suggested the owner.

"No," said Gabrielle squeezing out a few fat tears. "I wanted only those puppies."

"They went to a very nice home. I think that they will be very happy there," said the owner in a comforting tone.

"Happy? I want them to be happy. But I am very sad. Mommy, maybe the puppies will come back for my birthday. Do you think so, Mommy`?" A stream of tears came down Gabrielle's face.

"Maybe, perhaps something special will happen on your birthday. Let's go home now sweetheart and why don't we draw the puppies," I said holding Gabrielle's arm.

"Okay, Mommy. But I am so sad. No puppies."

I thanked the owner as we left the shop. We walked down the street to Old Faithful, patiently waiting for us in the parking lot. Gabrielle's crying jag was almost over. I could hear her sniffling in her kiddy seat.

I didn't think that I heard the last of the puppy story. I had better be really lucky and think of something brilliant for her birthday or I was deep muck. Meanwhile, I was the proud possessor of a first class wardrobe. Maybe I would let the receipt lie around for my mother's sharp eyes. The tut-tutting would be excellent. The dresses were lovely, and my new Italian sandals were just exquisite. How about a manicure before the party? Nice idea. It wouldn't be overkill. This party talk was getting me giddy and excited. Maybe, I would even stop being mad about Leif. Now that would be really funny.

We turned down our street and into our driveway. The elms were fully leafed out and our house looked warm and friendly. I was so glad to be back home.

Chapter 17

"...so Winston supposedly was caught, pants off, the whole nine yards, with Tabby Dodd by Philip. Can you image, finding Winston in your bed. Actually, can you image finding Tabby in your sheets? I never understood what he saw in Tabby. She always reminded me of an ugly red cat; flat face, nasty yellow eyes and —. Oh my God. Look who got out of that car. Haven't seen her in years. Sheila, isn't that Vivi. You know. Vivi what's her name. She use to be Vivi Bartlett, then married some guy in California. Got divorced. Very messy I heard. Supposed to be some artist or designer. Probably back home looking for a husband. A rich one. Can't have too much money, I mean look at that old car."

I walked up the stone path. Nice evening for a party. Maybe someone would kiss me tonight. Goodness, it was Barbara and Sheila, the Gorgons protecting the entrance. *Okay, Vivi, en guarde.*

"Hello, Barbara. Hi, Sheila. It's Vivi, Vivi Bergstrom. Long time. Winston's new home looks lovely. I heard he got married to Tabby Dodd. So how are you doing?"

Yikes, pounce on me immediately, why don't you. The two cats started to update me on all forms of irrelevant gossip. Linda with Michael, Michael with Lisette, Charlie and Cosi, Cosi and Cathy (who is Cathy?) and it went on and on. I had better get moving before they decided to put their claws into me.

"Well, this is fun. I haven't been back for fifteen years. It seems that although nothing feels the same, it's still the same place with the same people. Anyway, got to run. Must be a polite guest and say hello to Winston. See you in a bit. Ciao," I said while taking advantage from a break in the conversation.

I left the two pussies to chat and chew over the tidbit of my re-entry in to Princeton society. Old age was not treating them kindly, their faces were turning into stone. *Oh, Vivi, you are starting to sound like them.*

Winston had a lovely house. Unfortunately, I couldn't take it all in because of the many people attending this event. Must be several hundred. I elbowed my way through the crowd in the living room. Winston must be near the bar. Right on target, there he was pouring the champagne.

"Vivi, Vivi, come here and give me a big hug. So what do you think of the place? Nice! Tabby-girl has done a great job. There is not a chair in the living room that I am allowed to sit on. Not that they're comfortable. But here you are. You look lovely. Some of the gang is really going to be mad when they see you. You haven't aged at all. So who have you met so far?" asked Winston looking like a large blond bear.

"Barbara and Sheila. Winston, I love this house. For all your teasing it is wonderful. By the way, Mom says hello," I said taking a seat near the bar.

"Did Barbara and Sheila get you up caught up on my past indiscretions. Tabby girl has me on a tight leash now. So I can't take advantage of you as lovely as you are. Who will be the lucky man?" said Winston winking.

"Oh Winston, you're still a horrible flirt. Give me a chance. This is the first time I've been out since the divorce. I've been really gun-shy. I'm lucky if I can manage to string a sentence together when talking to someone of the opposite sex."

"Ah, Vivi, the most gorgeous woman here and still knocking yourself down. Well, I will protect you from yourself. Hey, Woody, over here. This is some you should meet," said Winston while preparing a tray of glasses filled with mojitos.

Winston, you old dependable yenta. There was no possible way with Winston, that I would marry someone that was not from Princeton. Winston and my mother would make sure that didn't happen. It was probably for the better. Woody came over, tall, bespectacled and with graying hair.

Presentations were made and conversation began. Winston politely edged out, and old acquaintances entered our group. By the time I made it to the kitchen, I had re-met many faces that I swear I never knew before. We were all great friends and I was pleased with myself with the ease that I was circulating.

“Hey Vi, how’s the house,” piped up a new voice.

I turn around and it was Tuesday McKinley, my realtor. “Oh it’s lovely, and I enjoy working on it. You should come over and see it. It really is a different house than the one I bought. What’s new with you?” I asked.

“Business is okay. I could use a few more clients like you, paying in cash. Talking about money, do you know what’s being said about you? It really is a pisser,” said Tuesday in a conspiratorial voice.

"What’s being said? Spill the beans. I’m as curious and egotistical as the next person,” I said somewhat amused.

"Well, the talk is that you’re divorced from some Swede; that you’re penniless, and that you’re on the man-hunt for a very rich one. It’s your car. When you came up in it, everyone naturally assumed that you’re broke. Especially since you’re an artist. Do you want me to tell them that you bought your house with cash? I’d love to see their faces when they hear that Vivi Bergstrom bought a house in the old Hun School area for cash. Please Vivi, I’m dying to do it," said Tuesday with a grin.

“No way, Tues. It’s best that they think that I’m broke. After all, we don’t want any fortune hunters after my gold, do we? Anyway, kidding aside, I want to thank you again for doing such a great job for putting the house deal together. I know I gave you little time, and I’m really thrilled with the place.”

"Trying to get off the subject, Vivi? Anyway, I'll protect your secret. But it really is funny. Penniless, what a joke. And about the house. The pleasure was mine. It was the fantasy deal of the year. Closing and cash in ten days. I loved it. Listen, I'll drop by soon. I'd love to see what you've done with the old place. Oh, there's Johnny. Looks like he wants to leave. Must have run into his ex-wife. I'll give you a call. And give my love to Gabrielle," said Tuesday while she quickly joined her husband and headed out of Winston's house.

I looked out of the kitchen window and saw the swimming pool. It looked enticing just to sit nearby. I grabbed my wine glass, exited through the sliding doors and walked over to the pool.

It was a glorious June night. The mosquitoes weren't yet ready to pounce on the occasional night stroller. The air was calm and clear with a hint of humidity. Fireflies were everywhere, twinkling in the dark and above the swimming pool. I took a seat in a lounge chair close the pool and closed my eyes for a few minutes. I remember being in my late teens and going to parties in homes like this.

There'd often be parents, with their own group of friends, and us kids, waiting for some excuse to go swimming. Usually the parties were in July and August, when the heat and humidity were most oppressive. Around eleven in the evening, one boy would throw another boy in the pool, and then the party would really begin. We would come home afterward, around two in the morning, soaking wet. Our parents shaking their heads in disgust of our wanton behavior. I wonder if someone will be thrown in this lovely water tonight.

"Vivi? Vivi Bartlett?"

I was awaken from my memories by a deep, pleasant, male voice. I opened my eyes. It was hard to see the man with the voice. There was a torchière in my line of sight and the light was in my eyes. I sat up straighter. Good heavens, it was James Greenwood.

Stud muffin of my Spanish class. I sat behind him and tried to concentrate on my lesson. Concentration was useless since I had a mad crush for the back of his neck. Actually, the mad crush was for all of him, but all I would see from my seat was the back of his neck. It was in great vain. He never saw me in high school. I was a non- existent geekette while James spent his junior and senior years going steady with a tall brunette cheer leader. I always felt that I was privilege to have my crush and to be able to gaze upon this immortal of physical perfection.

Life got more and more amazing. James Greenwood spoke with me? Will my heart palpitate as it once did during Spanish Class? Or will he bore me with his marital or prostate problems? This was such fun. I was so glad that I came to the party.

Chapter 18

“The name is Bergstrom now.” I replied. “How are you, James. I haven’t seen you since high school. What are you up to?”

"Oh, I’m living in town and have my own law firm. And you?

I’ve returned from California with my daughter, Gabrielle. My mother is getting older and Princeton is a nice town to raise kids. Nothing very exciting. So catch me up on your life,” I asked.

“Let me see, I’m divorced with two kids, who I never see due to their mother’s incessant need to travel to Palm Beach and the Riviera. I worked in New York for years, got tired of competing for partnerships at a prestigious law firm, and moved back here. Life’s been great being back in Princeton. I like the work and I can get away on holidays and weekends. Got a nice ski place in Vermont and a house in town.” James took the seat next to me.

“Congratulations. I just moved back on a whim about six months ago. My daughter loves it here. I’m doing art work which keeps me busy. Illustrating children’s books and stuff like that,” I said noticing his maturing facial lines and nice graying hair.

“Heard you got out of a terrible marriage. Your mother, like the rest of the mothers, has kept the bridge club informed of your activities.” James smiled at me. Good teeth.

Oh no, that means everyone at this party had the play-by-play interpretation of my divorce. Also that they probably believed in the Tin Cup Mary story. I was getting cooked about this. *Get a grip*. Everyone had been too busy with their own divorces to remember much about mine. And being thought as being poor could be beneficial. I thought my face was turning red, but hopefully, it was too dark for James to see.

“James, I am surprised that after what you’ve heard about me, you’re willing to speak to me,” I said in a teasing manner.

“Now Vivi, money isn’t everything. For most of the women here, cleaning out their former husbands with settlements and alimony payments has been a duty and something to keep score with the other divorcees. I find it quite noble of you not to accept anything from you husband, but just to walk away from the whole deal. However, you should have demanded child support. It really is too bad that you didn’t come to me for a consultation,” said James using his best lawyer voice.

"Oh, James, I don’t want to talk about my divorce on such a lovely night. My lawyer was excellent and tried to talk me out of my bizarre requests. So let’s change the subject. Tell me, how is it to do business in town,” I said somewhat peevishly.

Regroup. Time to cool down. James was happily telling about some divorce law deal. I was not listening to him, but making the obligatory vocal sounds. I really needed to get myself together. Ah, the bathroom.

“James, if you could excuse me, I need to use the ladies room. Be back in a few minutes, “I said needing a break from the “Poor Vivi”conversation.

"You promise, I’ll be waiting here,” replied James flashing his beautiful, perfectly aligned teeth.

I smiled and left. *Now where did they hide the bathroom. There should be one on the second floor*. I quickly maneuvered myself through the crowds, then to the landing and walked up. The bathroom faced me as I reached the second floor. Quickly I entered, walked past the twin sinks and open the door leading to the toilet. I close and lock it. Trapped but safe for five minutes.

Suddenly I heard footsteps of two women. They began opening their purses and seemed to be freshening up their makeup. Their voices got louder. I could hear their conversation through the locked door.

“I am pissed. I’ve given him all of our family’s legal business and some referrals, and what does he do. He goes and sits down and spends the evening talking to that little nothing of a woman, “exclaimed Woman A.

“Humor me, whom are you talking about?” said Woman B.

“James, James Greenwood and Vivi Bartlett. That was her maiden name, I don’t know what she goes by now. You probably don’t remember her. She went to the public high school. She was cute in those days, but nothing special. The guys use to be crazy about her hair. Her mother’s French and her father was a photographer. No money. I once caught her wearing a dress for the cotillion that I gave away to a thrift shop. Of course, I would never embarrass her by telling her about it. But there was no money in that family. I think that they were trying to pretend they were something else. But you know that sort of thing is always found out,” squawked Woman A

“So what has that to do with James?”

°°Well, it burns me. She disappears for fifteen years, comes back divorced, with a kid and from what I hear, penniless, and James, who I have had my eyes on, makes a beeline for her. It’s not fair. He’s one of us, and she isn’t. She’s some sort of artsy-fartsy intellectual and James is an active man. Golf, soccer, sailing and the rest. What does he see in her?” Woman A’s voice was getting more and more piercing and I winced thinking who could be hearing this crap outside of the bathroom.

"I don’t know. She’s kind of attractive in that petite way. Bill thinks so. She still has beautiful hair,” said Woman B weakly.

"Oh Patty, you’re no help. You just don’t understand. After all, you’ve been married to Bill for years. It is tough out there. And the hair is probably dyed. I’m not taking this lying down.”

“Are you finished, Lily? Let’s get out of here before the party is over. Bill has probably gotten shit-faced while we’ve been in here gossiping,” replied Patty.

"Okay. I'm going down to the pool to talk to him. Maybe I can invite him over for dinner and maybe something will happen. With that body, he's got to be a tremendous fuck. Let's go." Lilly quickly shuffled around what I believe to be her purse and both women went out of the powder room.

I had better get out soon before the next wave of gossip comes through. I didn't think that I could handle much more. Well, seemed that I've made instant enemies. The funny note to this situation is that I found James to be a bit stiff and boring. *Oh, be nice, Vivi.* Maybe underneath that old preppie facade lay a wild and crazy guy. *Time to get back.* Maybe I could even meet the evil Lily and jerk her chain. A girl has got to have fun.

I left the bathroom, descended down the back staircase, and walked out to the pool. James was at the same spot, speaking with a tall woman with a large butt. Must have gotten it from all of the riding lessons.

"Hi, James. Hi, I remember you. You were to be Lily Blalock. I'm Vivi Bergstrom, formerly Bartlett," I said cordially.

"Hello, of course I remember you. Winston says that you moved back in town. With a daughter. I hear you do illustrations of adorable little fairies. How marvelous. We must have lunch. I just adore talking with you creative types. I was just telling James that he must take off more time. He's always working so hard. Did you know that he is absolutely brilliant. He pulled together this fabulous real estate deal for Daddy. We are turning our land in Montgomery Township into a luxury condo development. The demand is amazing. Everyone wants to live near Princeton, but there just isn't enough space. Not everyone can afford to live here. Are you living in town, Vivi", said Lily with a steely tone in her voice.

"Yes I am out ...," I never was able to finish the sentence, old Lily Bitch Queen did that for me.

"Well, I know how it is, moving back in with the folks. But at least it gives you time to settle in and save a bit of money. James, you will come to dinner on Wednesday. I'm dying for you to try out the new tennis court. My brother, Fred will be there with his wife. Maybe we can play doubles."The lovely Lily gave her most charming smile, and flashed her expensive bridge work and stained caps. *Charming.* I smiled back.

"James, Lily, it really has been a pleasure. I've got to be going. You know, the baby-sitter. Do give me a call. Let me give you my card, Lily. I'm not listed. Lunch would be fun." I turned around and started to head out through the garden to the driveway.

"Wait, Vivi. I'll walk you to your car. See you on Wednesday, Lily. Doubles it is." James quickly caught up with me. It was a long walk down to my car and the company would be appreciated. As we got beyond hearing distance, James leaned over and whispered in my ear.

"You don't think you're going to leave me with the man-eater, do you?" It's going to be bad enough being at her house on Wednesday. She's always trying to get me in her bed," confessed the poor James.

"Ah James. I'm quite sure that you can easily wrap old Lily around your finger. I know you'll come out of the lair alive." The picture of the two of them in bed was quite amusing.

"I'd rather it be you. I must have been blind in school. We never did go out together, did we?" asked James.

No, in those days you were too good looking and I was just another cute girl. Now, twenty year later, all those beauties are well past their prime, and I'm starting to look good in comparison. "You know how it was. You were madly in love with Beth, and I was just a kid in your Spanish class. Here's the car."

"Vivi, do you think this car is old enough. I know that you're broke, but couldn't you at least have gotten a new car out of your divorce. You need someone to take care of you. I'm going to London to close a deal but I'll be back in three weeks. Let me take you to dinner. Please," begged James.

"Great. Give me a call when you're back. I'll give you one of my cards." It was somewhere down in my purse. *"*Listen, I don't need any help, James.

It's kind of you, but I really don't need any help." I handed my card to James, who took a look and tucked it into his breast pocket.

"Oh Vivi, you're so sweet. So innocent in the ways of the world and so sweet. I just want you to know I'm here for you."

James leaned over and kissed me. It was a good initial kiss, professionally executed, just what I expected out of him. But it was not a kiss that would send me over the edge. Little stars didn't go off. I was not hearing the 1812 Overture. Heck, in high school I would have died for one of James Greenwood's kisses. And here I was, twenty years later getting kissed by him and analyzing his lip skill. Oh well, it was probably for the best. Maybe what I needed was a relationship that would develop over time instead of instantly falling in love. James and I made our good byes and some promises for his return in three weeks. I started up Old Faithful and left the estate.

Well, Vivi. You got your wish tonight. Someone kissed you. It wasn't so bad after all. And you made it unscathed through the den of vipers. I got my wish. Maybe poor old Lily will get hers. I started giggling on the way home. I was picturing Lily's large white, naked butt being heaved up in the air while having sex with poor James sent me into a fit of laughter. I wondered if she hears Bolero while getting it on.

Chapter 19

"Mommy, telephone," called Gabrielle from the second floor landing.

"Who is it Gabrielle? Can you please ask nicely?"

"It's Lena. Mommy, it's Lena. Is that Lena who sends me presents?" asked an enthusiastic child.

"Must be. I'll get the phone. Why don't you go out and play on the new jungle gym?" I suggested.

"Okay, Mommy. Don't take long. I want lunch. Wieners, please," requested Gabrielle. Gabrielle went out through the kitchen door. I picked up the kitchen phone.

"Lena? Good God. Where are you? You're in the States? How soon before we can get together? You'll be in Princeton tomorrow? Good, of course, come over for lunch." I said dying to see my best friend and catch up on old times. "My house. So what has happened? Richard quit the bank? He's starting up an investment capital firm in New York City? Wonderful. You're looking for a house to rent in Connecticut? You'll have to get me up to date. I can't wait. My house is the only white Cape Cod on the street. A dèmain, Lena."

I hung up the phone. Lena. I haven't seen her since her wedding to Tom. This would be fun. I'll make Gabrielle her wiener and then we'll go shopping at the McAffry's. I opened the French door, poked my head outside and shouted, "Gabrielle, come in. Help me make your lunch. We're going grocery shopping afterwards. Lena's coming tomorrow and I'd like to have some food in the house."

"All right, Mommy. But first you have to watch me do this trick."

I stepped outside, watched Gabrielle hang from her knees and gave a big round of applause. We ran into the house and Gabrielle started setting the table. Thank God for the microwave. Zapped up two hot dogs, pulled together a quick garden salad, and took out a plate of cookies. Gabrielle had completed her chores including setting out the condiments. Her taste was a bit strange at the moment. She wanted to try peanut butter on her hot-dog. We both sat down at the breakfast nook.

"Lena is your best friend, right, Mom. Is she a bigger friend than me?" asked Gabrielle.

“No, Lena is my best non-family friend. She is like a sister to me. It’s different than you and me, or Grandmère and me. Whitney’s your best friend isn’t she?” I replied.

"I think so. I’m finished. Can I have a cookie, please.”

“Why don’t you take two, one for now and one for the trip to the grocery store,” I suggested knowing that Gabrielle would be hungry in an hour.

“Okay, Mommy. Here is your bag, Mom, let’s go.”

We quickly closed up the house and hopped into Old Faithful. Gabrielle popped herself into her car seat, I buckled her in and got into the front seat. The engine turned over after a couple of tries.

"Mom, is Old Faithful sick?” asked a worried Gabrielle.

“I think Old Faithful is getting tired. She’s very old, Pumpkin. Maybe we have to find a new home for her. Oh, here we are,” I said as I pulled into parking spot and turned off the ignition. We scrambled out of Old Faithful and walked to the entrance. Every time I entered this place, it was like a trip into the Twilight Zone.

A long time ago, Princeton society was based on family and having the right things, such as beach homes, country clubs and certain neighborhoods. Today,it was more democratic; the rich have gotten poor, the poor were now rich, and the geniuses from the University were finally recognized (since the Einstein days). You only needed one of three things to make it in this town; money, brains or art. We fell in the artistic clan.

Lena was from the brains group. Her dad was a mathematician at the Institute, and Winston's gang was dumb and rich.

Since Princeton had become more liberal on its views of society, there were two major ways that the women gathered together during the day, bridge or the McAffry's grocery store. My mother was a champion bridge player and a master at the meat sales. But this store was special. This McAffry's was Ghislaine Bartlett Nicholson's bastion, her citadel and whenever I entered its glass and metal doors, I needed to be prepared for the onslaught of questions from her friends. They probably also would tell my mother which cuts of meat I purchased. The first time I put my foot in here, I was ill prepared.

It goes back to the bridge game. Men and women play differently. Men make up a bunch of archane rules at the last moment, inform their partner briefly, and then would have a screaming rage when they lost the rubber, or game. Women on the other hand, were more devious. They calmly played the hands, scarcely looking at their cards, chomping on the peanuts, and sipping through a lot of alcohol. Gossip was part of the game, and my mother used it like a maestro. Mom would casually drop a gossip tidbit when she was finessing a trick or to see if the opposition was alert. It had the effect of an atomic bomb, and Mom, being the victor, quickly collected her winnings. This also meant that everyone she played with, passed the tasty piece to another bridge game in town. Gossip took a maximum of three days to get around. I always felt sorry for Mrs. Harriet Forsythe. She was usually the last to hear the news, and tried to use it in her defense strategy. She rarely won a game.

I took a cart, plunked my little wonder into the kiddy seat and we veered off to the produce section. Quickly, I gathered up romaine, a nice melon, chicken for tonight and Asiago cheese. Blessed that Princeton was fairly adventurous with food, I found pine nuts and those nice hard almond cookies from Italy. Down a few more aisles and I would be home free.

No such luck. Zelda Worthington saw me and raced her cart to meet me. Mom loved Zelda because she was very rich and very crazy. The stories she told at the bridge games were first class smut and titillating for the ladies. Zelda was welcomed everywhere.

"Oh Vivi, Vivi dear." Zelda was almost six feet tall, with dyed red hair - whore's special - and a deep booming voice. Today she was dressed equally strangely. She was wearing a horrid raincoat, playing with some object in a greasy pocket, no stockings to cover up a pair of white, hairy legs, and pink bedroom slippers. All I could make out, was that she must have traded her good raincoat with one from the homeless. I didn't want to get too close and be able to identify the stains. Zelda also believed that body odor brought out her natural woman.

Her cart was full of dented cans and meat that had been reduced in price. She was famous for being incredibly cheap. Once it was rumored that her kids ate oatmeal for breakfast and dinner. They grew to be equally as strange as their mother. Mom never ever brought up their achievements to me. They must have been borderline murderers, drug addicts, and thieves.

"Hello, Zelda. This is my daughter Gabrielle. Gabrielle, meet Mrs. Worthington, a friend of Grandmère," I said.

"Call me Zelda, honey. No one calls me Mrs. Worthington and actually at the moment there is no Mr. Worthington. You know, he ran off with that trashy little secretary of his. I wouldn't let him back in the house, not even to collect his coin collection. That'll teach the little bastard," said Zelda gleefully.

He probably was tired of oatmeal and body odor. Zelda was not what I wanted Gabrielle to use as a role model. Gabrielle, on the other hand, was fascinated and smiled a lot. I was more and more taken by Zelda's strange attire. I couldn't hold back my curiosity longer.

"Zelda, what are you playing with in your pocket? And, excuse me for asking, but are you wearing anything under that raincoat?"

"Oh honey, it is just a ring," and Zelda took out an immense diamond solitaire out of her pocket. "I lost it a few days ago, I was wondering where I put it after going to the hunt. And yes, I must confess, I am naked under this. It's because of Khalid, the renter I got from the University."

"Khalid?" I asked fascinated and repulsed at the same time.

"Oh, honey, those Indians are the best fucks. We've been in bed all day long, and I had to put on something to run to the store. He's in the car. I don't think that we can hold out all the way to the house. Maybe we'll do it again in the car. You should get an Indian, honey. They really send you to Hindu Nirvana, or whatever they have for an Indian heaven. Got to go. Kisses to your mom."

"Bye Zelda." Again, it felt like I had been hit by a hurricane. Probably the whole store felt the same way. After all, they most likely heard Zelda's news broadcast.

"Mommy, what does fuck mean?" Gabrielle was giving me a wicked little grin, knowing that whatever "fuck" means, it was really bad.

"Pumpkin, I'd suggest you forget that word and anything else that Zelda says. Okay?" I suggested.

Gabrielle knew not to test me. "Sure, Mommy, I was just wondering."

A woman in her fifties with graying dark brown hair approached me. She looked like she just stepped out of an Orvis catalog: Cutesy cotton sweater with embroidered with strawberries, a navy blue cotton golf skirt, stockings, tasteful pumps, and of course, the required string of pearls.

"Excuse me? Were you talking to that poor woman who was here?" she asked in a concern voice.

What is this all about. "Do you mean the woman with the red hair?" I replied.

"Yes, that's the one. Was she asking you for money? She looks poor and probably homeless, but really, we must draw the line at allowing the unwashed in Princeton."

"Are you new in town?" I asked.

"Why, yes. We just moved from Darien, Connecticut. What's that got to do with that person?"'

°'Well, when you've been here for a while, you'll know Zelda. She's probably the richest woman in town," I said.

"You're joking. Harry said that there were some democrats with strange ideas here. Well, I never," and she huffed off. Give her a month and she'll be dying to invite Zelda to her house. And Zelda was a dyed-in-wool republican.

I bought a few more items and went to the front of the store, for a cashier. The lines were fairly long. Gabrielle was leafing through a children's magazine that I always picked up for her. There were two carts ahead of me and a woman getting her purchases totaled at the checkout. The two women ahead of me began talking to one another.

Two women in their early thirties. Career-type women. They reminded me of a day in January, a dark rainy day in a similar supermarket that caused our exodus from California.

Damn. I could remember it like it was yesterday.

Chapter 20

I was standing in line at the local Whole Foods with a cart full of groceries. Gabrielle was in the cart's seat. Two attractive women were in front of me, speaking in loud voices. Out of boredom, I eavesdropped.

"Shasta, just the person I've been dying to call. How are you doing? And the love life?"

"Oh, Lora. Wait until I tell you. Did I meet a great man. Total love," said Shasta.

"Do tell. No one here knows us," replied Lora.

"Well, I met him skiing in Tahoe. I was at Squaw Valley, skiing in the morning with Nancy Johnson. That afternoon, Nancy decided to take it easy and go shopping so I skied alone. It was the beginning of Christmas vacation and the lift lines were awful. You know how it gets," said Shasta.

"So what else is new. Go on. Go on," prompted Lora.

"So I said "to hell with this" and got into the singles line. This man nearby asks me if I'm single and if I'd like to ride with him. So I did," boasted Shasta flicking her long perfectly maintained dark chestnut hair.

"And?"

"And he's gorgeous. Stark raving gorgeous. Blond, green-eyed, a build like you can't believe. He is an architect in the city," cooed Shasta."Well, I went out to dinner with him, got a bit high, and I never came home that night. It was wonderful. Now we've been seeing each other steadily for the last three weeks. He sends me flowers all the time. We go out and have a marvelous time. I think he wants to get married. He really is serious. He wants kids. And Lora, you should see his house in the city. It is awesome. Really."

“So about this paragon, Shasta. Where is he from, is he married, was he married, are there any kids?” questioned Lora.

He’s originally from Chicago. He’s divorced, like years ago. He said his wife was a real arty type that got weird on him. He hasn’t seen his kid since the divorce. Seems that the wife disappeared, but now he is going to get an investigator and start legal action to get full custody.”

“Is the kid a girl or a boy?” asked Lora.

“Lora, I don’t know. I don’t think he mentioned it. He gets quiet if I bring up anything that has to do with his ex-wife,” replied Shasta.

"If there is a custody battle, it will be ugly. And remember what my granny always said to me. It takes two to tango. After two husbands, I know there is no perfect male,” said Lora.

“Oh, you’re such a pessimist. This guy’s great. He’s the real thing. I’ll support him through this legal stuff. He’s worth it. His ex-wife must be a real nut to ruin such a good thing,” explained Shasta.

The store clerk leaned over and announced, “Ma’am. That will be fifty-seven dollars and eight-five cents. Would you like paper or plastic?”

“Plastic, it’s raining. Listen, Lora. I’ll give you a call this week. Maybe we can all get together for dinner. Then you can meet him and decide for yourself.”

“Sounds good. Do give me a call, Shasta, I’ve missed hearing from you,” replied Lora.

“Ciao.” And my brunette bombshell walked off. I was stunned. She had to be talking about Leif. No way was he getting any part of Gabrielle. No way was he going to upset our lives. What could I do? I would move far away. I had better get Gabrielle home and think about this.

Move. But where to?

I could move back home.

Chapter 21

"Ma'am. That will be fifty-seven dollars and eight-five cents. Would you like paper or plastic," said the register clerk.

"Mommy, get with it." Gabrielle was tugging on my sleeve and snapped me out of my flashback.

"Oh sorry, I was daydreaming. Paper, please. Here we are, sixty dollars," I said somewhat embarrassed. The clerk handed me back my change and placed the bags into the cart. We wheeled out of the store and into the parking lot.

"Mom, stop daydreaming. It's embarrassing," begged Gabrielle as she wiggled in shopping cart seat.

"Okay, Gabrielle, I promise to try harder." I really meant it, these flashback weren't healthy for me. They often made me depressed and angry. I got my keys out of my purse, unlocked the car and opened the rear door.

"Can I have a gummy bear?" cajoled Gabrielle with several flutters of her long eyelashes. No need for mascara in that girl's future. Quickly I lifted her out of the shopping cart seat and placed her in her car caddie. Gabrielle did the honors of locking herself in.

"Sure, I'll get you the bag. Is Grandmère coming to get you today?" I asked while placing the bags in the back seat. Quickly I shut the door, walked over to the driver's side and got into the Old Faithful.

"Yes, Can we go to her house first? It will save her a trip," asked Gabrielle chewing away on a gummy.

"Fine." I started the engine, got out of the parking lot, and drove to Mom's house which was located near Carnegie Lake. I could see they were both home. Richard was outside cutting the lawn and Mom was weeding in a flower bed.

"Hi, guys. Is it okay if I drop Gabrielle off a bit early? We were in the neighborhood," I asked once out of the car.

"Parfait," exclaimed Mom. "Gabrielle, get a hat on and help me in the garden. So what is new?" said Mom with a tinge of expectation in her voice.

"Lena's coming over for lunch tomorrow and I ran into Zelda at the A&P. Lena's husband is starting a new business, and she's house-hunting in Connecticut today." I shouted from the driveway.

"Oh, Lena. How nice to have her back in the States. That will be good for you. And Zelda, nuttier that ever?"

"Yes, she was wearing a disgusting raincoat in the grocery store and nothing underneath," I replied while walking on the grassy lawn.

"You know, her husband left her for the secretary," said Mom while pulling out a dandelion.

"Yes, she told me. She has a new friend, a graduate student from the University," I said.

"Oh, you mean the tenant. She hasn't shown up for bridge in days. It must be the first time she has had sex in years. What man would want to get near her anyway? Hi, Poupée, see this awful weed. Let's pull it out. Has James Greenwood asked you out yet?" queried the French general.

"No, he should be back anytime." We were getting into dangerous territory.

"He has done very well for himself. Don't be an idiot this time. You're not getting any younger, you know." Mom looked like she was winding up for one of her grand statements on my husbandless condition.

"Yes, Mother, got to go. I'll pick up Gabrielle in a couple of hours." I started moving back toward the Volvo.

"No need to do so. Richard wants to help you paint the house. We'll be dropping over after diner. Is that okay?" Good, Mom had dropped the subject and I could have an easy escape.

"A tout à l'heure, I'll see you later," said Ghislaine, now focusing on the verdant chickweed.

I sneaked a kiss from Gabrielle, walked over to the car, and zoomed off. I drove past Carnegie Lake, through the back of the University and up Alexander Road. Then I cut through the Seminary and the Graduate College to get a glimpse of the annual beauty pageant of rhododendrons that were growing in massive clumps lining the roads. They were in bloom; huge bouquets of red, fuchsia, pink, rose, pearl and white. Absolutely magnificent. I then headed off to Battle Road area and meander along the roads leading to my house.

The house looked ugly. I should consider painting the outside. Actually, what would look lovely was to strip off the old paint and have a white stain effect. I didn't know if it could be done since there may be years of paint on the shingles. The front yard was looking picturesque, the fence needed to be replaced, but the wisteria was magnificent as I had once remembered. A little pruning went a long way. I parked the car in the driveway and brought in the groceries just as the phone began to ring. Quickly I dropped the groceries in the kitchen and picked up the portable phone.

"Hello."

"Vivi, is that you. It's James Greenwood. How are you doing?" His voice was nice and deep, like I remembered.

"Fine, how was London?" I replied, trying to get the groceries out of the bags and into cupboards.

"Excellent, got a lot of work done. Getting financial backers and satisfying them in this real estate deal. But that is fairly dry. Listen, how about going out for dinner with me tomorrow night? I'm sorry about the short notice, but I came in last night from Heathrow and I'm leaving on Thursday for Phoenix."

"Tomorrow sounds fine. I should have no problem getting a sitter." What would I do without Mom and Richard at these times.

"Good, then I'll pick you up around seven thirty. Do you like French? There is a new restaurant that just opened up in New Hope that has great reviews."

"James, of course I like French cooking. My mother is French,' I said with a light touch.

"Oh, that's right. It slipped my mind," confessed Mr. Perfect.

"New Hope would be lovely. See you around seven-thirty." *Get off of the phone, Vivi, you have a dinner to get ready.*

"Bye, Vivi."

"Bye, James and thanks for the invitation," I said.

My first date in years. This should be funny. Hope I could manage not to spot my white dress before the evening's end. It was nice of James to call. I hoped that he wasn't pushy. I was not ready for a full-board relationship yet. Yikes, once again sex raised its proverbial head.

I walked through the kitchen French doors to the terrace and ignited the grill. One nice addition to the house was to extend the gas line from the kitchen to an outside grill. I took a good look at the back of the wall. Yes, it was time for a facelift and new gutters. The roof still seemed solid. *That's enough Vivi. Time to get the chicken and some vegetables on the grill. And after dinner , you should take out the patio seats and umbrella and give them a good scrubbing. Let's impress Lena.*

The chicken was cooked in forty-five minutes and I sat down outside to dine on chicken breast, some vegetables, a small salad and a glass of wine. After I cleaned up the table, I started scrubbing the cushions and umbrella.

Halfway through the project I heard a knock at the door, followed by Mom's voice.

"Out here, Mom. On the patio," I shouted.

"I brought you back the princess. She behaved like a little dolly. Richard is here to talk about the house paint. So what is new?" said Mom as she walked out on to the patio.

I decided not to tease my mother with anticipation. "James Greenwood called."

"For what? Polite conversation? Did he ask you out? I hope you were nice with him?" said Mom sounding anxious.

"Yes, Mom, I was very nice with him. He asked me out on a date. Tomorrow."

"That's not very much time. Do you have something nice to wear? By the way, you have been dressing much better. O zut. I can't help you. Richard and I are going out tomorrow dancing with Mimi Schaffield and her husband." Mom seemed disappointed at the thought of not being able to get the low down immediately about the date.

"Don't worry, Mom. I'll call Loretta and see if her niece is available. There should be no problem getting a sitter for Gabrielle. And I have a lovely new dress, Mom. I even have shoes to match. Gabrielle can vouch for me," I replied in a dreamy way since I was seeing myself in the dress.

"Grandmère, we went to a pretty store uptown and I made sure that Mommy looked nice," Gabrielle chirped up.

"You bought a dress in one of those shops, Vivi. My God, it must have cost you a fortune. I've never found anything in my price range there," admitted my mother.

"Don't worry Mom, I won't make it a habit."

Richard came out on to the terrace to join us. Mom turned to him and said, "Richard, why don't you talk to Vivi about painting the house. Gabrielle and I are going up to her room." Mom and Gabrielle went back inside the house, probably to discuss strategy and tactics. Richard picked up a scrub brush and helped me clean the cushions.

"Richard, do you really want to paint? We're just getting in to the summer season and I don't want you having a heart attack," I said worried about the possibility of Richard working in the heat.

"Y our mom thought it would be a good idea. Keeps me busy and saves you some money. Man, is there a lot of work to be done on the exterior. You are right, though. It's going to be hot," admitted Richard.

"I have an idea. What I want to be done to the house will take a lot of time. I need the shingles to be sandblasted, stripped and stained white. Also I want to replace the gutters. That's too much work for you. But Gabrielle wants her bedroom wallpapered. So why don't you go with her to the hardware store, pick out something she likes and paper her room. It would help if you could do that since Gabrielle and I have been locking horns recently. And the house is air-conditioned so you won't get over-heated."

"Good idea, Vivi. But I think that Ghislaine wants me out from under her feet for two weeks. I need some more work," begged Richard.

"Well, could you help me with the dining room? I want to hang paper in it which has been ordered. It is a beautiful paper but because the background is black, it's a hard job," I admitted.

"I've always liked a challenge. Let's go tell your mom," concluded Richard.

We tramped upstairs to Gabrielle's room and explained the situation. Mom thought that helping Gabrielle with her room was a great idea and wanted to help pick out wallpaper with them. Gabrielle was in agreement and excited about the prospect of being in control. Hopefully, Mom will steer Gabrielle's developing taste buds in the right direction. Richard was a bit weak in the good taste department and a real pushover when it came to Gabrielle.

"But the house still looks terrible from the outside," complained Mom, "and it could be so lovely."

"Mom, don't worry. A fat check came in from the book publishers for the new set of illustrations. I've enough for a new fence. How about a dark green picket fence? It will set off the white house.

"Sounds parfait. I'm glad you're making some money. I hope that you have another job soon, so you can pay your taxes. Life is expensive here. And your car is terrible," reminded Mom.

"Don't worry Mom, it will all work out," I said.

"I hope so. I hope so. Come Richard let's go. Be nice to James, Vivi. Gabrielle, come over and give us a big kiss. I will pick up Gabrielle after your lunch so that we can pick out wallpaper," concluded the French commander. Kiss, kiss, and away they went. Gabrielle and I climbed up the stairs and we went to her room to play dolls.

I felt like I was in high school again, preparing for the big date. The thought of going out with a man gave me the shivers but I needed to get over this hurdle. Oh what would be the worst that could happen. Let me see. I would be unable to talk and would stutter through the conversation. I would spill each glass of wine on my dress. I would get drunk and throw up all over James in his car. That would be the worse.

No, the worse would be that everything goes fine and he falls in love with me.

Chapter 22

"Mommy, Mommy, look. Do I look nice for Lena?" cried Gabrielle. Gabrielle had never met Lena and only knew her from the presents and letters sent from Europe. She was beyond excited and I hoped all went well with my little one or else she would burst into tears.

"Honey, you look lovely. Now calm down and help me set the table. I think we'll use the orange tablecloth, yellow napkins and those blue plates. Here, why don't you take out the tablecloth outside and come back to get the napkins?"

"What about the plates? What if I drop one?" said Gabrielle using a worried tone.

"Why don't you take out the silverware?" I replied hoping to placate her.

"Okay, Mommy." Lena should be here any moment. I had flowers everywhere; inside and out. Lunch was a snap to prepare, and I found a wonderful white wine that would be great with our meal. Oh, there was the doorbell. It must be Lena.

"Gabrielle, can you open the door, please?" My hands were full bringing out the plates and silver to the terrace.

"Okay, I got it." I could hear Gabrielle's little legs running down the hall, opening the front door and the sound of Lena's voice in the background. Lord, it had been so long. It would be wonderful to have her so close again.

"Hello, you must be Gabrielle. I had no idea that you would be so tall. Well, I am your Tata Lena. Come and help me. I brought you something from Europe. Vivi, I'm here," sang out Lena.

Quickly, I put down the plates and ran to the front door. *Lena, you haven't change. Sure, there were a few wrinkles, but you looked like the same Lena to me.* I went up to her and gave her a big hug.

"Seems like you missed me. Well, I missed you, too. Living in Holland was fun, but I really missed my friends and family. You know, Gabrielle is your spitting image. I see some of Leif in her, but she looks like you," said Lena once we had finished hugging each other.

"However she acts like Ghislaine. I'm getting back everything I ever did to my mother with this kid. I'm being tormented by both sides. You know, she and her grandmother are best friends. So how do you like my new place?" I asked taking her bags.

"Well, from the outside, the garden looks great, but the house looks ready for demolition. Why don't you give me a tour? I'm dying to see everything you've done."

We quickly gave Lena a tour of the house. Gabrielle became the docent, filling Lena in on all the changes to the interior. Lena made all the proper cooing sounds and Gabrielle was very pleased, acting as the proprietress. Then Lena gave Gabrielle her present, a beautiful pair of wooden shoes.

"I think it is time to start lunch. Gabrielle, will you take Lena outside and show her to her chair? I'll just bring out the rest of the food." Lena and Gabrielle went outside and I soon followed, with a tray containing the melon wrapped in prosciutto, filet steaks, salad, and a bottle of sangiovese wine. The steaks were tossed on the grill and I sat down at the table with Lena and Gabrielle.

"This house is heavenly. I love what you've done so far. Gabrielle told me that her bedroom is next on the list. When are you going to give the outside a well needed facelift?" asked Lena while sipping her wine.

I chatted about the next set of improvements and asked her how the house search was coming along. We spoke about the homes she's seen, how happy she was to be back in the States and her nervousness about Tom's entrepreneurial spirit. We then moved on to the subject of children, Lena had two girls, and the search for a good school.

"You've got it made, Vivi. At least in Princeton the public school system is excellent. And talking about school, have you seen anyone from the old high school day? Oh, Gabrielle. You should have seen your mother and me in high school. We had a blast," confided Lean while I served the steaks. For a few minutes we made inroads into our lunch. The ripe melon exploded with flavor in my mouth while the salty prosciutto sent me to food heaven.

"By the way, I have seen someone from the old days. Remember James Greenwood. He was one year older than us and I'd sit behind him in Spanish class. You know, the hunk," I admitted while helping myself to the salad.

"The one we use to swoon for? The guy that you would make kissing noises behind his back? Oh, this is good. Tell all to Lena." Gabrielle was bored with us and went off to her playhouse in the back yard.

"Well, Lena. He looks as good as in high school. He's divorced with two kids. I don't know much about his past. He opened his own law practice in town and seems to be doing well. I met him at Winston Harrington's party. Anyway, I have a date with him tonight," I confided.

"A date with a past high school crush. Isn't this your first date since Leif? I'd be in a total panic if I'd ever have to date again," admitted Lena. "By the way, this meal is sublime."

"The concept of a date is somewhat daunting to me. In fact, I am dreading the beginning and the end. The middle part should be fine." I went for seconds on the salad.

"What do you mean by "beginning and end"? I don't understand," said Lena intrigued by the idea of dating again.

"You know. The beginning of a date is always uncomfortable, trying to start up a conversation, finding subjects that you are both interested in. The end is the worse, like are you going to be kissed, groped, all of that stuff," I admitted while having a bit more of the wine.

“You mean are you going to bed with him on the first date? I know. And what if he is a great guy and really kisses well," said Lena.

“That’s part of it. I’m not worried about having sex on the first date since I have to deal with bringing my baby-sitter home. I’ve planned ahead. But he is a little, how should we say, patronizing and he kissed me at Winston’s."

"And, come on Vivi, spill it.” Lena was dying for more information.

"Well, keep in mind that I haven’t been kissed in years, his kiss was very professional but there’s no chemistry. I think the problem is that he reminds me of Leif, another great looking guy, very successful, wanting to take charge of my life,” I confessed.

But then, it’s only one date, and maybe there is nothing to worry about,” said Lena.

We chat more about life. Mom showed up to get Gabrielle and to scold Lena for living in Holland all these years. They all left and I was alone, reminiscing about this morning. Mom was right. It was good to have old friends back home.

Chapter 23

I made it! I was smooth, charming and intelligent. I didn't lose my temper, but stood up for myself. And it was over, the date was over.

We had a very nice evening. The drive to New Hope was lovely. James made reservations at an excellent restaurant. The meal was superb and service was impeccable. James ordered a mediocre wine, and almost insisted on ordering for me, but I managed to quietly change his mind. Then we strolled around the little picturesque town with its river walk and went home.

He was very nice, bit too controlling but otherwise a nice man with good manners. He was as polite as he could be. I knew he thought that I live in an awful rundown house, with a rundown car and that I should move to a nice townhouse. I must admit from the outside, my house and Old Faithful were not looking their best. He also made a comment about the color of my living room but what does one expect for a man raised by a woman who used the Sears decorator. For now he will do. I didn't think that Gabrielle liked him. She didn't seem comfortable around him. She said that he was shiny. It was true, his Mercedes was immaculate, he looked like Mr. Perfect and his personality was a bit forceful. She did question me daily about him.

"Mommy?" Gabrielle began her interrogation of the date night while I was working on a painting in the studio.

"Yes, sweetheart. What is it?" I didn't really feel like talking to a four year old about the date or the painting.

"That man you went out with. Are you going out with him again?" she said while working on her own puppy drawing.

"Yes, I will be going out with James again. Why?" This painting might be heading for the trash bin since it didn't look like fairies, more like little nasty demons.

"He's not going to be my daddy, is he? I don't want him to be my Daddy," said Gabrielle adamantly and making strong black lines on her drawing.

"He's a nice person, Gabrielle. But I'm not thinking of marrying him. Why, I thought you wanted me to find you a daddy for Christmas."

"I think you should go out more. He's shiny." Gabrielle was definitely in a bad mood. Maybe I could derail this conversation.

"What do you mean by shiny?" I asked.

"Oh, like when I get a doll. Some are shiny. Not real. No good," explained Gabrielle. Then like a little angel herself, she stopped talking and concentrated for a while on her puppies.

Actually I was in the midst of casually dating. After Winston's party, I had become the acceptable single woman for diners. Most of the hostesses knew that I wouldn't go off and steal their spouses. My social life was developing, and although there was no strong contender for my heart, I was having a good time. More importantly in the grand scheme of things, Ghislaine was having a great time with my social success. She called me her late bloomer. She was very optimistic about my chances for a good match.

Progress was happening to our house. The outside paint was being stripped and the shingles were being sand-blasted. The windows have been re-hung and the gutters should be installed tomorrow. It all looked splendid, much like a beautiful, comfortable home that had aged well over the years. Not bad for a first time decorator. Gabrielle's room was a dream of violets. Her grandmother found the wallpaper in a fabric pattern and was making a bedspread and curtains to give to her on her birthday. I hadn't solved the puppy art problem, and prayed for some miracle to occur. Otherwise, life was fine except that it got hotter and muggier each day. We were not use to this weather and were reluctant to leave the air conditioned house and venture outside.

Richard had finished his chores here. Not only did he wallpaper Gabrielle's room to perfection, but he also papered the dining room. The walls were covered with exotic birds and flowers on a black background, mirrors everywhere to reflect light. A large oval mahogany table and chairs with cushions that were the same yellow color as the living room. Mom wanted me now to do her house. She still had this idea that I should be a decorator and she would sell my talent. I had told her that I was not at all interested, but she was not listening. She had decided to show her friends my work and so I was the sponsor of her next bridge game.

Lena found a house on the Long Island Sound. It sounded great and we had an invitation to join her. Gabrielle will have her birthday in three weeks. We should leave soon for Long Island and return for her party. Hopefully it will be cooler at Lena's house.

Damn. The air conditioner, which had seen better years, just died. This didn't forebode well for us wimpy Californians. I picked up the phone and dialed.

"Mr. Antonelli? This is Vivianne Bergstrom. Yes, it did finally happen. The monster's dead. How soon can you come over and replace it? In a week? No sooner? Well, all right, please replace it as soon as possible. Thank you." I gasped at the thought of spending a week in this heat without the damn air conditioner.

I remember summers as a kid living without air conditioning. Since the house no longer had the attic and ceiling fans, the nights would be miserable until the air conditioner was fixed. The large trees on the property helped to shade the house, but between the humidity and no breeze, the thought of staying here was not attractive. *I'll call Mom.* I picked up the phone and dialed her number.

"Mom, it's Vivi. Listen, my air conditioning system just died. Yes, I am using Antonelli. He can't repair it for one week. He has to order a new system. I can stay with Lena but someone has to let Antonelli and the painting guys in the house. You and Richard can? You are a doll. I think that the sea air will be good for Gabrielle and me. We'll be back in time for her birthday. The second of August. I'll send the invitations from Lena's house. I'll call her now. Big thanks. I'll talk to you later." From despair to exhilaration, this could be absolutely great. Time to spend with Lena, and be near the water. One more call to make: Lena.

"Lena, it's Vivi. How are things? Yes, that is what I want to talk to you about. My air conditioner died. Funny, it's always happening just at the worse time. The plumber won't be able to do anything for a week. As soon as possible. What is easiest for you? Sure, we would love to there tonight. You are an angel. Yes I have a map and your directions. Thanks again. It will be wonderful to see you, Tom, and the girls. Gabrielle should have a great time with the kids. Right, I'll leave shortly to avoid the rush hour traffic. Kisses. See you this evening, about five-ish. Ciao bella." I hung up the receiver and tried to get my thoughts together.

Okay, let's start packing. Mom and Richard were coming over to review the situation and Gabrielle was at Whitney's until one. That meant we would be able to leave by one-thirty and should be there no later than five-thirty.

I descended into the basement, grabbed the suitcases (a dumb place to put them with the basement's humidity) and headed back up to the second floor. The house was getting warmer and warmer, and the thought of running away from the heat gave me energy to continue packing. I filled the suitcases with summer clothes, rain gear, beach towels and a few "just in case" items. Old Faithful just got a tune-up and a clean bill of health a few weeks ago, so there should be no problem on the highways. I heard knocking at the door. Must be Mom and Richard. I went downstairs. It was them. I met them at the door.

"Hi, come in. Thanks for saving me. Otherwise I would have spent a week or two in a hotel. Awfully warm isn't it. Would you like something to drink? I have iced tea or lemonade. Let's go drink in the kitchen." We headed to the kitchen. I got out three glasses from the cupboard and handed them to Mom, who brought them to the kitchen table. I pulled the pitcher of lemonade from the refrigerator and joined Richard and Mom.

While sipping our lemonade, I went over the schedule for the painting, repair of the windows, and the air conditioner. Richard would handle all of the details and meet with the contractor. Mom was going to make sure that the maid came to clean up the mess. I heard a car in the driveway. Must be Loretta bringing Gabrielle home. Gabrielle came running into the house.

"Hi, who's home? I'm hot. Mommy, where are you?" she shouted.

"Hi, Gabrielle. Hi, Loretta and Whitney. We're in the kitchen. Thanks for bringing Gabrielle home. Have some lemonade," I shouted back.

Whitney, Loretta and Gabrielle walked to the kitchen and sat down.

"Hello, Ghislaine and Richard. Hi, Vivi. Gabrielle was an angel today. She always plays so well with Whitney. Lord, it's awfully hot, Vivi. Thought you had air conditioning," said Loretta, moping her brow with her hand.

"I did, Loretta, until today. The guy can't fix it for a week, so we're going to stay with friends on the Sound for next two weeks. Sorry for the short notice," I apologized.

"I'd do the same if I were you." I handed Loretta a cool wet paper towel to mop off the sweat.

"Mommy, am I going to miss my birthday party? I want a big party. With all my friends," asked my concerned moppet.

"No, we'll be back in time for your birthday and we we'll send out the invitations from Lena's."

"'That sounds good Mommy. I like the beach and I like Lena. She has kids, right?" continued the concerned one.

“Right. I’ve got everything packed in the car and we’re ready to go. Why don’t you say good-bye to Whitney, Loretta, and Grandmère and, of course, Papi Richard. I’ll close up the house and give Richard the keys.”

All went smoothly. Whitney and Gabrielle hugged each other. Gabrielle gave Loretta a big kiss then Gabrielle kissed her grandparents. I too, gave out hugs and kisses, we got into the car, fastened our seat belts and waved bye-bye on our way out the drive way.

Gabrielle screamed out, "I’ll miss you, Grandmère. I’ll miss you all.” In five minutes she was fast asleep. We were on our way.

Chapter 24

"I want to know everything about your love life. Everything down to the littlest detail," demanded Lena. We were on the beach, under an umbrella, watching the children playing in the water.

"It really is boring. My life was more interesting in high school than it is now," I admitted.

"Listen, old chum, I'm a happily married woman with two kids. I've got a husband who I never see except late at night when he comes in exhausted from his day in the city. We don't go out, he is too tired, and I've seen all current movies on Netflicks. So, if you want to talk about boring lifestyles, honey, yours looks like a page from the National Enquirer to me. Just try to bore me." Lena took a sip of water from her glass.

°'Well, as I've told you, I've been seeing James Greenwood on and off." I moved into the shade of the umbrella. My skin never did well with large blasts of sun.

"Why on and off?" questioned Lena glancing out over the beach to check on the kids.

"His business takes him out of town for long periods of time. Anyway, he's a nice man. There are times I find him to be condescending and patronizing."

"Like Leif?" Lena opened the sun protection lotion and squeezed a dab in her hand.

"Just like Leif. But James, even though he's good-looking, doesn't resemble Leif at all. He's very kind, doesn't push me. I think he's kind of lonely; he calls me whenever he's out of town. For all I know he may be in love with me. I can't tell."

"And you, how do you feel about him?" The lotion was being well massaged into her arms.

"He's nice. That's about it. I'm comfortable around him, except when he gives me lectures about improving my stake in life. I'm not in love with him, and I don't know if I can deal with the intimacy issue. Lena, I don't hear music when I kiss him," I confessed.

"Not a good sign. However, if you're looking for companionship and a steady partner, maybe this is the one. Do you want some cream? This stuff isn't bad."

"Lena, I don't know. I like being in love with my partner. On the other hand, look where it got me the last time. Then there is the situation of improving my stake in life, whatever that means. And more importantly, Gabrielle doesn't like James. Yeah, please pass me the cream." Lena nodded her head and handed me the tube. My turn to get greased.

"Most children don't like the new husband. Don't make that an issue. But I do have a question. What do you mean by "improving your stake in life"? I thought that you were doing well financially. After all, you bought the house and have been making changes to the property." I started putting the cream on my nose, face and ears.

"It's funny, Lena, you're the first to ask. Everyone has assumed what they want to believe. See, when I got divorced, I got back all that was mine; stocks, company options, retirement and Gabrielle. I never took anything away from Leif. Personally, I thought he was leveraged to the maximum. And then there was the drug problem. Leif thought that the stocks and options had no real value. I didn't say much, not wanting to upset the apple cart and then Leif gave away his custodial rights. I lived frugally and quietly since I didn't have any large needs. Mom assumed that I am broke and stupid since I never took money from Leif. I think that I got off with everything I wanted. Did I get the cream in all the right places?" I asked.

"Vivi, I've been in your house. The house and the furnishings are really lovely and expensive. We're talking more than a half million. You must have made more money. What happened after the divorce? By the way, you need some cream around your left ear."

"Oh, I really started to invest in the market. New issues, hot companies. Most of them were clients of mine. When I saw that the management was good, I invested. I would at least double my money. One year I tripled, and the other year I made four times the money. But I never told anyone about the money since I never felt it was real, just some sort of game that I was good at playing. When we moved out here, the money became a lot more real since I used it to restore the house. There's enough for me to live off of if I am careful," I admitted.

"Lord, Vivi. You've got that much money? Hell, the whole town should try to marry you. Why does everyone think that you're broke?" Lena was stunned by my financial confession.

"I guess that Mom discussed my divorce over a bridge game, and the story made its way around town," I said while starting to boil from the heat.

"You've got to be joking. What a hoot. And the admirable Mr. Greenwood?"

"He's the worst of all, always giving me helpful advice on how to make three percent interest on my investment. And his advice is lousy. Why do all men think that they are financial geniuses and wine connoisseurs? I think James really needs a woman who will always be grateful to him for saving her and dependent on him for the future. That is not the real me," and beads of sweat started forming on my face.

"I don't know the answer. I think that because of your looks and build, everyone thinks you're a delicate flower."

"More like a weed, Lena. Enough, I'm getting too hot. I need a dip. I'll race you to the water."

"You're on. On your mark. Get set. Go!"

We ran down to the beach and jumped into the water. I found Gabrielle, who was making a sand castle with Lena's daughters, Tara and Alexandra, grabbed her and tossed her in the Sound. Great screams emitted from her mouth as I grabbed her again and waded out into deeper water. She got upon my back and we bobbled in the waves. Lena did the same with Tara who had decided to start a water war with us. Alexandra, the eldest girl, ran after her mother in the waves and helped with the merrymaking.

After five minutes, the moms had it, and deposited their sopping daughters back at the sand castle. Lena and I ran back to the umbrella and collapsed on the beach towels.

"I don't understand it, Vivi. How could Leif think you were a little idiot? I saw the way he was with you before the marriage. He was great and he really loved you, or else he put on a great show. What happened?" asked Lena.

"Hell if I know. As soon as we came back from the honeymoon, it all went downhill. And then his mother showed up. What a bitch. At first, I thought the problem was me. Finally I decided that I wasn't the problem. Leif, for some reason, had decided that it was time to settle down and get married and picked me from the lineup of "wifey" material. Then, especially after discussing it with his mother, he decided that he didn't want the family package. Lena, the guy cheated on me several times. And then the abortion idea."

"So Vivi, why did, you stay with such a jerk?" Lena sounded incredulous once hearing about Leif.

"Well, like I said, I was trying to figure out what I'd done wrong nor could I admit what a disaster I had on my hands. You know. Was I too fat, or lousy in bed, or a bore to be with, or really unattractive? I was still wondering that stuff when I divorced him. Divorce was the only way to keep the baby. One day I decided that the problem was his, not mine. Plus, he had a lot of skeletons in his closet and a little drug problem which confirmed my diagnosis."

"Yeah, Doctor Vivi."

"So, let's get off talking about Leif and instead let's dissect James." I really wanted to move away from the Leif disaster story. It was still too close to me and uncomfortable to dissect.

"Your Leif story so far is more interesting. James sounds like another white, preppie, prosperous lawyer looking for an acceptable mate. You'll end up as a country club wife with him. And you'll have to have chintz living room slipcovers in your livingroom."

"You know Lena, sometimes you hit it so well on the nail that I hate you. Now I am hungry from all of this man conversation. Let's set out the lunch. The girls must be starving."

"You're right. I'll get the drinks. You clear out the basket. Girls. Gabrielle. Alexandra. Tara. Lunch is ready. Come on," shouted Lena, waving at the threesome around the sand castle. Alexandra, Tara, and Gabrielle came running up, their faces glowing from the sun. Quickly, they settled down and ravenously attacked the sandwiches and potato chips.

"Hey, girls. Let's get on those hats," cautioned Lena. "I don't want to see any sun burns today." The girls, faces stuffed with food, grabbed their large brimmed cloth sun hats. After the food frenzy attack, Alexandra, Tara and Gabrielle decided to play in the sand and dig for treasure.

"Vivi, can you believe the appetites of our delicate daughters. Who would think that creatures that small and slim could eat so much," said Lena while trying to tidy up.

I rummaged through the beach bags. "I know, I am trying to find us something to eat. They cleaned out the chips. Aha, found it. Here's a sandwich and a peach. I've got one for myself."

"Thanks. So when is the wedding`? And will I be your Matron of Honor?" Lena was looking a bit too comfortable and smug with her questioning. There should be a bottle with ice water nearby. Found it.

“Me? Consider getting married again. No way, not till Hell freezes over. You know, like this,” and I poured the icy water on her stomach. Lena, electrified, leapt up in the air, howling, with a glass in her hand.

“Jesus, Vivi. I’ll get you for this,” and started to chase me around the beach umbrella, waving her glass in the air. The three girls, hearing the commotion, ran over to watch what was going on.

“You asked for it. Don’t think for a moment I’d let you get away with that marriage stuff,” I shouted. Lena’s longer legs were gaining on me. In one swift move, she lunged, grabbed my swimsuit, and poured the water down my back. The girls, looking like little mushrooms under their wide hats, started giggling. I grabbed Lena’s ankle and we both fall over into the warm sand. We took a look at each other and burst out with laughter.

“Well, Vivi. Guess I was a bit premature about the wedding idea. But you know, I’d look so good in chintz,” quipped Lena.

“Mmmm. I wonder if they make chintz straight jackets for the bride,” I mused.

“With a chintz mouth gag,” added Lena.

“Definitely, no self-respecting mad bride could be without her matching gag. That would be tacky.”

“Actually, I hope you don’t get married for a while. It’s so nice having you around again. Like the old days.”

“Yeah, like the old days,” I murmured. I looked up and saw Gabrielle, Alexandra, and Tara staring down at us with little smiles. "No, not like the old days. Too many changes. More like a new page in my life.” And I grabbed my little poppet, wrestled her to the ground, and smothered her with kisses.

Chapter 25

"Great dinner, Lena," I groaned as I tried to get out of my chair. "The bouillabaisse was superb." We've made pigs of ourselves feasting on Lena's creation. The girls have already been excused to play dolls in their rooms.

"Amazing," said Tom. "But let's put off desert for a while. How about retiring to the porch. It is starting to cool down outside and there is a nice breeze."

"Oh, that's a great idea, Tom. I'll bring out the coffee out there," voiced Lena. Tom and I slowly lumbered out to the porch and took our seats. It was a beautiful warm night with a full moon. From our rattan chairs we could see the ocean and the waves breaking. I turned my head to speak.

"Tom, are you going to rent this house for the winter? It's a nice place."

"I think so. At least for a while. We are on a month-to-month. We'll see how it is in the winter," said Tom.

"And business. How are you doing?"

"So far, so good. Lena told me that you've done quite well for yourself with the technology stocks."

"I've been very fortunate. Are you getting venture capital for technology start-ups?" I asked.

"No, not as of yet. Mostly the companies that I have been working with are in service industries. However, I hope that I can get into the technology area soon. The returns are much higher," confided Tom. "Ah, here comes Lena with the coffee." We rose from the comfortable old seats to help Lena set the coffee on the table.

"Nice evening. And the weather's been great," exclaimed Lena. "Vivi, has Tom been boring you about his new business?"

"Yes, but I like to hear investment shop talk," I admitted.

"Lucky you. I can't do anything that deals with math. Tom has to balance my check book ..."

"Which wouldn't be bad if Lena just would remember to write down all the checks in the register," interjected Tom, smiling.

"All right. I admit it. I'm almost, almost perfect," confessed Lena.

"Listen Vivi, not to change the subject, but I'm curious about some stuff. It's about Leif. Do you mind talking about him?" asked Tom.

"No, it's okay. Go ahead."

"Well, I always felt it was strange that he asked me to be his best man. I mean, I met him a few weeks before we ran into you," Tom confided while looking at the ocean.

"Tom, I didn't realize it at the time, but Leif didn't have any friends, just business acquaintances. There was very little, except his mother, from his past," I confessed. "I didn't realize that until much later."

"He use to have swing moods, and although his work was superb, often he was late on a project. That's why we never used him again."

"Oh, Tom. That's because he had a coke habit," I admitted.

"He had a coke habit? And you married him? Vivi, were you nuts?" Lena shrieked as she poured the coffee. "Cream?" she added as she lift the creamer.

"Yes, thank you." I took the cup from her. "I didn't know about it. I don't know if he was using the stuff when we were together or on our honeymoon. But one day, I was cleaning the garage and I found a leather bag. When I looked inside of it there were a set of weights, like something the pharmacist would use. And a large bag of talc. I thought he was dealing in the stuff. Figuring out that Leif was on coke explained a lot of his behavior: the moods, his "allergies", and the paranoia about the state of his finances. You know, I never knew how much money he made. He was really secretive about money."

"And yours, Vivi? Did he know about your state of finances?" Tom asked with a puzzled look on his face.

"No, he felt that since I was a designer, I wasn't making much. And that part is true. I made a comfortable living, but nothing to boast about. He would always look down at anything I achieved at work. You know, raises, promotions, stock options. So I gave up and did my own thing. At the end, there wasn't much there to keep us together," I sighed.

"Strange. You know, I would have never thought that he was like that. Or that he would let go of Gabrielle. Sounds like a guy totally different than the Leif I knew," said Tom while sipping his coffee.

"Let go of Gabrielle," I replied indignantly. "Tom, he wanted me to abort her to save our marriage. I figured the marriage was dead if that was his way of thinking. You may not know, Tom, but at the divorce, Leif turned down all custodial rights and any responsibility toward his daughter. He was so paranoid about his precious house and holdings, that he didn't even want me to have them investigate. So he gave me my options, retirement and all the savings that I had accumulated. You know, he even smirked when he said that I could keep them," I said getting a bit agitated.

"He must have thought that you had peanuts and he was getting off scot-free," interjected Lena.

"The joke was on him. My portfolio was substantial. Can I have a refill?" Lena passed the coffee pot to me.

"So, Vivi. What did you do afterwards?" inquired Tom.

“Easy. I rented a townhouse, worked at my company until my maternity leave, and was able to freelance after Gabrielle’s birth. That’s how I found out about the good stocks. If I saw that one of my clients had their act together, I would invest.”

“And why did you come back to Princeton?” Tom and Lena were all ears.

“Something weird happened to me in San Jose. I was in the checkout line at my local market when two women in front of me started to chat. One was dating a really good looking, blond architect from San Francisco who was going to set his lawyers after his ex-wife to get custody of his kid. Sounds familiar?” I asked rhetorically.

“Holy shit. So you moved?” replied Tom.

“Yeah, I went into a panic. I wasn’t going to lose Gabrielle to that jerk or to blow my nest egg on lawyers, no way. I felt that if I moved, Leif would have an expensive time trying to get Gabrielle. So in ten days, I bought a house, had a garage sale of our old junk, and moved back.”

“I don’t blame you. I would have done the same. I don’t know how he can live with himself, not knowing about his own flesh and blood. What a jerk,” muttered Tom.

“Well, what I want to know, now that we are trashing Leif, is why didn’t you get married in Princeton at your house. You know. Under the willow tree. Your mother was so upset that the wedding was being held in California," asked Lena.

“Like a fool in love, I let Leif talk me out of having it back east. But it was beautiful.”

“Oh, it was one of the prettiest,” cooed Lena. “I remember it being great weather, and that old adobe house, up in the hills of Napa, was a perfect location.

You looked ravishing. I must say though, I didn’t look bad myself,” I said in my usual self-deprecating way.

"And what about me. I thought I cut quite the figure," Tom interjected.

"Of course, my beloved. You were most dashing, and if you recalled, seduced me that evening. But I'll never forget when we were on the terrace that overlooked Napa Valley. We were having dinner at our table, and the fog was coming in lightly. The evening light was soft and misty. From the trees, a herd of deer came out from the woods to feed in the field below us. It was so beautiful. Like magic," whispered Lena, her face aglow in the memory.

"Oh, I remember that. Even musicians stopped playing so that they could watch." I exclaimed.

"Oh you romantic women. All I remember is that the food was terrific. Didn't Leif get Raoul to cater the affair? And finally, I was able to ravage Lena," said Tom with an evil grin.

"You know what my mother said about the wedding?" I said with a smile.

"No, what did Ghislaine say?" replied Tom.

"Vell, at least I did not pay for zat foolishness. Zere is zometing rong vit zat man. I can't put my finger on eet but zere is zometing," mimicking my mother's accent and mannerisms. Tom and Lena burst out in laughter.

Still laughing, Tom asked, "So Vivi, has your mother finally forgiven you?"

"Yeah, I gave her a wonderful granddaughter, named her after my dad, and came home with my tail between my legs. Plus, I'm now dating a Princeton lawyer. What else could she want?" I laughed at the thought of it all.

"Sounds like penance to me. But to really get her off your back, you'll probably have to marry your lawyer and let her parade you around the town in your wedding dress," teased Tom.

"Just remember, Vivi. Chintz. The word for the day is chintz," added Lena.

That's it. I've had enough. Time to end this conversation.

"What did I do to deserve this? All this marriage talk makes me hungry. Lena, where did you hide the dessert? I hope it's chock full of calories. You know, fat gravitates to people who are cruel and wicked toward their friends. You'll see," and I wandered out to the kitchen.

Marriage. All this talk about getting remarried had made me nervous. It was coming from all sides. Mom. Gabrielle. Lena. Tom. I didn't know if it was in my best interest. I just didn't know anymore.

Too bad we were not having fortune cookies for dessert.

Chapter 26

Today we were leaving Lena and her family. Gabrielle and Tara were tearful at the thought. They had pledged undying devotion to each other and promised to get together regularly. Tom had taken the day off to make sure that we had no problems getting on our way. He also properly packed up the car. It seemed that Lena and I had done quite a bit of shopping during my visit and had emptied a good deal of the antique shops. Poor Old Faithful, packed to the brim again.

“Vivi, it’s time for you to start looking for a new car. This one’s beginning to resemble the one used on the Beverly Hillbillies. A little more capital consumption won’t hurt you,” teased Tom while tying down furniture to the roof of Old Faithful.

“You’re right, but Old Faithful has been so good to us. It’s been through a so many traumatic periods in my life. I hate to part with it. It’s been so reliable,” I admitted.

"Listen, here is an offer. My niece just got her driving license and is driving her parents crazy for a car. This would the perfect answer. Incredibly safe and incredibly ugly. There is no way she would get the idea in her head to try for the Indianapolis 500 in that car,” said Tom while giving a final tug to the rope.

“Other than hurting my car’s feelings about its physical appearance, I accept your offer and willing donate Old Faithful to your cause. Gabrielle, give Tara a big hug. You’ll see her at Thanksgiving. Lena. Tom. What can I say for such a lovely stay and for rescuing us from the New Jersey heat. I promise to call when we get home. Thank you again,” I said starting to tear up.

One more round of kisses and hugs and off we went. Gabrielle was sorry to leave Tara but looked forward to her birthday party and seeing her grandparents. I needed to get back to the drawing board and pay some bills. I placed a memo in my head to start paying bills online.

The drive home was tedious and uneventful. Gabrielle kept me busy by chattering about her birthday, her friends and the presents. I hoped I wouldn't disappoint her, but the only thing that could keep her spirits down was the thought of rain on her special day. Finally, around four in the afternoon, we were home.

Damn, the house looked good! The windows were repaired, the gutters replaced and the outside had been stained. All the plants were in full bloom and the front yard looked like my chaotic flower dream. Gabrielle read my mind.

"Mommy, look at the house. It's beautiful. Just like you said it would be. Look at the flowers. They're beautiful. Everything's beautiful. Hurry and get me out. I want to see my house."

I turned off the engine, got out of the car and unfastened Gabrielle from her seat. She climbed out of Old Faithful and began to run amok all over the yard.

"Come on, Mommy. Come on. Let's see the back," she cried as she opened the gate. We were greeted by the sight of a wonderfully romantic nineteenth century setting. The roses had taken over the arbor, Canterbury bells, foxglove, lilies and larkspur were towering in their clumps, daisies sprang out their happy faces, and masses flowers were blending with one another. The lawn had been newly mowed. It was a deep green carpet that complimented the flowers. Truly, it was my dream house and garden and I knew I could never leave this Eden.

"Mommy, let's go inside and call up Grandmère and Richard. Can they come over for dinner?"

"That's a wonderful idea, Gabrielle. Let's call them now. Afterward, can you help me unload Old Faithful?" We entered the house through the front door and walked to the kitchen. Gabrielle brought me the portable phone and dialed her grandmother's phone number. I took the handset from her and watched her bounce up and down. Too much energy.

“Mom? Hi, it’s us, we’re back. Yes, it was lovely. Yes, she does have a lovely house. They are renting, you know. Because Richard needs to make sure his new firm is going to be successful. They both look happy to be back. So, how are you?” I asked. “Well we missed you guys and Gabrielle really wants to see you today and wants to know if you would like to come over for dinner. No, it’s no problem. I’ve got salad from the garden and we can put a steak on the grill. You’ll bring bread and dessert? Great. I’ll expect you and Richard around six-thirty. See you,” I said and turned off the phone.

"Gabrielle, it’s all set. Let’s go unload Old Faithful.” We walked out the front door to the drive way.”

“Mommy, everyone is right. Old Faithful is tired. She said so. She talks to me. We need to get a new car. When, Mom? When?” asked my poppet while helping me unload the car.

"Soon. I was thinking on the way back that we should retire Old Faithful. I also thought that we should wait a while. I want to turn the space above the garage into my new studio and I thought that it would be best to buy a car after that work was done. But now, I am in the mood to go car hunting. Let’s go sometime this week. You can help me pick one out, sort of for your birthday,” I suggested.

"Yes, Mom. That will be fun. Can I pick the color?”

“Sure, honey, as long as it’s not pink. No pink cars.”

“No, I don’t like pink or purple cars, Mommy. Mommy, you said you’re going to move your studio. Why? I like it in the house,” asked Gabrielle.

°‘It will be bigger and the light will be better for me. The room downstairs is too small and we can turn it into a guest room. Like when Tom and Lena come to stay with us,” I said while dragging in some antique lamps.

“But Tara and Alexandra get to sleep in my room, right?” pouted Gabrielle.

“Right, Gabrielle. So what do you think about my studio idea?”

“I guess it’s okay. Can I come and see you?” said Gabrielle in a worried voice.

“Of course. And we can get a little bed for you in case you want to take your nap in the studio,” I reassured her.

“That’s sounds good, Mommy. I like that.”

“Fine, now help me with this package. I think it goes in your room.”

In an hour the car was unloaded. We drove out to the market to pick up provisions and were back by six. By six-thirty, dinner preparations were done since summer cooking was usually grilled meats and vegetable with a garden salad. At six thirty-five the doorbell rang and I went over to greet Richard and my mother.

“Bonjour, Vivianne. Bonjour, poupée.” My mother glided through the front door. “How are you? We missed you. Thank you for your cards. It was the only thing that we had to look forward to each day. Doesn’t this house look wonderful? The staining is a wonderful solution. It doesn’t give the house the newly painted look, but is much gentler. I never dreamed when you bought the house that it would turn out this well. I am jealous about your garden. Your earth is better than mine. Mine is like a rock,” said my mother with a tinge of envy in her voice.

"Hi, Mom. Glad you like the changes. Hi, Richard. Thanks so much for baby-sitting the repairs. Did you also cut the grass?” Richard nodded his head. "Thank you, you are an angel. I am so glad it is done. And that the air conditioner is working. I’ve got dinner started. Let’s go outside and relax. What would you like to drink? Gabrielle and I went shopping and we bought just about everything” I said.

"A beer,” said Richard.”

“Richard wants une bière and I want sweet vermouth with a twist.”Mom was such a trip. No matter what Richard said, she had to repeat it with added confidence as if we didn’t believe it the first time. Usually his request were given in French in case I didn't understand the English version of the word. I made the drinks; Gabrielle got a Shirley Temple and I had a rum tonic. We quickly took our places at the outdoor table.

"Richard, isn't the backyard lovely. I love the rose arbors. What about Japanese beetles? Aren't you having a problem with them? I remember when you collected them in a jar as a little girl." Richard was busy carving his steak and was not tuning into Ghislaine's conversation.

"No, the Japanese beetles don't seem to be as attracted to the old fashion roses as they are to the tea varietals. At least, that what's happened here. Maybe that the bugs avoided this year because there weren't any decent roses here in the past. But you are right. The arbors are lovely, especially on a moonlit night," I agreed and took another look at the garden.

"Ah. So romantic. And talking about romance, guess who showed up here?" Mom just gave me the big, all-knowing wink.

"Pray, do tell, Mom."

"James. You called him, didn't you, to tell him that you were going out of town?" she asked making sure that I followed proper dating protocol.

"Of course I did, Mom. I called everyone," I said slightly exasperated.

"Well, he came around. Luckily I was here with Richard. There's no telling what Richard might have said to him," said Mom confidentially. "So, he was very polite. He is very good-looking. You really do attract the handsome men, don't you. He asked me when you would be back. Then he took a look at the house and looked puzzled. So I asked him if there was a problem. It was strange."

"What do you mean by strange, Mom?" I asked somewhat perturbed.

Oh, he turned to me and asked if the owners of the house were doing the upgrade and I told him that you were the owner of the house. He then got red in the face and said that he didn't know that YOU were the owner of the house," said Mom.

“That’s true, Mom. Like everyone in town, he assumed that I’m broke.”

"Oh, that’s my fault, I think. I was talking to Myrtle Weber and the girls at bridge several years ago, telling her that you didn’t get any money out of your divorce and that you were living in a tiny townhouse. Unfortunately, it got around town,” said Mom airily.

Aha, my suspicions were correct. It was the bridge game. Who needed the Internet, telephone, and telegraph services when there was a bridge game in Princeton. Well, no harm done. It really has been somewhat amusing.

“Well, Mom. Did he say anything else?” I asked knowing that there was more to the story.

“Yes. So then he said, “Why is she driving around in that old hunk of junk?” I told him that your father gave it to you, and you are sentimentally attached to the Volvo. Then I told him that when you sell it, you will be over a very hard time in your past. James said something about an appointment and very nicely said his good-byes." Mom smiled and seemed pleased with herself.

“So, what do you think, Mom?” I asked politely.

"About what?”

“About James, Mother.” Oh dear, something negative was going to fall out of Mom’s mouth.

"Oh, good-looking, prosperous, divorced. You could do much worse. He would provide well for you,” said Mom in a conspiratorial manner.

"What about him personally? Do you like him?”

“I don’t know. He’s not my type. No soul. Leif had no soul. That’s what puzzled me about him. Smart, handsome, well-educated but with no soul. I couldn’t put my finger on it at the wedding but later it came to me,” mused Mom.

“So I should strike James off the list.”

"I wouldn’t say that. The reasons that you get married now are different from your first marriage. He’s a nice man," she concluded.

"I don’t want him, Grandmère. Too shiny," piped in Gabrielle.

“Ah. Ma petite ange. You are but a child. Come show me what you brought back from your vacation. We’ll talk about your birthday,” consoled Mom and blew a kiss to Gabrielle.

Richard and I were left alone after the commanders left the table. He laughed. "Well, now you have it, Vivi. You should but shouldn’t marry the guy. All I care is that you are happy. Talking about another subject, Gabrielle said that you’re going to change the garage so that your studio is above it. Why don’t we take a look at the space,” said the ever useful and practical Richard.

"Great idea. Leave the dishes, Richard. Let’s go see what is feasible.”

Through the French doors, Richard and I walked across the terrace to the back door entrance of the garage. I opened the door and we took a look at the empty space and the overhead loft. Richard always traveled with a flashlight and scissors on his key chain, and a measuring tape. He ran the tape in a few places and made a complete inspection of the building.

“Listen Vivi, you know how your financial situation has been driving your mom crazy. Like we always think you’re broke,” he said turning red. Richard didn’t ever like to talk about money and finance.

“Yes, I know. Mom thinks that any day I’ll be in the poor house.”

“Well, this is embarrassing. When you were gone, your Mom was in your kitchen and accidentally, pulled out the file draw with your financial papers and your tax returns. I didn’t see her. I was outside.”

“Don’t tell me. She read the stuff, didn’t she.” I had this real desire to giggle but I didn’t think that Richard would understand. Plus I was getting tired of the “poor Vivi story” and the effect it had on the community.

“Just a few statements from your broker and the last three years of tax returns. Well, she sat on the kitchen chair and was quiet for a few minutes. She called me over and showed me some numbers. I told her it wasn’t our business. She said, “You know Richard, for years I had thought my daughter was a nouille, a noodle, a pushover, just barely making it and now I find out she could support all of us in comfort. She’s just like Gabe, her daddy. In her own quiet and unassuming way, she amassed a small fortune without anyone finding out, especially not Leif. I’m so proud of her, so smart and protecting herself so well, but I can never tell her why.”

And then your mother told me never to tell you that we peeked, but I’m so ashamed about what she and I did.” Richard was looking down at his feet.

“Oh, Richard. Don’t be hard on yourself. I’m surprised it didn’t happen earlier. This finance stuff has been driving Mom crazy. I can’t believe that she’s been so restrained for the last six months,” I said reassuringly.

"Well, the other things is that she’s starting, not to brag, but to set straight the record at the .... ”

“Bridge club?” I interjected.

Richard continued, “Well, yes. I mean, she’s not saying that you are loaded, but she is correcting any impressions that she gave in the past about you being in the poorhouse.”

I really wanted to laugh now, but Richard would think the family was totally insane. I don’t know if I wanted Mom to correct her tell-a-bridge communications of the past, but I didn’t have a lot of control over her. With my luck, every stockbroker in town would start calling.

“Richard, I realize this has been sitting heavy on your mind. Please don’t worry about it. No harm has been done. It’s just kind of funny,” I said quietly.

"Do you really have that much money, Vivi? I mean all that money...”

“Yes, Richard, I do. I’m not rich woman but I am very comfortably off,” I admitted.

Richard’s face lit up. "Well then, let’s start talking about double sets of wood windows and some skylights for your studio. They’re a lot more expensive but will really bring in the light.”

Chapter 27

"Mommy, Mommy, are you asleep? Mom, I hear noises at the back door. Can you hear it?" Gabrielle whimpered as she stood in front of the door way to my bedroom.

"What time is it? Five in the morning. No, I don't hear anything. Go back to sleep," I murmured.

"I heard it again. Please Mommy," she pleaded.

"Okay, I'll go check out the sound. Let me get on my robe. Now, where do you hear it?"

"Near the back of the house, Mommy. Don't you hear it?"

I really hoped that Gabrielle was not psychic and was able to hear the voices of the dead, especially if they made noises at five in the morning. Wait a second. I did hear something. Quickly I put on my robe and fluffy slippers.

"I think it's outside of the kitchen. Gabrielle, I'm going downstairs and out to the backyard to investigate. I want you to stay in the house. Do you understand" I commanded.

"Yes, Mommy," she solemnly sweared.

I went downstairs, through the kitchen, got my flashlight, and flicked on the outside lights. I could hear a small sound to the left of the kitchen. Going through my head were several scenarios, none pleasant. It could be a skunk or a raccoon, mortally injured, with rabies just waiting to bite me. Or perhaps a mad serial killer with a new kick on death, or a deer, loaded with Lyme disease. I approached the sound with great anticipation. There it was in the bushes. Oh heavens, it's a little puppy.

“Mommy, Mommy, it’s a puppy, a little puppy. Oh Mommy, we have to take care of it.” Gabrielle’s head peeked out from around my robe.

“Gabrielle, didn’t I asked you to stay inside? What if it was something bad that could hurt you? Did you think about that?” I said relieved that my scenarios were untrue and furious that Gabrielle didn’t follow my instructions.

“Oh yes, Mommy, that’s why I sneaked around you. In case you got hurt. But you didn’t. A puppy, Mommy. A puppy.”

Nothing except fear, dirt and hunger seemed to be wrong with the puppy and I couldn’t bear for it to stay outside any longer. Gabrielle was wide awake staring at the poor little thing. I picked him up and brought him into the kitchen.

"Honey, it must be lost. Listen, we’ll give him some food now and a bath. You’ll make him a nice bed in the kitchen and we will put out some newspapers so he can go to the bathroom. He can sleep down here. Then we will go to the dog doctor in the morning and make sure that he’s okay.”

“Can we keep him? Oh Mommy, can we keep him?” pleaded Gabrielle petting the head of the puppy.

“Honey, I don’t know. He might belong to someone. They could be crying that they lost their little puppy.” We walked back to the house and entered the kitchen.

"You’re right Mom. What do we do?”

“Oh, we’ll put an ad in the newspaper and see if we get any phone calls, I said reassuringly.

“What if no one wants him then, Mom? What will we do?” Gabrielle eyes were starting to tear up.

"Let’s not worry about that. Help me feed him. I hope he likes what’s in the refrigerator.”

"Mommy, here's some chicken and leftovers from dinner."

I chopped up the chicken and placed it in a bowl."That should be enough. Put it on the floor here." Then I filled another bowl with fresh water. Like all puppies, this one was no different and in two minutes was licking the few remaining crumbs of food off the plate. Now time for the bath. The poor creature was caked in mud.

"Gabrielle, I'm going to clean him in the kitchen sink. Go upstairs and get some shampoo and a hair dryer for him."

"I'm going. Do you think he'll like my shampoo? It's strawberries smelling."

"I am sure he will. Now hurry up," I ordered. Knowing that Gabrielle would want to be part of the action, I brought her stepladder to the sink. As I heard Gabrielle descending the staircase, I grabbed the puppy and placed him in the sink. Gabrielle slid into the kitchen with her pink shampoo bottle and her orange hair dryer.

"Okay, you're ready. I'm coming," shouted Gabrielle as she ran to the ladder.

"Now, we're going to wash him, just like I do with you. Can you get some old towels out of the big drawer? We'll use those to dry him. I'll start rinsing him now to get some of the dirt off." The poor dear quietly whimpered as I sprayed his fur with water.

"I've got the towels. I'll put them by me."

"Fine. Now let's put some shampoo on him. That's right, Gabrielle. Put a glob on your hand and now rub it on the puppy. Oh what nice lather you're making. Good, around the ears, and watch out for his eyes and inside his ears." The puppy was now resembling a baby lamb with all the suds around his body and a long nose sticking out of the foam.

"Mommy, he's really dirty. Look how the water is black."

"Isn't it. Now let's rinse him and give him another shampooing. He should be clean after this," I said hoping that after the early morning excitement, I could go back to bed.

"See, Mommy. I pour the soap into my hand and now I scrub him. Mommy, He's shivering. Do you think he is cold?"

"No, he's probably scared. He's never seen us and the bath may be scary for him. Wouldn't you be scared if some strangers gave you a bath," I asked a very excited poppet.

"Yes, I think so. Is he clean now? The water isn't dirty any more. Can I hold the spray and rinse him?" begged Gabrielle.

"All right, but I will hold him. He's very wiggly and wants to get away." After rinsing the poor dear, I wrapped him in a large old towel to damp dry. "Gabrielle, go upstairs and get the old quilt in the closet, the yellow one with the daisies. He'll also need something warm and cuddly to snuggle up with, like an old stuffed animal. And my old hairbrush in the bottom drawer."

"I know Mommy, my old pig. He'll like that. I'll get those now. Can I help dry him?" asked Gabrielle.

"Yes, now skeedaddle." Gabrielle dashed out of the kitchen and scampered up to the second floor.

In a minute, Gabrielle was back down with brush, pig and dragging the old quilt. We set up the dryer and start brushing the puppy's fur. He was not appreciating our efforts, but at least he wasn't biting. Nice dog manners were a requirement in this house. In ten minutes, we had ourselves a very fluffy puppy, pointed face with white and tan markings.

"What kind of dog is he, Mom? Is he a wolf?" asked Gabrielle.

"No, sweetheart, he's probably a nice, little mutt that will grow as big as our house. Now I'm tired so let's put the blanket and pig over here in the corner, and some papers on the floor. That's good. We'll let him sleep there. Come Gabrielle, time to go back to bed," I mumbled needing desperately to go back to bed.

We returned to our bedrooms. In two minutes I was fast asleep. I thought I heard some noises, but I was too tired to do anything but sleep. I awoke at eight thirty, and went downstairs for some coffee. Damn, no puppy, but a small wet spot on the paper.

Good, our little mutt was housebroken. Then I ran up to Gabrielle's room. Just as I expected. Our visitor and my poppet were fast asleep in her bed, nothing but their little heads popping out of the blankets. I quietly closed her door. What a smart cookie have I. She knew better than to ask her mother if the pup could sleep with her. What will she think of next?

Chapter 28

"His name is Shep. He told me so. He doesn't have a home and, Mommy, he wants to stay with us," Gabrielle informed me while she ate her bowl of cereal. Shep was happily inspecting the house making little yippee sounds.

"Is there anything else he wants?" I sighed; sip my coffee and remembering yesterday when we were dogless and fancy-free.

"No, not now. You know Mommy. I think about God a lot. Do you think about God?"

"Yes, sweetheart," I replied, curious of the new track of thought being explored by my little pumpkin. Where will this lead us?

"Well, I think that God felt bad that I didn't get the picture of the puppies, so He sent me Shep. Don't you think so, Mommy? I am so lucky, I have my puppy. Thank you, Mommy." Gabrielle looked over at me and flashed a beatific smile. I gulped my coffee and held back a fit of laughter. Personally that atrocious piece of artwork was more from the Devil and I didn't want to think where the dog came from. "Well, first let's see if Shep has another home, honey. We would have to give him back if someone claims him."

"I guess so." Gabrielle looked crestfallen.

I had to be the mean one in this party, and remind her of the possible outcome. "Anyway, I've called the vet, the animal doctor, and she's going to see Shep in an hour, so speed it up, kiddo."

"I am not a kiddo."

°'Well you will be if you don't get going this morning. Gabrielle, you'll also need to take Shep outside so he can go to the bathroom. I'll show you how."

"Okay, Mom, I'm going. I'm going," shouted Gabrielle as she slid off of her kitchen chair, grabbed her spoon, cup and bowl, and took them to the sink. "I'm going to get dressed now, Mommy."

It seemed we were rapidly becoming a family of three. Gabrielle, Shep and I bounded up the stairs to get dress, or in Shep's case, to watch. I quickly threw on a summer dress, sandals, slopped on some make—up and headed to Gabrielle's room. She was practically dressed except for her shoes and socks, which were being engaged in puppy play.

"Gabrielle, get a move on. I've got a piece of rope for Shep for his leash and a ribbon which we can use as his collar. See, it looks perfect. Let's take him in the garden so he can go to the bathroom," I informed Gabrielle. She quickly extracted her sock from the puppy's mouth, slipped the pair on her feet, slide into her shoes, and grabbed hold of the makeshift leash.

We bounded down the stairs and out the back door to the far reaches of the garden. Shep properly marked the shrubs and did his business. Gabrielle gave his leash a tug, grabbed my hand, and we headed to the garage. It took a little bit of time, since Shep wasn't acquainted with Old Faithful, but finally I got Gabrielle in her seat holding Shep.

"Now I'm just going in the house to lock up and to get my purse. I'll be back in a minute." Shep and Gabrielle ignored me. The tug-of-war game with the leash was of greater interest. I took note that the car's upholstery was not going to last under these conditions. I closed the side car door, ran into to the house, grabbed my purse, locked the house doors and returned to the car.

We drove north of town, to the commercial area. In one of the centers, I saw the name of the veterinarian and made a right turn into the parking lot. I scored on a parking spot closest to the vet's office and parked Old Faithful. Mom would have been proud of me. One of her greatest joys of life was finding parking close to wherever she shopped. Handicap parking drove her crazy and was the temptation from the Devil. Heaven help us if we had to walk more than twenty steps from the car to her store. And Mom was lucky; she had good parking karma.

We tumbled out of the car and headed to the vet's office. Gabrielle and Shep quietly found a place to sit away from the lady with the Persian cat, while I told the receptionist that we were here. In five minutes our name was called. We were ushered to a clean room with a metal table in the middle. The doctor, Dr. Elaine, a brunette in her mid thirties, entered and smiled at Gabrielle.

"Hi, you must be Gabrielle and Shep. Don't we look happy? Come, Gabrielle. Can you bring Shep to me so we can see how strong he is?" asked Dr. Elaine while taking out her stethoscope.

"Me and Mommy found him this morning. He was yucky. We fed him and gave him a bath? Is he okay? Can I keep him?" pleaded Gabrielle with a worried look.

"Well, let me take a look. Seems sound. Good teeth. I like the strawberry smell of shampoo." Dr. Elaine smiled, made nice sounds about Shep's general condition and Gabrielle tension seemed to dissipate. Shep didn't seem to be too upset about the inspection.

"Gabrielle, we will need to give Shep some shots so he won't get sick and I will need to teach you how to take care of him," informed Dr. Elaine. "Also you must not give Shep sweets, especially chocolate, which could kill him. No onions, garlic, or grapes either."

"Okay. Okay, I will, I will," sang Gabrielle, skipping around the room.

"Dr. Elaine, this sounds stupid, but what kind of dog is he, or what mix do you think he is?" I queried.

"Gabrielle and Vivianne, your little puppy is a five month old male and is in excellent health. I've check out his lungs, eyes, hearing, heart and a few other things. He should live to a ripe old dog age. Funny, he looks a sheltie, a purebred, but how he got lost or why is a real mystery. Usually people don't abandon a valuable dog, especially not a puppy. Now, for his care, you'll need to brush him everyday, and once a week give him a really good brushing. Shelties have two layers of fur and it is really important that the shorter hair does not ball up or stay wet. He'll need a real collar and a leash. If you are going to keep him, then you'll need to apply for his dog license. I suggest you get a book on caring for dogs with a section on herding dogs such as shelties and collies. They are wonderful dogs, especially for children. And take him to puppy training. Now I'm going to give Shep his shot. This will sting him a little bit, and he'll give out a yelp, but he needs to take this medicine. I'll send you a card when he needs to get his next booster shot." Gabrielle squeezed her eyes shut, not wanting to see Shep getting his shots. It was over in a minute.

"Thank you, Dr. Elaine for everything, and for squeezing us in." I was thankful that we got such a competent and sensitive vet through my internet search.

"No problem. Listen, I'm curious. Were you formerly Vivi Bartlett?" she queried.

"Yes, I was. I left the area about fifteen years ago, got married, got divorced, and recently returned. Why do you ask?" I replied.

"Oh just curious. I was Elaine Robertson. I remember seeing you when I was a freshman and you were a senior. I have an older brother, Jason Robertson. Perhaps you remember him?" she inquired.

"Oh, sure, Jaz. He was one of the wild boys. I'll always remember him with long black hair, skipping classes and cruising around on his Triumph motorcycle. What is he doing now?" Heaven help me, was this a walk down memory lane. I had a huge crush on Jaz Robertson, and an even bigger one on his Triumph.

"He is not longer the wild man anymore. He's married with four daughters, absolutely petrified that they will bring home boyfriends that are anything wild like him. He lives in Seattle and is an engineer for a computer company. He's doing fine and gave up the motorcycle," she replied with a laugh. "I was always being watched by the high school teachers to see if I was a troublemaker like my brother, "she concluded.

"Tell him that Vivi says hi and if he's ever around, tell him to drop over with his family. I'd love to see him," I answered.

"I will. Well, you best be going. Gabrielle, I hope that you will take special care of Shep. He's a wonderful puppy and will become one of your most special friends."

"I will, Doctor Elaine. I promise," Gabrielle solemnly swore and she took Shep in her arms.

"Well thank you again, Dr. Elaine." We left the room, stopped by the reception area to pay the bill and left the building.

"Look Mommy, on the other side," screamed Gabrielle.

"What is it?" I responded alarmed by the scream.

"Cars, they sell cars. Let's go over and take a look. Please. You need a car Mommy and Old Faithful is tired," she said while still carrying Shep through the parking lot.

Her idea made sense. It was time to let go of Old Faithful and today was as good a day as ever. *Vivi, let's get the gang in the car and cross the highway.* I got everyone back in the car, turned on the ignition, and pulled out of the parking lot. Once on the highway, I started to turn at the first dealership.

"No Mommy, not this place. I don't like this place. The other place. Down there," commanded my backseat driver.

I drove into the car dealership. Actually Gabrielle's selection was good since this was the dealership selling the brand of car that I like. A salesman approached us. Poor man, we must look like the family from Hell to him. A woman, a kid, and a dog in a rust bucket of a vehicle.

"Hi, can I help you or do you just want to browse?" he inquired.

"You can help. I'm looking to replace my Volvo. I need something large, but not too large, that is practical but that has some pizzazz," I replied.

"Well, we have several options on the lot, and if you see a car you like but want some changes, we can special order it. Your Volvo looks like it's been a real good car for you. How many miles does it have?" he asked politely.

"Almost three hundred thousand. It's been wonderful but it's starting to show its age," I admitted while standing around the car lot. Gabrielle was running around with Shep and looking at the interiors of various models.

"Three hundred thousand miles. That's just a young puppy in Volvo time. Are you going to trade it in? I'd buy it for my son. It's the safest thing I can put him in while he's in his idiot driving years," he confessed, sounding a bit low about his son's driving skills.

"Sorry, another worried parent has claimed Old Faithful," I answered back.

"Too bad. Well, my name is Steve Guttman and why don't we just take a stroll and see if anything meets your needs." Quickly I introduced myself and explained my needs in further depth.

"Mommy, over here, over here," screamed Gabrielle while Shep made puppy howls. This is the one." She was jumping like a cricket trying to get my attention.

"Wait a second; I'm looking at this station wagon." I had learned not to quickly capitulate to Gabrielle's whims. She needed about two more minutes of jumping up and down. Actually none of the cars I saw was of any interest to me. They looked practical and very dull. Steve and I slowly walked over to Gabrielle's area. She ran up to us with Shep on the rope, and dragged me to her area.

"This is the one. We like it. It will look pretty against the house. And we could do neat things with it like go camping," she exclaimed with great enthusiasm.

Pretty good for a kid almost five years old. Gabrielle had picked out a white all-wheel drive vehicle, that had great gas mileage and great consumer reviews. Except for the white color, it was the car that I was considering. However I didn't know about this camping concept that she sprung on me. I was a bed & breakfast woman, and my idea of camping was a hotel without room service. Oh, maybe if she camped out in the back yard we could get over this new idea. Plus who would be crazy enough to take a white car camping?

"So Steve, seems like this may be the one. What can you tell me about this car?" This guy was nice and was taking his time to explain the features and benefits of owning this car. The car answered my needs and Gabrielle liked it. Then Steve dropped in the closing point.

"Look, we've had this one on the lot for a while. I can give you a price below book and throw in a dog gate, so that your puppy won't jump on the leather seats. It could be ready by this afternoon, even with a lease or with terms." Steve mentioned an acceptable sum. Sold. So what if it is white, at least it will reflect the heat.

"Do you accept local checks? I could give you a check for the full amount and you could get it approved by my bank with a phone call. I would need someone to bring the car to my house, if that would be possible?" I asked.

For a moment, Steve was stunned and needed to regroup himself. I guessed that he never expected that the family in the wreck would actually purchase a car in less than an hour and pay for it in cash. He pulled himself together quickly. "That will be great, Mrs. Bergstrom. Why don't you and Gabrielle step into the office where we can take care of all the paperwork? It should only take twenty minutes."

As we walked to the office, Gabrielle, still jumping, sang, "Oh, Mommy. This has been a bestest day. First we find Shep, and now we have a beautiful car for him. It's okay that we don't have the puppy picture, it's okay. I'm so happy. Come on Shep, let's go."

In the office, we quickly finalize the sale. The car would be delivered late this afternoon to the house. Steve threw in a few more goodies. He must have been feeling guilty about the ease of this sale and brought out a miniature racing jacket for Gabrielle. She gave him a big hug as we left the dealership.

After we got home and had lunch, Gabrielle went to her room for her nap. Damn, where was that dog. I headed for the most obvious place. Snuggled in Gabrielle's arms was Shep, and my two little ones were fast asleep with soft afternoon light filtering on the bed. I went downstairs, loaded my digital camera with film and returned to her bedroom.

There my little princess, you shall have your puppy picture.

Chapter 29

Big day today. It was the birthday party and the question that presented itself was whether I would live through this ordeal. I had foolishly invited fourteen children from one to three o'clock to destroy my house.

Actually it shouldn't be that bad. I had hired a magician and if this kid could just do a few card tricks, I would be off the proverbial hook. The house shouldn't get too damaged since the party was being held outside. Richard had been decorating the terrace with streamers and I had put out several umbrellas for additional shade.

Gabrielle was so excited. She was beyond anyone's control. She had been driving me nuts as the inspector, checking the details.

"Mommy, is the cake here? I want to see it," commanded Gabrielle with Shep following her little footsteps.

"It's in the refrigerator, Gabrielle. Go in and look for yourself." There, the little juice boxes were now in the cooler filled with ice.

"Mommy, did you get the party favors? Where are they? I need to see. Mom, did you send out all the invitations? Is everyone coming?" demanded Gabrielle as she ran back and forth from the kitchen to the outdoors in the summer Jersey heat.

It went on and on. Finally, Grandmère arrived and rescued me. Actually she had just rescued Gabrielle from a mother going postal. She was upstairs helping Gabrielle with her clothes and hair.

"Mom, can you come up," shouted the birthday girl to me while I was trying to get the plates, cups, forks and spoons out of the storage section of the kitchen.

"Vivianne, attendez. We are coming down," announced my mother. And down the stairs they came, Gabrielle and Shep flew down with Mom carefully taking her time as not to fall. My baby was turning five years old today and looked like angel, her long hair held back by a velvet hair band that sported a jaunty bow and wearing a Lawn of Liberty dress that I found at a garage sale. Little rose sandals encased her feet and a look of happiness glowed on her face. Mom and I smiled at each other and I secretly thanked her for her loving efforts.

Then the party began. Fourteen equally lovely children entered our home with chaperoning mothers. I had set up several parents' tables with food and wine. Quickly the children merged together and the parents sat at a good arms' length, merrily chatting, eating and drinking.

Two hours passed quickly. We played the standard party games, had cake and ice cream, and watched the magician. My fears were relieved. The high school boy I hired as the magician did a wonderful job and the children were mesmerized.

Money was coming out of their ears, baby rabbits out of a hat, and flowers out of his sleeve. Gabrielle was being a lovely hostess, sharing her new toys and making sure that her friends were having fun. Even Shep was on his best of behavior, letting everyone pet and cuddle him. *See Mommy, no need to worry*. At three-thirty, the last of the tiny invitees had left. It was a lovely day.

Gabrielle looked around the back yard and said, "Thank you Mommy. Thank you, Grandmère and Papi. It was the best birthday."

"It's not over Gabrielle," said Grandmère with a smile. "You have still the presents from your Mommy, Papi, and me to open. Why don't we go get them?"

"Oh, yes, let's do that now," agreed Gabrielle.

My mother and Richard went out to the Cadillac and brought several small boxes and two big presents in to the house. I went into the studio and carried out my offerings. We returned to the rose arbor and sang "Happy Birthday" to Gabrielle.

“Thank you, thank you, for coming to my birthday party. Can I start with this big present from Mommy?” piped up Gabrielle.

"I think that would be a good idea.” Gabrielle unwrapped the large box and let out an excited squeal. “It’s a tent. A real live camping tent. Like the big kids. Thank you Mommy.” She came over to me and gave me a big wet kiss.

"You said that you wanted to go camping. I thought that we could first start practicing in our back yard.”

“Can we do that tonight, Mommy? Can we?” said Gabrielle, her eyes alight.

"Sure. We’ll ask your grandfather to set up the tent and we’ll give it a go tonight. Now, I think you should open your grandfather’s present.”

Gabrielle attacked the next present. After wrestling with a good deal of paper and tape, she finally opened the box. "Wow, a sleeping bag. I’m going to be a real camping person now. Can I also keep this in my room?”

“Anywhere you want. Just make sure that you tell me where you’re going to camp,” said Richard. "I’ll be very sad if you go to Alaska and you don’t say good-bye,” he teased.

“Papi, I’m not going to Alaska. I’m going to the backyard. Let me give you a kiss. Thank you, Papi. Gabrielle ran over and kissed Richard. Now came the attack of the smaller presents, which she treated with great gusto. From my mother and myself she received some lovely clothes and wonderful books.

“Thank you, thank you, thank you. Now, Grandmère, what do you have hiding behind your back?”

My mother pulled out her the largest of the presents and handed it over to Gabrielle. “I wonder what this is? The box makes no noise,” asked Gabrielle. She ripped open the wrapping paper and peered inside of the box. “Look, Mommy, Look. Grandmère gave me a beautiful bedspread.

And curtains. Just like the flowers in my room. It's so pretty. Thank you so much. My bedroom is the prettiest in the world."

Gabrielle grabbed the next package. "Boy is this heavy, Grandmère. I wonder what it is?" she said while unwrapping the box. Her little hand reached inside and out came a pair of tiny figure skates. "Wow, Grandmère, real skates. They are so pretty. Thank you so much, Grandmère. Here is your kiss. When can I start ice skating, Mommy?"

"As soon as the skating rink opens, Gabrielle, which should be in four weeks."

"Do you know how to skate, Mommy? Can you show me? Can you do the turns, like the ladies on the television?" she asked.

"So many questions. Yes, I know how to skate. You can ask your grandmother. When I was about your age, your grandmother bought me my first skates. So when the rink is open, we'll go and I'll show you how to skate," I promised

"Okay, Mom. Thank you everyone for my birthday."

"It's not over, sweetheart. I have one more present. I don't know if you'll like it but let me go get it." I ran back to the studio and got the large flat present. "Here it is," I shouted as I dashed out to the arbor.

"Wow, it really is big. I wonder what it could be? It's not the puppies. They were sold." Gabrielle threw her last bit of energy to opening up the present. She took a look at it and smiled. "It's me. It's a picture of me with my Shep. It's my own puppy painting. Thank you, Mommy. Thank you for the best birthday ever. I love you."

Later, after setting up Gabrielle's tent, Richard and Gabrielle solemnly marched up to her room and ceremoniously mounted the picture. Richard then hung the drapes while Gabrielle placed her comforter on the bed. My mother and I were permitted in the room afterward as the viewing audience.

Later that night, finding myself in a tent with my snoring princess and her dog, I peeked my head out of the tent, looked up at the sky, dark and hazy with the moon trying to pierce the cloud covering.

"Thank you, God. Thank you for the best year ever.

Chapter 30

“We’re here, we’re here. Last one in is a rotten egg,” screamed Gabrielle as she headed to waves breaking on the shore. “Come on, Mom. Come in the water with me.”

"Wait for me, pumpkin. I’m coming.” I dropped my umbrella and beach bag on the hot sand and ran down to join Gabrielle who was madly hopping at the shoreline. “Okay, hold my hand and we’ll run in.”

It was mid-September and although the month had been hot, the beach was relatively empty. Since Gabrielle’s birthday, I had been working with my contractor and Richard on the studio and decided that it was time for a break. We had rented a cottage for a week at the Jersey shore and would stay until tomorrow. I had invited James and his two children, Erin and Sean, who were at the cottage changing into their beach clothes, and who would be joining us momentarily.

“Mom, do you like Erin or Sean? I don’t, they’re yucky,” piped up my picky hostess.

“Yucky doesn’t describe anything. Why don’t you like them? They seem to be very nice and well-behaved.” This was awful to say, but I didn’t like them either. They had little sly eyes and looked sneaky. Probably liked to tattle on each other. In fact, I found them repulsive. *It is only for a day, Vivi. Be nice. I will like James’ kids, I will, I will, I will.* Maybe a mantra would help.

“They’re mean. Erin tried to pinch me. Can I hit her?” asked the future warrior.

“No, I want you on your best hostess behavior. If they don’t behave we’ll never invite them again. But I want you to be nice. Like it was your birthday party,” I replied getting exasperated over the thought of a day ruined by shitty kids. Now I should throw in a bribe to sweeten the pot.

"And if you do a real good job, we can buy that collar for Shep that you've been eyeing."

"Okay, Mommy. I'll be perfect. But I don't like them at all," asserted Gabrielle.

"Listen, here they come. Wave and let's go meet them. Just remember what I said." We waved at James and his clan, and ran up to meet them. James was staking the umbrella into the sand. Erin and Sean looked displeased.

"I hate the beach," stated Sean. "I only like swimming pools. Mom says that the ocean is full of dirty water from toilets and there are strange things swimming in the water."

"Yes, the ocean is really dirty, Daddy. That cottage they are staying in is pretty ratty, isn't it. When Mommy took us to the Riviera, we stayed at the best hotels," added Erin.

"Now, come on guys. I want you to make an effort. It was nice of Mrs. Bergstrom to invite us and you can have fun playing here today. Don't worry, we'll be going home tonight," apologized James.

What charming children you have, James. Can I kill them now? Smile Vivi. "Why don't we inflate the rafts and you can take them out on the water." *And maybe they could sail off to Borneo.* "Come on James, start pumping," I said jovially.

We got the rafts inflated and forced them upon Erin and Sean, who sulkily took them to the water's edge. After a few minutes of hesitation, they paddled off in the waves. James and I set up the rest of the blankets, towels, coolers and beach chairs. Gabrielle was in the midst of trying to bury herself in the sand.

"Mom, can you help me. Please cover me up. I need more sand," begged Gabrielle.

"All right, I'm almost finished here. James, why don't you get wet. You look like you need a dip." It was true; James was getting red and sweaty.

"Right. I never thought that it was so hot at the beach this time of year. Look, Erin and Sean look like they might be having fun. I better not make a big deal about this. They're going out of their way today to be royal pains. The kids wanted to be at the country club where there's a large pool and they can order food to my account," he admitted.

"Go on. Maybe you can pretend to be a shark and scare them," I said deviously.

"Yeah, that will do it. See you in a bit." James gave me a peck on the neck and took off down the beach. *Nice body, Mister. Just lose the kids*. I went over and helped Gabrielle cover herself. She looked like a white powdered donut. The sand had made a fine dusting over her arms and body.

"All right, sand lady. I've covered you up the waist. If you lie down, I'll cover all of you to your chin," I promised.

"Do Mommy. Mommy, do you think that Shep misses us? He's locked up at the cottage," replied Gabrielle with her worried voice.

"No, I don't think so. He probably is taking a nice snooze on your bed right now and dreaming of snacking on Erin and Sean," I joked.

"Mommy, I love Shep very much. No one has called for him, have they?"

"No, no one has called and it has been at least a month since I started the ad. Shep is probably ours for good." I stopped covering Gabrielle with sand.

"I knew it. God sent him, like I said. God sent me my Shep. Mom, I'm hot. Can I get out of here? I'm thirsty. Can I have something to drink?" I took a paper cup from one of the bags and filled it with water

“Here is some water. Not so fast. Now let’s go play in the water.” My powder sugar daughter got up and we quickly went to the edge of the water.

The water was perfect, warm with nice wave action and little undertow. I lifted Gabrielle on to my shoulders and we frolicked in the waves for a good hour. Gabrielle made great squealing sounds so it was always fun getting her wet. I then extracted her off of my shoulders so that we could run into the small surf. The sun was overhead and it looked about the noon hour.

“Come on pumpkin. It is time to get lunch ready. Get a move on it or I will kiss your fanny.” Gabrielle took off like a greased pig and headed up back to our umbrella. I scampered after her and we set out the plates, cups, napkins, plastic utensils, chicken, salads and chips on top of the coolers. I had another cooler filled with lemonade for all of us to drink.

James and the enemy came to join us. Erin and Sean were actually smiling and looking pleasant.

"Wow, do you see that last wave I took, Dad. It was the biggest,” said Sean, red in the face from the sun.

"Looked like a mean one. You did really well riding it.” James seemed less tense. He must be relieved that his brats were finally enjoying themselves.

“Listen, I don’t want to be the mean one of the group, but before eating I want everyone to get recoated with sunscreen. If we do this now, and let it dry, you won’t have to put on another coat for the rest of the day.” Surprisingly, there were no protests and everyone complied.

“Okay, everyone. Let’s eat.” Either the food was great or else our party was ravenous - I suspected the latter of the two. Before I knew it the chicken has been devoured and the cole slaw was gone. Sean and Erin were actually behaving well at this moment. Oh, maybe they weren’t so bad, it was their upbringing.

"Hey, Dad. Can Erin and I go back to the beach? Please," begged Sean.

"Yes, but stay out the deep water. You need to digest your food. Why don't you play on the surf with these flat boards that Mrs. Bergstrom brought?" James was starting to mellow out and allowing his kids to experiment with wake boards.

"Yeah, they look like fun," said Erin. Come on, Sean. Follow me." They grabbed the boards and headed back down to the water.

"Mommy, can I take my nap in the chair. I'm tired," complained Gabrielle. I got Gabrielle comfortable on the lounge chair and covered her with a towel. She should sleep well in the shade. Gabrielle fell asleep in a few minutes.

James cleared his throat. "Finally, I have you to myself. I thought this would never happen today. I thought that I'd first have to kill my kids, which at certain parts of the morning, did seriously enter my mind. Christ, can they be a pain. But they are having a great time. Thanks for inviting us and putting up with us, Vivi."

"You know, they're not bad kids, James. They were rather sweet during lunch." I replied.

James continued his apology while running his fingers in the sand. "They're not in a good environment. Karen has them in boarding school during the year and drags them around Europe if I don't take them. The problem I have is my business. It takes up all of my time and I just don't get to see enough of them."

"James, this is my lecture of the year. If you don't act now, your kids are going to turn out to be real shits. Even worse, they'll be strangers that you don't even know or like. And later on when you need them, when you'll want to see grandchildren, the connection will be broken." I spoke my piece and too bad if that was uncomfortable.

"You're right, Vivi. I need to do something. It's just that my business demands long hours and travel. You're lucky. No one will pay me to stay home and paint." *Don't lose your temper, Vivi. James doesn't realize that he just put you down.*

"James, let me be candid. There's nothing, not business, love interest, money whatever, that's more important than what you do with your children. Your kids are the only things that count in this world. The only things. I made a lot of changes and some sacrifices in my life for Gabrielle. At times it's been hard. But she's worth everything and more to me," I declared.

"Karen isn't going to change. I guess I'll be the one. I'll talk to her about having the kids next year during the summer," replied James in a heavy voice.

"And James, don't just stick them at the country club and leave them for the day. Make sure you spend time with them, like going to the Delaware Water Gap, or mix some of your travel with Sean and Erin. But be WITH them." *There, stop blaming Karen and spend some time with these kids or else you're going to have problems in the next couple of years.*

"Okay, I'll try, I promise. Not to change the subject, but there's something that I have to apologize for. About a month ago, when you were with your friends in Connecticut, I dropped by your house. I saw some men working on the place and decided to be nosy. Your folks were there and I introduced myself. Your Mom told me that you were getting the exterior of the house repaired." James' face was turning into an adorable shade of red.

"Looks nice, doesn't it." *Let's not try to help the poor guy. Go on James, I want to hear this.*

"Well, I assumed that you were fairly broke, trying to live in a nice part of town for the good address. At Winston's party, there were rumors to that effect. You know, you're an artist, you have a rust bucket of a car, your house looked neglected and you never received child support or alimony.

It all added up. Then when I saw the work on the house, I realized that maybe I was wrong. Maybe you're doing fine and you don't need help from anyone. Any way, if I've said anything or done anything that was, um, uncomfortable or..."

"Thank you, James. I appreciate and accept your apology. This whole money thing has been really embarrassing. Anyone that talks to anyone assumed that I was broke when I moved back to town. People will believe what they want to believe so I never set the record straight," I replied.

"I still don't understand. Being a designer, and not having child support or a settlement, how did you do it?" James looked at me confused.

"Stocks. Stocks and company stock options. Since I was in California, I knew which companies were hot, and which hot companies were going public. I gambled on a few theories and it paid off. I'm still gambling, but only with my play money. I've got the rest tied up in blue chip stocks and bonds. So your assumptions are correct. I don't need help from anyone, but that doesn't mean that I might not want it. And I do need some good friends." James coloring started to cool down and so did my temper.

"Thanks, Vivi. Now I want to have a serious conversation with you about us. I know you're a bit hesitant, well that you had a really bad time in the past with your husband and are gun-shy, but I really care for you and would like for our relationship to develop. I know that I'm to blame for not getting this show on the road, my business takes up to much of my time, and I've been traveling a lot. In fact, after I drop the kids off tonight, I have to pack for a six-week trip to London. But when I come back, I want to be with you more Vivi. Maybe we can get away for a week. You and I," said the stud muffin across from me.

Okay Vivi, you knew that this would happen, that you can't spend your whole life just dating men. What are you going to say to this man? Make a decision, you idiot. Darn, James is looking at me with puppy eyes. He is a good and caring person, great looking, and nice buns, so what's the problem. I'm just missing some chemistry. Maybe with a bit of sex, the chemistry will develop. I better get over this hurdle.

"You're right, James, about all of it. About my divorce, my marriage, and being gun-shy. I'm still scared as hell, but it's time for me to get over the past," I admitted.

Then James leaned over to me and started kissing me, nice long, lovely kisses and I was starting to feel warm all over. *Hell, so what if I'm not hearing music or seeing stars, I could grow to like this a lot. And maybe I could grow to love you, James.*

Chapter 31

Brilliant October, the pinnacle of autumnal beauty. Cold, cold mornings and hot crisp afternoons. Black and orange football games and yellow pompom chrysanthemums. Intoxicating winds carrying smells of freshly mowed grass, leaves and bonfires. The windows were open in the newly completed studio and on days like today, a capricious and arbitrary mood captured me. Concentration on pixies and fairy illustrations had been broken.

“Gabrielle. Grab Shep and meet me on the front lawn," I yelled from the window. I was so pleased with the windows in the studio. In fact, I was in love with the studio with its marvelous light that poured in every day. Richard was right. The windows turned a little modest garage into a cathedral of the arts. It was a little over dramatic statement on my part, but my soul got religion whenever I saw the light beaming through the windows.

I ran down the stairs and out the back door. Somewhere on the side of the house was my rake. *Ah, there it is.* I grabbed it and ran to the front of the house where I began raking the first of fallen leaves into a sizable pile.

“Hi, Mommy. What’s up?” Out came Gabrielle wearing a strange concoction of clothing. Mademoiselle was wearing my pink full slip over her clothes along with a summer straw hat. She had attacked my make-up drawer and created lip lines that the most daring model would never sport. She resembled a miniature Folle de Chaillot. Shep seemed to be part of this carnival. He sported a tiny hat and had flowers stuck in his collar. I looked to see if my neighbors were watching.

“It’s time to test the leaves. I’ve made you a pile. Now it’s up to you to jump in it and test them to see if autumn is really here,” I dared the short mad woman.

"Okey-dokey, Mommy. Let's go, Shep," and Gabrielle took a running leap into the pile; hat, slip and all. Shep was one step behind her. "Fall is here," shouted Gabrielle as she got back on her feet. "Do it again, Mommy. Do it again," she begged.

I piled up the leaves again, raking more leaves from the side of the house and watched while Gabrielle and Shep slammed into the pile again.

"That was a good one, Mom. Can I help with the leaves? Shep wants to help too."

"Sure, there is a small rake on the side of the house near the trash can. May I ask, what is the reason for your fine attire?" I queried Gabrielle who was putting herself back together from the leaf jumping.

"I am wearing fine attire because Shep and me are having my birthday party. I am going to have a birthday party all the time. I want one at the skating rink. Do you think so, Mommy," shouted Gabrielle as she galloped and grabbed the kiddy rake.

"Well, that sounds lovely. But the ice skating rink is closed on your real birthday. Maybe we could have it at the roller skating rink?" I asked.

"Okay, did you know that I am the best skater in the class? Mrs. Carol says so. Jimmy Michaels can't even stand up. I am learning to go backwards, like this," and Gabrielle demonstrated her new steps on the front lawn."

"Maybe when James gets back from London, we will all go ice skating together," I suggested.

"I guess. He's okay, I guess. But not his kids," and Gabrielle started raking in earnest.

"My pile is made. Why don't we put yours and mine together so it will be bigger?"

Gabrielle threw down her rake to the side and started to dance while I merged the piles. “Higher, Mommy, higher,” screamed Gabrielle with her blond pigtails hopping around her head. “Get more, faster.”

The morning coolness was beginning to evaporate in the inevitable warm fall day. This weather change unfortunately was slowing down my raking ability, since I was getting damn hot. My leggings and long sleeve knit shirt were fine for the morning, but would be soaked with sweat shortly if I kept up the activity level. *Okay, I'll be the obliging mother for a few more jumps and then, lunch time.*

Raking leaves had never been my forte and was one aspect of life that I was glad to escape from when I moved to California. Every year, my mother and father assumed that I would naturally enjoy a hearty workout raking leaves. To me, either the leaves hadn't settled and there was more to come so why rake now? On the other hand, if leaves were all on the ground, they had probably been rained on and were now too heavy to rake. Today, I found myself acting like my parents, happily spending my weekend pursuing the never-ending raking task and allowing my daughter to make a mess of my work. *So, get with it, Mom, and rake up some more leaves.*

A car slowly passed and parked one house down from ours. Gabrielle jumped into my lovely pile of leaves with Shep closely behind. I was always watching the cars passing by. Maybe I was afraid that Leif would show up after all these years.

“Do it again, Mommy. Do it again. One more time,” demanded Gabrielle throwing me kisses. I started piling up the leaves. A tall dark haired man got out of the car. It was not Leif. I turned around and raked up all the leaves that were spread by Gabrielle's last jump. The pile was ready to be pounced on again.

“Your turn, Mommy. You do it,” demanded Gabrielle as she ran around the pile with Shep.

"All right. But then you have to kiss me.”

“Okay, Mommy. Can Shep kiss you too?” squeaked Gabrielle now skipping.

“Sure, he kisses everything anyway,” I admitted.

“Mom, on your mark, get set, GO!” I jumped and landed majestically in the leaves, collapsing into my newly scattered pile. Lying down I saw the elm trees with a background of a lovely robin’s egg blue sky. “Kiss, me,” I begged, throwing my arms to the sky and shutting my eyes. “Kiss me.”

“I’ll kiss you if you insist but I’m afraid that you will box my ears if I grant you your wish,” said a deep masculine voice.

I opened my eyes and looked up. Standing above me is the tall man. I looked into his eyes. Standing above me was the face of a fallen angel.

Chapter 32

I jumped up as if hit by lightning.

"Do you remember me, little Vivi? Do you remember me at all?" he asked softly.

"Now I should box your ears for being so silly. How are you, Robbie? Nice to see you. It's been so many years. Give me a big hug." One thing good about Robbie was that he always obeyed orders. *I see some things never change.*

I stepped back from the hug and took a good look. The face of a fallen angel disappeared and taking its place was a good-looking man with blue eyes and brown hair, thinning on the top. No longer skinny, Robbie's body, had comfortably filled out, eradicating all signs of gangliness and colt-like movements of youth.

"You look wonderful. You filled out. You don't look like you're not going to make it to your next meal," I said laughing.

"Yeah, I must say that I'm no longer skinny and starving. What is it, being a teen-ager, that you can eat all day, and never have enough food? But you, Vivi, you look wonderful.*" Flattery will get you everywhere, Robbie.*

"Thank you, thank you." I gave a little bow. "I owe it to my hairdresser. I'll send her your compliments."

"Hi, I'm Gabrielle. Vivi is my Mommy." Gabrielle stuck out her right hand.

Robbie bent down, got on one knee and shook her hand. "It is a pleasure meeting you, Gabrielle. I'm Robbie. You know, you look just like your Mommy when she was little.

"I know, my Grandmère keeps telling me that. Are you here to have lunch with us?" I'm floored. My daughter had just invited a man she met seconds ago to lunch.

"Yes, we were about to go in and eat. Do you have plans? Would you like to join us?" I added trying to remember if the house was somewhat tidy.

"Yes, I would like that. I would like that very much." Gabrielle grabbed Robbie's hand and led him to the front door.

"My Mommy got us this house. It's the house of her piano teacher long time ago. It was very old but now it's almost all fixed up. It's my favorite place. Oh, this is my puppy, Shep. He's special. God sent him to me. One night Mommy found him outside crying. I'm five now. I'm a big girl." Gabrielle smiled at Robbie pleased with her dissertation of our current status.

I could not believe my little chatty Gabrielle, the child that wouldn't say two words to James, was babbling away at Robbie as if he was her long-lost best friend. Gabrielle, Robbie, and Shep went into the house and awaited me in the living room.

"Vivi, this house is beautiful. This living room has a great feel to it. You were always so good with colors." Robbie looked around the living room and smiled when he saw my Dad's photos on the wall.

"Thanks, I am proud of it myself. It's been my first adventure in interior decorating. Redoing this house was a fun project. Come, let's go into the kitchen and we'll make up a tray of food to take outside." We walked into the kitchen. "Gabrielle, can you show Robbie where he can find the flatware, cups, plates and napkins. Is everyone in agreement for bacon, lettuce, avocado and tomato sandwiches? I even have some fresh tabouli salad." Everyone, even Shep, nodded and in ten minutes lunch was ready. Robbie carried out the tray and I brought out the beverages. Gabrielle set the table and we sat down to eat on the terrace, overlooking the backyard in its fall splendor. Gabrielle broke the ice by starting the conversation.

"Do you have any kids?" asked Gabrielle sweetly while grabbing a sandwich.

"Yes, Gabrielle. I have a son. His name is Connor and he's seven years old. He's at his grandparent's house right now," answered Robbie amused by the Social Miss.

"Your parents, Robbie? And how are they doing?" I asked.

"Oh they are fine, thank you. They moved to Griggstown about four years ago. But, I meant my wife's parents who are living in Pennington. I lost her in a car accident two years ago, and he's all they have. She was an only child," explained Robbie quietly.

"Oh, Robbie, I'm terribly sorry," I said horrified at the news.

"Yes, it's been hard. Connor and I've been two sad guys for a while. It's been an especially difficult period for him. They were very close. She was a wonderful person." I never know what to say when someone loses a great love. I waited a few minutes so that Robbie could gather his composure and continue the conversation.

"I'm dying of curiosity - pass me the tabouli, please - what are you doing here and how did you happened to drop by?" I spooned some tabouli on to my plate and took a sip of water.

Robbie took a second to gather his thoughts and started, "I've been thinking of moving back to Princeton. I had a computer company up in the Boston area and after Anne's death, Anne, that was my wife's name, I decided to sell. The business was taking up a lot of my time, and Connor really needed me. I was approached by a major company the year before the accident, and called to see if they were still interested in buying me out. So four months later, we closed the deal. Then I realized there was nothing holding me to the Boston area; Anne's parents and mine live here and would like to see Connor more often, the schools are great in this area, and my childhood memories of growing up in Princeton are really strong. I liked it here as a kid. So for the last couple of weeks, I've been house-hunting and staying with my folks. Then a couple of days ago, I ran into Tuesday, who was showing me a house. She said it was funny how people were starting to move back and that you moved here recently and bought a house from her. She gave me your address. I was thinking off giving you a call, but you're not listed in the directory. So I decided to drop over and see if you were home. Your green salad is excellent, by the way."

"Garden grown," I answered while taking a long look at him.

"Mom, can I be excused and go play with Shep." Gabrielle was beginning be look bored with our conversation.

"Sure, honey." Gabrielle slid out of her seat, picked up a tennis ball nearby and started playing fetch with Shep.

"Nice kid," said Robbie. "Pretty as her Mom."

"You're doing great with the flattery, Robbie." This was a new development, the old Robbie was never known for his tact.

"So what about you? Husband - yes or no? Your parents, are they well? Where have you been for the last twenty-some years?" asked Robbie turning the tables on me.

"Let me see. Dad passed away about sixteen years ago. Mom met Richard five years ago, and is married. They're very happy. I ran away from Princeton and ended up in San Francisco as a graphic designer, fell in love, got married, got pregnant. Was given an ultimatum - to choose him or the unborn child. So I chose having my Gabrielle, got divorced with full custody, lived in San Jose for four years, and moved back to Princeton in the latter part of January."

"Why now," asked Robbie.

"Oh I heard something to the effect that my ex might want to challenge the child custody issue, so I fled. I'm still looking over my shoulder. That's why I am not listed in the phone book. Lena, you remember Lena? Well, she met her husband the same time I met mine at a health club in San

Francisco. They now live in Connecticut, still in love with each other, and have two kids. They'll be spending Thanksgiving with me," I added trying to get the conversation off of my marital disaster.

"So what are you doing now? Working in the graphics field?"Robbie inquired while munching on a sandwich.

"No, working fulltime for a firm or company is too time intensive. I wanted to be with my daughter, so now I'm an illustrator. Mostly children's books. I wrote and illustrated one called *The Alphabet Fairies*."

"I know the book. You did that? I bought it for my sister's kid last year. The illustrations are wonderful. Are you also painting?" Robbie loved to hang out with my Dad and I when we were messing around with photographs and paint.

"Somewhat. From time to time I get a request for a child's portrait. Whether I take the request depends on how much I like the child." Between the work, taking care of Gabrielle and the house, it keeps me pretty busy." I really liked talking with Robbie. He still had beautiful dreamy eyes and the beautiful hands. *Oh, forget it, Vivi, he's probably still in heavy mourning for Anne.*

"It has been so good to see you. I always wondered what you were doing or how you turned out. Listen, I don't want this to end, but I promised Connor to play football with him this afternoon. Are you doing anything this evening?" Robbie's eyes were bright blue and inquisitive. I wonder if he's still a great kisser.

"No, nothing in particular. In fact, Gabrielle is going to sleep over at her girlfriend's house."

"This maybe sounds silly but will you go out with me this evening? Like a date. We could go to that little Italian restaurant on Nassau Street, and then take a walk through the University. I think they're having some to-do at the art museum. We could pop in and take a look." *Oh my God, he's asking me out on a date.*

"I don't think it sounds silly. Rather nice. I'd love to be your date. What time?" I asked trying to be nonchalant.

"Oh, around seven. I'll pick up Connor and spend a couple hours running him around. If he doesn't get a lot of exercise, he doesn't sleep well at night."

"Don't I know that problem. I have the same problem with Gabrielle. Thank heavens for Shep. He's got endless energy to play with her," I replied.

"That's a good idea. Maybe when I find a house, we can get a dog. That might also help Connor work through the death of his mother. By the way, any chance of you selling your house to me? It really is wonderful," added Robbie while filling his glass with more water.

"No way, Robbie. But you know, this house was on the market for months. No one wanted it. It was really run down. You should have seen it then. So keep an open mind at house-hunting," I said.

"Maybe you should help me. I'm starting to hallucinate this stuff and I'm not the greatest shopper."

"Sure, you're on." I smile at the thought. Shopping with Robbie. This could be fun.

"Well, I better get going. Let me help you with these dishes in the house." Robbie got up out of his chair. We stacked the plates and cups, placed them and all the remaining bowls, flatware, and trash on the tray. Robbie picked up the tray and carried it into the kitchen. I turned around to call Gabrielle.

"Gabrielle, Robbie is leaving. Would you like to say ...," and quickly I was interrupted.

"Mommy, I'm coming. I want to say good-bye. Don't let him leave. I'm coming," screamed Gabrielle from the under the big elm tree that marked one end of our property. She broke out in a run, with Shep galloping at her side.

I entered the kitchen, carrying the luncheon remains. Gabrielle raced through the door and ran up to Robbie with her sidekick.

"Robbie, I came to say bye-bye. And Shep wants to, too." Gabrielle looked straight up at Robbie and smiled shyly. Robbie bent down and gave my poppet a hug and a pat on the head for Shep.

"We'll walk you to the door, Robbie." We escorted Robbie through the living room to the front door. '"Thanks so much for dropping in. It has been lovely to see you."

"If you come back, can you bring Connor to play with me and Shep? We could go down to the brook," pleaded Gabrielle sweetly.

"Don't worry, Connor will be here the next time, if we are invited."

"Oh, you are, you are. Aren't they, Mommy?" begged Gabrielle.

"Of course, they are. Thanks again and I'll see you later." Robbie then leaned over and quickly gave me a kiss on the check. "Later," he said hoarsely and sprinted out to his car. We waved as he drove off and then returned to the kitchen to finish cleaning up.

"Mommy, what did you mean when you said that you will see him later?"

"Oh, he's taking me out tonight." This kid didn't miss a step. I had better watch it around her.

"That's good. I like him very much. He's very nice. I hope Connor is as nice.

I'm sure that Connor is lovely," I replied and Gabrielle started talking softly to herself, tossing her head back and forth. At this time, I didn't want to know what she was plotting or what she was going to tell the Supreme Commander. All I knew is that I was humming a tuneless song and that my cheek was still feeling warm from his lips. Very warm.

Chapter 33

"...Robbie, Mom, Robbie Terhune. Yes, that's what I have just been trying to tell you. Robbie dropped over to say hi, and we're going out to tonight. Dinner and to the Museum. The Art Museum on campus. Yes, the one with the Picasso sculpture in the front. He's widowed with a little boy. He's changed a lot. Filled out, no longer skinny. Gabrielle is spending the night at Loretta's house. No, I don't think he will take advantage of me. He's still in mourning. Mom, he's just an old friend. No, I won't do anything stupid. Yes, I know, James is a very nice man who cares for me. Yes, I'll get Gabrielle on the line. Gabrielle, it's your Grandmère," I shouted to Gabrielle, who was running up the stairs.

"Mommy, I'll get it in your room. Thanks. Grandmère, it's me. Hi. Mommy, hang up, please."

I turned the handset off in the kitchen and sat down with a cup of coffee. Can that woman interrogate. I had better anticipate a more stringent crossfire after my date. I wondered how the two commanders were making out on the phone. I probably would be devastated if I overheard their conversation. I had better interrupt them. Loretta will be here in ten minutes to pick up Gabrielle, and we still needed to pack her things.

"Mommy," shouted Gabrielle from the second floor. "Grandmère wants to know if I can go to New York and see Mr. Monet's paintings."

"Let me speak to your Grandmother." I seized the telephone. "Mom, what's up? Next Saturday? You're staying over at Jeannette's? That sounds wonderful. I'm sure Gabrielle will love it. You know how much she loves her book about Linnea at Monet's garden. All right. I'll have a nice time. Thank you. Je t'aime aussi." I hung up the telephone and headed out of the kitchen and up the stairs.

"Gabrielle, honey. Get a move on it. Loretta will be here shortly. We need to make you an overnight kit." I entered Gabrielle's domain, a vision in violets. Spread all over her room was every single outfit she owned. "Honey, you don't need to take all of this. Just a nightgown and tomorrow's change of clothing. May I help you?"

Gabrielle was looking depressed by her activity. "Mommy, I don't have anything to wear. Can't we go shopping?"

"You have lots of nice clothes, pumpkin. Let's pack your green corduroy pants and top combo. They will look nice with your new jacket. And you'll need some socks, those blue ones are nice, a t-shirt, and a pair of panties. Now we will need a toothbrush and toothpaste, your towel, pillow and wash cloth. Do you want to take a doll or an animal? No? Why don't you get Shep's blanket and your sleeping bag? Now you're ready." This idea of not having a thing to wear was new and perhaps a nasty indication of life with a teenager.

"Oh, Mommy. Thanks. I better help you clean up. I get so confused. It is my first time over night. Are you going to get fixed up to go out?" Gabrielle wrinkled her little nose at my leggings.

"Of course, to uphold the family honor, I will change my clothes. I'll even put on make-up," I promised while packing up her things.

"Good, I like Robbie. He's nice. Do you think he's nice`? Was he nice when he was little?"

"Yes, he was a very nice boy and he seems to be a very nice man. I think I hear Loretta's car in the drive way. Come on, let's go down and meet her." Gabrielle and I ran down the stairs with Gabrielle's pack and met Loretta at the front door.

"Guess what, Loretta. Mom's got a date with Robbie. He's nice. She knew him when she was little," explained Gabrielle.

Loretta grinned, "Childhood sweetheart. And just think that Gabrielle won't be here tonight. Perfect timing. So are you going to do IT?"

"I haven't done IT in years. The idea terrifies me. We can forget the big IT," I admonished her lightly.

"Mommy, what is IT?" queried Gabrielle as she entered Loretta's station wagon. Whitney was waiting for her with a shaved-head doll that had been the recipient of too much love and attention over the years. Gabrielle climbed into the extra car seat and awaited an answer. Shep jumped into back of the wagon and found a comfortable area near the girls to curl up.

"Have a nice time pumpkin. Remember to help Loretta and be polite so you can come back." I locked Gabrielle's car straps and gave her a kiss.

"Mommy, what is IT?" demanded Gabrielle.

"Bye, I'll miss you. Tomorrow, let's go for a bike ride. Bye." I waved at Gabrielle as Loretta maneuvered the car out of the driveway and into the street. That was a close one. Hopefully she will have forgotten her line of questioning by tomorrow.

It's time for me to take a shower and get my act together. I walked back to the house, and headed upstairs to my bedroom. Off with the clothes, into the bathroom, turned on the water and stepped into a lovely warm spray. I squeezed a dab of the current protein miracle shampoo into my hand, patted it into my hair, and created lather sculptures on my head. Wonder what Robbie was thinking right now? Maybe he's was the shower, too, washing his hair. Wonder what his body was like now, in the shower? How much he had changed? *Vivi, get it together, and get rolling. At this rate, you'll still be in the shower when he comes.*

Okay, towel off, deodorant on, moisturized and brushed my teeth. Blow dried my hair and put some make-up on my face. There, I was starting to look human. Now for the clothes. Nothing too formal. I know; slacks, a cashmere sweater and a sweater-jacket for when it cools down. This all needed an accent; my Hermes scarf and my pearl studs. I looked in the mirror. Not bad for forty, not bad at all. I hoped Robbie was not disappointed that I didn't look eighteen years old and destroying a secret fantasy. *Yikes, the doorbell. Quickly, get some lipstick and perfume*. Okay, I was ready. I hurried down the staircase and opened the door for Robbie.

"Hi, Vivi. You look lovely. And you smell good. I always remember how good you would smell in school."

"It's that French upbringing. You look nice, too. Would you like a glass of wine or anything?"

"Actually, since it's Saturday night, I made reservations so we should be going," said Robbie shyly.

"Let me get my purse and jacket and we can leave." What was with me? James would get beautifully dressed in silk ties, cashmere sweaters, and jackets, and here I was moon-eyed over a man wearing a striped flannel shirt and a polar fleece vest. We were so talkative yesterday and now it was like the cat's got our tongue. I gathered my belongings and we headed out to Robbie's car, a Volvo, albeit one of a newer vintage than Old Faithful. I saw that Robbie hadn't gotten his ego wrapped up in his car.

"I know, I should get a new car, but this station wagon has been so dependable and is really practical," apologized Robbie. He turned on the ignition and we took off toward Nassau Street.

"Robbie, just before my dad got sick about twenty years ago, he bought a Volvo station wagon. He gave it to me when he could no longer drive. Just a couple of months ago I finally bought a new car. The Volvo's in the garage waiting for Tom, Lena's husband, to bring it to Connecticut for his niece. So don't apologize." Robbie nodded and grinned. The remaining segment of the ride was held in silence until we parked the car.

"Well, here we are. I wonder if this restaurant is as good as it was when I lived here? Vivi, are you all right? You're so quiet." Robbie hadn't been motor-mouth himself. Maybe he was regretting making a date with me?

"I'm fine Robbie. I was just thinking, after all these years, how nice it is to see you." I got out of the car and as we started walking toward the restaurant entrance, Robbie took my hand. Warm and firm.

"I was really surprised to hear that you moved back to town. Here, let me get the door. I never thought that you would come back." The hostess approached Robbie. I scanned the restaurant and saw no one that could report back to the Commander.

Robbie spoke to the hostess, "Reservations for Terhune, seven-thirty." The hostess scanned her seating chart, checked her reservation list, and nodded. "Your table is waiting. Please follow me," she gestured and placed us at one of the tables by the window.

Once seated, Robbie looked up at the ceiling. "Same old art work. Maybe the food is as good."

°'Well, they've classed up the place a bit with white linen napkins and table cloths. No more plastic red and white checks."

"That's usually an indication that they've seriously raised their prices," Robbie smiled at me. I'm doomed.

"Oh, Robbie, you're terrible. Well, I know what I want without looking at the menu."

"And what is that, Vivi. Some rare and exotic meal from the ancient Etruscans."

"Nope, eggplant parmesan and a glass of red wine."

"You're easy to please. And I'll have lasagna," replied Robbie.

The waitress came to take our order. Robbie recited our requests and ordered an excellent Italian wine.

"Good choice, Robbie. I didn't know that you were into wine."

"Anne and I took a trip to Italy about ten years ago and visited some vineyards. Actually, I had quit my job and we went on a lark. All we could afford to do was to visit vineyards and drink free wine. We had a wonderful time," and cleared his throat.

"Lucky you. I haven't been to Europe for years. Maybe next summer I can take Gabrielle and show her off to the relatives. It might be a lot of fun and maybe she is old enough to travel overseas and remember something of the trip ten years later," I mused.

"Gabrielle is a lovely kid. You've done a good job raising her alone. Don't you hear anything from her father?" I shook my head. "What a fool. She's beautiful. She looks just like you. Who wouldn't want a little girl like her?" Robbie looked confused about Leif's action.

"I don't think that Leif wanted any kid, let alone her. Maybe it's better that way. She is all mine. So, let's get off my most disliked subject, my ex, and on to you. What are you going to do, now that you've sold your business?" I asked.

Robbie was happily telling me about his new project, which was writing programs and tools for on-line security. I was trying to focus on the conversation, which was difficult since he did have the most beautiful eyes. Tonight they were dark blue.

".... So when I quit my job, I was asked by the father of a classmate, to write a program protecting their mainframe from hackers. That job was the foundation of my old business and it grew like crazy. The company that bought my business asked for first rights on any new programs I develop. It really works out well. I can design software, without staff and once it has progressed to a certain level, I turn it over to the company. They pay me a fee plus my royalties. Now I don't usually need to be away from Connor and I can spend time with him after school. He's much more reclusive since Anne's death. I'm trying to line up activities like soccer, where he can meet kids his age," Robbie concluded.

“Didn’t you use to play ice hockey? Is Connor going to enroll in peewee hockey? I’m enrolling Gabrielle when she’s six,” I said.

“They’re taking girls? Times have changed. That’s a great idea. I forgot about hockey since Anne thought it was an unnecessarily violent sport. Thanks Vivi, for mentioning it. I’ll check it out. Aha, dinner.”

It was a perfect dinner. At any moment, I expected that the owner would come out with his accordion and begin to sing *That’s Amore*. I wasn’t not worried if my eggplant fell in my lap or if I spilled the bottle of wine. For once, I wasn’t worried at all. We drank our cappuccinos and shared a delicious tiramisu. Robbie took care of check, helped me into my jacket and we left the restaurant. The evening was definitely cooling off.

“You don’t mind the walk to the museum, do you Vivi? I mean, we could drive?” asked Robbie.

“Robbie, it’s only five minutes away. And after that lovely meal, I certainly could use the exercise. When was the last time that you were on campus?” I replied.

"Seems like decades ago. I came here once to deliver a speech on a security issue, but that’s all. Lovely, isn’t it? Stars and the crescent moon.”

“It is the smell in the air that I love. I missed it in California. But I was really glad for the respite from raking. Funny, I must be over my leaf trauma. I seemed to enjoy raking the stuff this afternoon," I said crossing the street with him.

“You know, you threw me for a loop. When I first passed by in my car and saw you, I thought I was back in a time warp. You looked like the Vivi I knew from high school.” Robbie reached out and held my hand. If I was a cat, I’d be purring.

“Yes, and then for every step you took to come closer, five years were added to my face until I became an old hag. Like a piece of morphing software.” I teased as we went thru the front gates of the university.

"Vivi, funny as always. No, you really haven't changed. In fact, I think you've gotten prettier. Maybe it's because you have Gabrielle. You certainly are nicer." His eyes were bluer than ever and twinkling as we strolled toward the museum.

"Pardon me Sir, I always was nice to you. You were just impossible."

"Madam, I reserve the right to return to this subject. Here we are." Robbie ushered me into the Museum, where our coats were collected at the door. We ascended the short staircase and received a brochure about the new collection from a volunteer.

I loved museum and gallery openings. Over the years, the art of an opening had become quite refined. Museum and gallery openings meant good finger food, excellent wine and superb coffee. This event was no exception, and I was happily holding a glass of wine while munching on a lovely mini-napoleon. Robbie had piled quite a few sweets on his plate. I would have never believed that only a while ago, we were stuffed from our dinner.

"Vivi, what do you think of the new collection? Personally, it's not my taste. I'm not really fond of neo-medieval."

"When I look at it up close and see the intricacies in the designs, I really like it, but from far away, most of it leaves me cold. It's too much for me. Like the Victorian age. When you look at each Victorian piece separately, they're lovely, but when it's a room full of that stuff, it's heavy; it is too oppressive for my taste. What I really like best at this opening are the desserts." I grinned and took another bite from my tasty little napoleon.

"Some artist you are. However, I agree. Especially about the desserts." We walked around the museum which was a perfect size. Not too large to become overwhelmed by art, but not too small to be frivolous. Closing time approached and we made our way back to the entrance to claim our jackets. The witching hour approached.

Robbie assisted me with my jacket and then put on his vest. We started walking back to the car.

"Damn, it's cold. I guess winter is on its way. Vivi, are you all right?" said Robbie concerned that I was freezing.

"Oh yes, if we walk fast. I forgot about how cold it can get at night, this time of year. I think I've just burned enough calories to kill one marzipan. By the time we make it to the car, I think that the napoleons will be gone, too." I started picking up the pace which was harder for short me than tall Robbie.

"After what I ate, I don't think anything will help. But walking quickly will warm us up."

There was silence for the duration of the walk. Not out of not having anything to say to one another but due to the cold and the need to concentrate our energy. Several minutes later we arrived at the car. Robbie unlocked the Volvo, and we quickly entered, shutting the doors. Now it was time to gracefully say adieu. Darn, I really didn't want this evening to end.

"Robbie, it really was a lovely evening. Thank you for the dinner and the museum opening. I had a great time."

"No, I have to thank you, for listening to me talk and ramble on. It's been a long time since I've anyone to talk with. I know I'm rather rusty at this social stuff, but I'm glad that I decided to drop over today to see you."

So was this the kiss-off or do I get to see you again? Maybe I had to think of something, fast. I wanted to see this man again. I liked him a lot.

But Robbie took the plunge."Listen, Vivi, maybe you're not ready for anything, who knows what condition I am in, but I want to see you again. Connor and I are leaving early tomorrow morning since we need to get some things done back home, but we'll be back next week. What are you doing next Saturday?" he asked earnestly.

Think of something, Vivi. Be clever. Non-threatening. "I have an idea. Why don't you bring Connor skating next Saturday at Baker Rink? It's open then for the public and I can bring Gabrielle. She's going to New York City for the night with her grandmother, but she will be free for the afternoon. She's very curious to meet Connor. Don't ask me why."

"That's a great idea. Connor will love it. I'll come pick you and Gabrielle up. What time?" asked Robbie.

"One o'clock. Skating will last until four. I'll bring the cocoa and munchies."

"You're on. Here we are," and Robbie brought the car up to the front of the house. We got out and walked to the front door. I scrambled through my purse looking for my keys and unlocked the door.

"Excuse me for leaving, but I do need to get up early tomorrow morning. I'll pick you and Gabrielle up on Saturday. Thanks again for being such good company." Then Robbie kissed me on the forehead, murmured something incomprehensible to me, and returned to his car. I waved good-bye, until his car was out of the driveway, then turned around and went inside the house.

Damn. I had a wonderful evening. It was better than I hoped for and yet I want more from the night. Much more. Was I ready? And was Robbie ready? I ran upstairs to the mirror in my bedroom. Funny I looked like the same old Vivi, but I felt different, tingling, and alive.

I peered out my window and saw a shooting star. *Make a wish, Vivi, make a wish. I wish, I wish, I wish that Saturday was here.*

Chapter 34

Saturday came finally. I wanted so many times to pick up the phone and call Robbie but I had manage to restrain myself. Actually, the latter part of the week was bearable. Maybe the magic was wearing off and I could go back to my life. *Don't get your hopes up, Vivi.* Last weekend may have been a cosmic phenomena.

Funny, everyone had left me alone. There had been no questioning from my mother or from Gabrielle. However Gabrielle was very excited to meet Connor and was ready to go. She had her skating clothes on and her skates were on the kitchen table. Beside her, a suitcase was ready for New York containing her favorite dress. We were in the kitchen finishing our lunches. The quiet was deafening.

“Mommy, I hear a car. Do you think that is them?” she inquired apprehensively.

"I don't know. Why don't you go look outside?" I said tired of tension level in the house.

“Okay, Mommy,” and Gabrielle hopped off the chair, ran over to the living room window with Shep and peeked through the curtains. “They're here. Come on, Mommy. Let's go.”

"Wait a second. Wait until they come to the door and please show them in." I got up from the table and took dirty plates to the kitchen sink. I stared out of the window above the white sink. This day could be a disaster, a real disaster. *Oh well, here goes.*

“Hi, Robbie. Hi, are you Connor? I'm Gabrielle and this is Shep. He's my puppy. I found him,” piped up Gabrielle at the door.

"Hi, can I pat him? He won't bite me will he?" said Connor timidly

“No, he’s really nice”, interjected Gabrielle, “Sometimes he might nip, if we are playing a rough game. Mom says he does that because he’s only a puppy.”

“Hi, Gabrielle. Where’s your mother?” I heard Robbie’s deep voice in the entry way. Maybe this will work out.

"She’s cleaning up and getting the food in a bag.” Quiet. It was time for me to make my grand entrance. I grabbed the food bag and headed to the living room. Robbie was sitting on the sofa watching the kids play with Shep. I took a look at Connor. Déjà vu, a younger red-head version of Robbie and so cute with those little auburn curls. Of course, Connor will think those curls to be the bane to his existence once he turns thirteen.

“Well, I hate to break things up, but why don’t we get going. Hi, Connor, I’m Gabrielle’s mom. You can call me Vivi”, and I brought out my right hand. Connor nicely put his hand in mine and looked me shyly in the eyes.

“Mom, can we take Shep?” asked Gabrielle after Connor I shake hands.

“No honey, sorry. He’s better off at home. There’s no place for him at the skating rink and then we’re driving you to your grandmother’s house. ”

“Okay, let’s get going. Can I carry the bag of food?” asks Robbie.

“Sure, and Connor, can you help Gabrielle with her suitcase? Thank you.”

It was a clean exit. So far, no disasters. The house was locked. Gabrielle had all her belongings, and I was still in one piece. We tumbled into Robbie’s car. Conversation was pedestrian, the kids were mostly talking about ice skating. A few minutes later, Robbie dropped us off in front of the rink with all of our skates and paraphernalia while he searched for a parking space. He quickly spied a spot, parked the car and joined us. We entered, en masse, the skating rink. The kids were in a rush to get on the ice. It seemed that I could not lace Gabrielle’s shoes fast enough, but despite the groans, she was finally ready.

“Connor, I’m not too steady. Can you hold my hand until I’m on the ice? Mommy usually does it but she’s slow today.” Connor nicely obliged my princess and the two of them set foot on the ice.

“Talk about beating a path to the door,” said Robbie with a smile.

"Well, Gabrielle has been doing nothing else today but talking about ice skating and meeting Connor. Look, they’re holding each other’s hand while they skate.” They looked adorable. The tall red-headed boy, holding the hand of a tiny bit of golden fluff. Damn it, where was my camera.

"It’s a precious time, isn’t it? I’m so lucky to be able to see my son playing. Today, so many parents don’t have this opportunity,” said Robbie wistfully.

"I know, we’re lucky. Listen, I’ve finally got my skates on. Are you ready?” I said wanting to get moving. The ice was calling my name.

“Race you, but slowly. It ‘s been a while.”

No pressure, it was just for fun today and we were having a great time. Everyone got to skate with one another and sometimes we skated all together. At break time, while the Zamboni circled the ice, we sat down on the cement bleachers and had cocoa and cookies. Then, back on the ice. The time passed quickly. Gabrielle decided she wanted to practice her new steps in the center of the rink and asked me to watch. Connor and Robbie skated off with each other.

“See Mommy. Watch me do my figure eights. Are you watching?” shouted Gabrielle to be heard above the din of the skating music.

“Yes, Gabrielle, I’m watching” Gabrielle demonstrated a wobbly figure eight and repeated the step several times on each side.

“Now that is looking lots better, pumpkin,” I said encouragingly.

“Now watch me do an arabesque, Mommy.” I watched and noted that Gabrielle’s arabesque, or whatever they call it in skater’s terminology, seriously needed work.

"Honey, you need to practice more."

"Show me, Mommy. You use to do them." If there was anything I learned from ballet lessons, was how to do a perfect arabesque. I started to glide and then executed the perfect step. Gabrielle was impressed.

°°Okay Mom, let me do it. Like this?" It was still wobbly.

"You need to pretend that you are being pulled with a string. One piece is in your hand. And one piece is tied to your blade that is on the elevated leg. Now try it." It was a definite improvement on Gabrielle's part.

"Now Mom, do the arabesque where you bend down," commanded the mini-general of my life.

"Oh honey, I'll try. But I'll probably end on my fanny. It's been a long time," I replied hesitantly.

"Come on, Mom. For me, please. Try it," she begged.

This would probably put me in the hospital. What a way to end the day. But I was my daughter's fool and hero. *Here goes nothing.*

I took off with a glide, got into an arabesque and started to bend over. Whoops, I landed on my fanny. It must have been a sight. Gabrielle was giggling.

"Wait Vivi, I'll give you a hand." Robbie must have seen my acrobatic attempt. Where is Connor? Oh, there he is, skating with another boy.

"Thanks, I just felt my forty years on that landing." I reached out to grab Robbie's hand. It was gloveless and felt strong.

Robbie drew me to my feet. I looked up into his soft blue eyes and once again saw the face of the fallen angel. He pulled me into the warmth of his chest where I could feel his heart pounding. The face of the angel leaned over and kissed me, a kiss radiating from his heart and soul, a kiss that went on and on as we slowly revolved on the ice.

And like a moon circling the earth, my tiny daughter skated around us, turning and twisting, spinning and twirling, oblivious to the event that was shattering her mother's precious world.

Chapter 35

"Dad, that was a lot of fun. Can we go skating again?" Connor's exuberance was contagious.

"Yes, Mom, when can we do it again?" Gabrielle's eyes were bright and shiny. The children had a wonderful time at the rink. And, if I know my daughter, she'll fall in a deep sleep in ten minutes. That was perfect for the trip to New York.

"Whenever you want to go. It was a lot of fun. I'm glad you liked it, Connor." Such a difference from James' kids.

"Yes, I did. I had a very good time. Thank you for inviting me," he said politely.

"Our pleasure. Gabrielle loved skating with you. It was nice of you to take care of her."

"You know, she really is fun. I didn't know that five year olds were so much fun. I thought that they were like babies," replied Connor.

"I am not a baby," protested the wunderkid. Connor apologized and the two conversed about the highlights of the day. We, in the front seat, were very quiet. Robbie held my hand from time to time. Ever since the kiss at the skating rink, we had scarcely spoken a word to each other. The silence was comforting, each of us deep in private thoughts, aware of a new direction, a new possibility in our lives.

"That's Grandmère's house. The one with the yellow mailbox. Turn here, turn here, please," shrieked Gabrielle. Robbie followed her instructions, turned into my mother's driveway and parked the car. I slid out of the front seat and assisted Gabrielle with her seatbelt. Robbie and Connor got out, went around to the back of the car, and unloaded Gabrielle's suitcase. My mother stood at the front door of her house, waved, and came down to greet us.

"Hello, poupée. Hello, Vivi. This must be Robbie. It has been many years, over twenty, hasn't it? Very nice to see you. Bonjour, you must be Connor. You look just like your daddy. Oh Richard, I want you to meet someone." Richard walked out from the back yard.

"Richard, I would like you to meet Robbie, it's Terhune, isn't it, and his son Connor. This is my husband, Richard Nicholson. Vivi knew Robbie in high school" The men solemnly shook hands.

"Well, Mom, I've brought Gabrielle's suitcase with one set of play clothes and her good dress for the museum. We went skating today, so Gabrielle should fall asleep as soon as you get her in your car. Okay, pumpkin, can I have a big kiss?" I bent down and got a big wet one planted on my cheek.

"Can I hug everyone else good-bye, Mommy?" I nodded my head. Robbie swings Gabrielle up and gave her a miniature bear hug. He then deposited my little fluff on the ground near Connor. The kids gave each other big hugs.

"We'll go skating soon, Gabrielle," promised Connor.

"Connor, don't worry. I'll see you soon." And Gabrielle blew him a kiss as she went to the front door of my mother's house.

"Robbie, it is lovely to see you again. I hope you come back when there is more time. I'll make you a famous French dinner." Robbie seemed to have gotten my mother's approval. She didn't make dinners for just anyone.

"I accept gratefully. In fact, I'm counting on it. Well, are we ready? I have to get Connor to his grandparents? We moved toward the Volvo and slid back into our seats. Robbie started the ignition.

I leaned out the front window and called to Gabrielle, "Be good, sweetheart. I'll see you tomorrow night."

My mother, Richard and Gabrielle waved good-bye. Then my mother shouted, "Merde, Vivianne, merde."

"What's that about, Vivi?" asked Robbie.

"Nothing, just a little French humor on her part." Basically my mother had just told me to break a leg.

In fifteen minutes we were in Pennington. Connor had been our social host during the ride once his initial shyness had worn off. Today he could match Gabrielle on chattiness. We drove up to a brick house with black shutters on a tree-lined neighborhood. Robbie parked the car by the curbside and in a flash; Connor was out of the car, running toward the front door. Robbie grabbed Connor's overnight bag and we followed. Connor's grandparents opened the door and gave Connor hugs and kisses.

"Hi, Betty. Nice seeing you, Bill." The men shook hands and Robbie gave Betty a hug. He turned around and introduced me. "This is Vivianne Bergstrom. We went to high school together. We took our kids skating today."

"It was great, Grammy. I went skating with Gabrielle. She's little but very cute," added Connor.

"Hi, Vivianne. Nice to meet you. Come in, come in. Bill, why don't you get these folks something to drink? I'm sure they can use it. Now, Vivianne, how old is Gabrielle?" asked Betty as she walked me to her living room. The men went off into the kitchen and we sat down in the cranberry velvet armchairs.

"Call me Vivi, please. No one calls me Vivianne. Gabrielle is five going on twenty. She's at her grandparents," I said.

"Oh, do they live in town?"

"They live in Princeton. Perhaps you know my mother, Ghislaine Bartlett, I mean Ghislaine Nicholson? My mother remarried five years ago."

"Oh, yes, I've played bridge with her many times at the YMCA. So you're the daughter who's come back from California. How do you like living here again?" *Oh shit, what did Betty remember of my mother's conversations?*

“We do. I loved the weather in California, but I have been appreciating the seasonal changes. My daughter loves it here, especially being near her grandparents.” I glanced around the room. Placed on most of the antique bureaus and tables were photographs of Anne; Anne with Robbie, Anne and Connor, Anne growing up. Pretty woman. What a tragedy for her family. "I’m sorry about your daughter. I never knew her, but knowing Connor and seeing her picture, she must have been a lovely person.”

“Thank you, dear. Yes, it’s been a hard time for us. Anne, you know, was our only child. She was a delight from the day she was born. Well, thank heavens for Connor. It’s a little easier now since Robbie is thinking of moving back. We’ve been very fortunate having him as a son-in-law. Anyway, enough of that sad part of our life. What would you like to drink? We have just about everything; beer, wine, scotch, soft drinks,” offered Betty.

“A glass of wine would be lovely, Betty.”

"Bill, can we please have two glasses of that nice cabernet," she shouted to the kitchen. “Cabernet’s all right with you, Vivi?”

“Oh, that will be fine. Thank you.”

"So how did you meet Robbie, after all these years?” inquired Betty.

“Well, he was looking at houses with the same real estate person who sold me mine. We all were in school together as kids. He decided to drop over and say hello. Personally, I think he was curious to see if I became ugly and fat. We use to get along as well as two Siamese fighting fish sharing the same bowl,” I laughed.

“Well, dear. I don’t know what you’ve done but Connor and he look happier than they have in the last two years. It’s time that Robbie gets over Anne. He still is young and has his whole life in front of him.” I didn’t know what to say to Betty at this time. Luckily the men had just entered the living room and joined us.

"A glass for you, Betty, and one for Vivi." said Bill.

"Grammy, I'm going ice skating again. Maybe next weekend if we come back down. And when we move here, Daddy says that I can join the peewee hockey team. That will be so cool. Gabrielle's learning how to figure skate, and for a little kid, she's really good. We can practice on Saturday." Connor was now talking a mile a minute.

"That sounds wonderful. Did you know that there is a very good pond here that freezes up every year? Your grandfather would to take your mother skating on that pond when she was a girl. Sometimes, when there was a full moon, we would take her out at night and skate by moonlight," reminisced Betty.

"Can I do that, Dad, can I?" Connor curls were bouncing all around his head. He really was adorable.

"Sure. Listen. It's getting late and I need to drive Vivi back to Princeton. Would it be all right if I come around tomorrow early afternoonish to pick up Connor?" asked Robbie.

"No problem Robbie, you know you can leave him here as long as you like," replied Bill.

We're always so happy to have him." Betty then smiled at her grandson.

"Well thanks for taking such good care of him. Vivi, are you ready?" I got reluctantly out of the very comfortable armchair that was so kindly cushioning my sore butt.

"Yes, thank you, Bill and Betty, for your hospitality and for the glass of wine," I said.

It was a pleasure meeting you both." Betty gave me a little hug and we walked to the door.

Connor, Bill and Betty watched as we got in the car and started the engine. "Bye," they said in unison. "Drive carefully," added Betty.

The Volvo roared away. "Nice people," I commented.

"Really nice people. The best," said Robbie. The atmosphere in the car was reflective and quiet. I presumed Robbie was thinking about Anne. Maybe he was sorry that his emotions got carried away today at the skating rink. I wasn't sorry. It was the nicest feeling I've had in years. Five minutes pass in total silence.

"Vivi?"

"Yes, Robbie."

"I've been giving this a lot of thought. Especially at Bill and Betty's place, seeing the pictures of Anne."

Oh, dear this could turn out poorly. "I know, she seemed to have been a wonderful person."

"She was. But she's been dead for two years and it's time for me to go on with my life. Since I've seen you, I haven't felt this good in a long while. I'm happy. What I'm trying to say, Vivi, is that I want to be with you. It's like fate. You and I separated years ago. We were too young for each other, too immature. We went our own ways. We fell in love with other people, married, had children, and now we find ourselves together again. Vivi, I don't want to lose you, again. I want us to be together. I wanted to call you all this week. I need to be with you. Do you follow me? I can understand if it's just too fast —"

I turned to face this wonderful man. "Robbie, it's okay. I don't want to lose you either. I, too, want to be with you. I don't know where it's going to take us, but I'm ready to give it a try."

Robbie was silent for a moment. He decelerated the car as he turned onto my street. It was a cold, crisp evening, and the stars were beginning to appear in the inky sky. We approached the house, went up the driveway and park the car. Robbie's hand was on the ignition key. He turned and looked at me with his soft eyes.

"May I be with you tonight? May I stay the night?" he asked.

Vivi, your turn to make a move. I leaned over and kiss this dear, beautiful man, my boy angel.

Chapter 36

"Robbie, let's do something different. Why don't we have dinner in the living room? We'll eat on the coffee table, Asian-style." I needed time to get my balance back and to stop shaking inside. Dinner should lessen the intensity of the prevailing mood.

Robbie looked relieved. "What can I do to help?"

"Why don't you take care of the music, choose the wine and make a fire in the fireplace. You can find the wood on the north face of the house. I'll fix omelets aux fines herbes and a salad." I left for the kitchen.

I opened the refrigerator and pulled out the carton of eggs. Timing was going to be crucial. I didn't know how to do it, but I wanted this evening to be very special for both of us, not an orgy of ripping clothing. A nice light meal with wine, good conversation and ambiance should be relaxing. I haven't been with a man for five years, and Robbie hasn't had a woman for two. We needed to take this slowly. *Now where were that head of fresh romaine and the goat cheese? Maybe I should add a few strips of bacon to the salad.* My arms were full with provisions, so I used my foot to close the fridge and waddle to the kitchen island.

Don't turn on heat high. Slowly melt the butter and clarify. I tapped an egg on the side of the bowl, cracked the shell and emptied the contents into the bowl. I repeated until all the eggs were gone. I quickly mixed the eggs and poured them into the hot pan.

Robbie walked into the kitchen. "Has anyone told you recently what a wonderful person you are?" and gave me a big hug. "I was getting lonely out there and decided to come in and pester you."

"Pestering is good. Can you pass me the salt and pepper?"

"Ah, a woman committed to culinary excellence. Where can I find the wine and the bottle opener?" he asked while snooping around the kitchen looking for tasty tidbits.

"There are a few whites in the fridge and the rest are in the closet near the kitchen table." I quickly microwaved the bacon and placed the clean romaine in a large wooden bowl. I crumpled the goat cheese over the dark green lettuce.

"Got it. Nice wine collection, Vivi. How come none from California?" Robbie inquired.

"Robbie, I'm French. I was raised on French wine. I was taught at an early age, the famous castles and wine areas. You can't break an old habit. Okay, I just need to add the bacon to the salad, pour on the vinaigrette, and let the omelets cook for one more minute. Then we're ready to feast," I said.

"Do you have a tray to bring out all this food?"

"You can find one in the tall cabinet on your right. The plates, cups, and flatware are also in that general area," I directed.

In the kitchen flow, we were mismatched. Robbie was constantly under my feet, positioning himself in the way. We seemed to be saying "excuse me" and "sorry" quite a number of times to each other. Oh well, life was never perfect. I asked Robbie to bring Shep a fresh bowl of water and food to his dog house. Finally, supper was ready. Robbie carried the tray out to the coffee table in the living room where a fire was merrily crackling away. I lit two candles in their silver holders, placed them on the table, and dimmed the electric lights. We took our seats across from one another and Robbie poured the wine.

"To the Fates," toasted Robbie.

"To the Fates." I took a sip. "Tell me, what else have you been up to since high school?" I asked. Robbie took a bite of his omelet.

"Oh the usual. Worked like a dog at MIT, backpacked through Europe, tried a few drugs and became a dweeb working for a computer company."

"Why did you quit?"

"The company was under new management and was being reorganized like crazy. In two years I had eight bosses, none of them competent. I figure it was a matter of time before the company would lose its marketing edge so I sold my stock and quit."

"What happened to the company?" I picked up the oversized tongs, tossed the salad, and placed some on Robbie's and my plate. Robbie reached for his glass of wine.

"It took longer than I predicted, but now they are a quarter of the size of when I was there. It was a good move to say adios on my part. I was able to start a company and successfully run it the way I saw fit. Running a company has been a real challenge and ego boost to me."

"And now?" Great salad, Vivi, should have made more.

"I don't need the headache. I have new priorities. Anne's death made some issues come to the forefront, like having a life and raising a child. Money is of no importance. I've enough socked away, and the work I get now keeps my mind active. Talk about socking it away, looks like you did very well, but as a designer, how did you do it`? On the whole, graphic designers aren't the new tycoons," inquired Robbie.

"Well, I didn't get it from a divorce. It actually started out of fear and damn good luck. You know, ever careful with money. We never had a lot of money before Dad's illness, but afterward, we were exceedingly cautious. Once he passed away, I was in the habit of living frugally and was able to save a little bit of money. I always kept an account at a New York discount broker and would invest money regularly. Then I got hired by a high tech company in Silicon Valley as the graphic manager. As part of the signing bonus, they gave me stock options. Later I was promoted and received more options. Leif thought the options were a joke and that they were worthless. By the time I decided to get a divorce their net value was about three hundred and fifty thousand dollars. At the divorce proceedings, Leif was so protective of his own net worth, that he ignored mine and let me have it all, my savings, options and retirement. I started heavily playing the technology stocks. It really paid off. So I have peace of mind for my future and for Gabrielle. I never have to worry that I will be poor again even if I get sick," I said.

"Was your husband exceedingly stupid, Vivi?" Robbie was stunned that Leif overlooked such large assets.

"Actually he is a very bright, talented architect. But with personal finances, he's an idiot. I think he believed that since I was an artist, there was no possible way that I had any financial acuity. Part of it was my fault. I was fairly insecure in the relationship and let him push me around," I admitted.

"I remember you in chemistry class. You aced the section about quantum mechanics and barely managed to pass the rest of the course, especially lab," joked Robbie.

"Robbie, I stink at the day-to-day, stuff. I got so bored with putting chemicals in little beakers and having to be so precise. For what? You can't even eat the stuff when you're finished." Robbie muffled a laugh.

"Vivi, you slay me. So what else can't you do? Come on, fess up."

"Well, I almost flunked geometry - after all what do I care about fences, triangles and proving that it is a square but I passed calculus with flying colors. That was interesting, bombs and abstract thought. I can't balance my checkbook to save my life, but on a super year, I can quadruple my income. I write tons of letters, but it takes me years to get them to the mail box. And as Gabrielle has commented, I do space out a lot. Robbie, stop laughing. Here, have more salad. And wine." I passed Robbie the bowl of salad and the wine bottle.

“Yes and yes. This meal is excellent. You know, I never knew where your brain was going when we were kids. It was a challenge keeping up with you,” admitted Robbie.

"I haven’t changed, I’m only worse. And by the way, you were also a complete challenge.”

“Aren’t we all? Anyway, I like you the way you are. I like who you’ve become.”

“I like the man that you’ve become. I never gave it a thought when I was a kid, you know, what people would be like when they’re older. You’ve turned out really well,” and I smiled at Robbie.

“And losing my hair, and getting fatter.”

“No, Robbie, you’ve filled out nicely. And since you are so tall, I can’t see your hair loss. So it’s not an issue,” I said.

Robbie laughed "Ah Vivi, soothsayer of aging men. By the way, the excellent wine is beginning to work its magic charm.”

“Then, do I get a kiss?”

"You get many kisses.” Robbie pushed the coffee table toward the sofa, grabbed our wine glasses and the bottle, placing them at the foot of the hearth, and drew me into his arms. We slipped to the floor, on to the Turkish rug with its golden and rosy colors. "Many, many kisses,” he whispered as he started kissing me in front of the fire.

I don’t think I’ve ever wanted a man this much. Just to lie in his arms gave me a sense of love, a sense of security. If we spend the entire night kissing and holding each other, I would be satisfied. I’ve never felt this peace, this tranquility with another person.

It seemed like minutes that we had been together, yet several hours had passed. I was drunk from his kisses; I was tingling at the back of my neck, my ears, and around my collarbone. Robbie held my head and scanned my face. I gazed into his deep blue eyes, the color of a summer's night sky and was lost in the reflection. My body instinctively arched toward him.

The lights from the fire glimmered on Robbie's face, constantly changing in its patterns. Slowly the candles flickered and sputtered. It was getting late and I didn't want to spend the night in this room. "Come," I murmured. "Come with me."

I rose and grasped Robbie's hand. Silently, we left the living room and slowly went up the staircase. I opened my bedroom door, turned on a reading light, and moved toward the fireplace. Robbie stood at the foot of the bed. Quickly, I started a fire, tossed in two logs and walked to Robbie's side.

"You're the same boy I knew, you're a different man. I need to see how and where you've changed. I want to know your body." Robbie bent and kissed me on the side of my neck. "Oh, Vivi," as his voice thickened.

I cautiously began unbuttoning his sea green flannel shirt. I could feel Robbie trembling. I pulled off his shirt, and placed my hands beneath his undershirt. Slowly I explored my way over his chest and lifted the undershirt over his head. Many changes, wonderful changes. A large growth of dark curly chest hair and solidness to his frame had developed over the years. I closed my eyes and kissed the side under his ribs, running my tongue over his skin, to taste him, to savor his transformation. I opened my eyes and looked up at this marvelous man.

Robbie kissed my forehead lightly. Carefully, he drew my turtleneck sweater over my head. It softly dropped to the floor. He lightly placed his hands on my breasts, unclasped my bra, and pushed it off my shoulders. Robbie gently explored under my arms and sides, my breasts, my stomach. He got on his knees, and began sucking my breasts, lightly, slowly at first, then harder, more demanding in time. It had been so long since a man cared, since a man wanted me, that I was lost to his invasion. I was shattered.

I looked down at Robbie. Our eyes meet and Robbie stood up. In unison, we unburden ourselves from our remaining clothing. Robbie stood naked in the moonlight while the fire dances its patterns on his legs and thighs. I could see his erect penis surrounded by the thick mass of curly black hair. I could even smell his dusky odor.

He was no longer my tall, thin boy; a magnificent man had replaced him. But the boy wasn't not gone from me tonight. At times, the fallen angel reappeared in his face and I was taken back to another time, equally as wonderful, when we were innocent children hiding from the moonlight. Now we were grown, and the moonlight was our friend, highlighting our new sensuality to each other.

"Vivi, you're so beautiful," and Robbie carried me to the bed. We lay in each other arms for a minute, just to catch our breath, just to recapture our equilibrium. Then Robbie and I turned to each other, to begin the dance of love.

I had no idea what I was doing, my body had taken over. I could not think; I had lost my balance. I just reacted to the onslaught of my senses. Robbie had entered me and I pulsated to his body rhythm, and was taken through the waves of exquisite pleasure. The bed had become my enemy; it held me down and I wished to soar from it. His body would not stop assaulting me, it would not surrender, and it would not allow me to re-gather my sensibility, my tranquility. Instead, I rose and fell to Robbie's explorations, to his pursuit, until at last, on an incredible wave, I exploded with millions of tiny colors bursting before my eyes.

Trembling, I looked at Robbie. He was completely still and his eyes were shut. Suddenly, they open, soft and blue as the color of the sky after a winter storm, and he smiled, like a child. There was no need to talk; there was nothing to be said. I knew that this was the man that I was destined for, that I must weld my life to, and that there would be no other.

Robbie took me in his arms again, and with his body, rocked me, rocked me to the rhythm of our subsiding current gently, and we entered a deep and profound sleep of lovers.

Chapter 37

Morning. The light coming through my window awakened me. I opened my eyes, looked over to my side, and smiled. He was sleeping like a child. I leaned over and kissed him. His eyelashes fluttered and those blue eyes appeared.

“Morning. How long have you been awake and abusing my defenseless body?”An evil little grin escaped his lips.

"Oh for two or three hours. Are you hungry?”

"I’m hungry but I’m hungry for something else. Something right here. Right next to me.”

“I can’t imagine what you are talking about.”

“Then image this.” Robbie began kissing my collarbone and the back of my neck. His hand reached down and started caressing the inside of my thigh.

"No fair,” I groaned and rolled over on top of him. I placed my mouth near his ear and with my tongue began exploring the area around his ear lobe; down the side of his neck; down further until I found his nipple. My mouth started to play, to suck, to stroke, to tease. I looked up at Robbie. His eyes were close with the heavy black lashes splayed on the utmost part of his cheek bones. Slowly his eyes opened again. He took his hand and placed it on my cheek. With his free arm, he brought my body in line with his, and his mouth deliberately plunged upon my lips. Swiftly, he entered my body which was now possessed by his cadence, with his pulsation. Once again, I was no longer in control of the moment. I was lost and betrayed by my senses’ quest for pleasure. I felt like the butterfly with wings pinned to the bed, and knew that there was no escape, only the inevitable surrender of my body. Though I anticipated and I awaited my deliverance, it came far too swiftly, too cruelly and I shuddered from my release. The climax was simultaneous and we held on to each other as our heartbeats gradually subsided.

"Damn Vivi, let's do this all day long."

"I don't think I'd live. Plus the kids would be mortified and stunned, "I said imagining Gabrielle's reaction.

"True, but the idea still tempts me. We can send out a note. Dear gentlemen and gentle ladies. Vivi Bergstrom and Robbie Terhune are holding court in Madame's bedroom. Please call to make an appointment."

"It's funny to think about, especially when dealing with the plumber and electrician. Anyway, thank you. I feel like I've been run over by the love machine," I groaned.

Oh, the pleasure was all mine. What time is it?" inquired Robbie.

"Nine-thirty. It's strange in a way."

"What is? The time?"

"No silly. When I make love with you, for a brief instant I recognize the Robbie I knew in high school. And I really love seeing that boy, but I'd rather have the man," I explained.

"I know. I've often thought about that night of the prom, down at the Institute. It's one of my sweetest and most personal memories. You don't know what it is to enter manhood and go off to school. The stupidest things worry you," admitted Robbie.

"What things?"

"Oh, about the opposite sex. Will you ever get laid? Will it be awful? Will she ever speak to you again? That night was like magic, it was wonderful and I was able to move on in my life without the nagging thought of sex in the back of my mind. You have no idea what a gift of freedom and trust you gave me. For the first time in my life I felt secure," he continued.

"You, Robbie? The school genius?"

"Yeah, I had a terrible image of myself. Low self esteem. It's part of that age."

"And to think that most of the time I thought you were an obnoxious idiot savant."

"Careful Vivi, cruel words."

"You know that I was crazy about you. But we met at a too early age."

"And we're lucky to have found each other again. Really lucky. Listen about the initial offer for food, will you take pity on a starving man?" begged Robbie.

"Gladly, kind sir. But first, I'm taking a shower," I declared.

"But first, we're taking a shower. Here, I'll help you with the sheets," and Robbie rose from the bed and pulled back the covers. I hopped out and straightened my side. Covers were returned to their proper places, pillows were fluffed, and the comforter was back on my bed. Last night and this morning's activity were now obliterated. Maybe Robbie's scent will still be on the pillow tonight.

"Stop daydreaming, woman and come play water games with me. Aha, a bathroom of noble proportions and a decent size shower. Did I tell you that your taste is excellent and, besides the fact that you're a wonderful person, you have a hell of a good bed," joked Robbie.

"No, but I'm taking compliments today. Now, here's your towel and wash cloth. The water is ready" and I walked into the shower. Robbie followed with his washcloth and soap in his hand, ready to do battle. As in the kitchen, he was in my way. His height and build blocked out half of my spray and his soap lather got in my eyes. Plus he was determined to scrub me clean from head to toe

"Robbie, be kind. Not again, I need at least a ten minute break," I groaned.

He grinned, and we swiftly finished taking our shower. Minutes later a very clean Vivi and Robbie descended the staircase and went into the kitchen.

"So chef extraordinaire, what are your plans? This humble male wants to know what culinary delight you intend to prepare."

"Wrong, Robbie. I don't do breakfast. I do coffee and then there are tasty treats from store like Danish, bagels, lox, cream cheese, cereal and fruit. If what you're requesting are eggs, potatoes, waffles or pancakes, I suggest you be in charge," I proclaimed. I'd better get the rules down right at the beginning of this relationship.

"Bravo. Actually I do make great pancakes and waffles and will avail you my services next weekend. I'll set the table. Is most of the stuff in the fridge?" Robbie walked over to the counter area.

"Yes, I'll make coffee. There's juice in the fridge along with some lox. I'll get the breads and cereals. Fruit is on the table. About next weekend, how are we going to arrange it with the kids? I'm not really comfortable with the idea of us spending the night together while Gabrielle or Connor is here," I admitted.

"No, it would upset Connor too much. I guess we'll just have to be flexible and take whatever opportunities we get. It was wonderful waking up with you this morning, but for a while that will just have to be a forgone luxury. Before I sound presumptuous, may I have the privilege of your company for the next, Um, let's say, twenty week-ends, with renewal rights?"

"You know the answer is yes. The water's boiling for the coffee. How do you like yours?"

"Black. And you?"

"With milk." I grabbed the mugs, placed the boiling water into a drip beaker along with a filter and some grounded beans. Coffee was ready in a minute and I poured the black liquid into the oversized red mugs. Carefully, I brought the mugs to the table, sat in a chair and waited for Robbie, whose arms were full of cereal packages and juice. With more attention to the contents in his arms than to his stride, Robbie hobbled to the table and instantaneously unloaded the food.

“Vivi, I try not to think about it, but it’s going to be very hard to be without you this week. If there wasn’t the question of kids, I’d move in with you immediately. Of course, only if you asked me.” He smiled at me and his eyes were twinkling.

“I know. But my mind and heart are moving so fast, having space and time really should he beneficial. I don’t think I could deal with the thought of you moving in and later moving out. It would be too destructive. I once was rushed, and it was a disaster. I hate the time, but I need it. Plus the kids couldn’t handle it,” I reminded him.

"You’re right. But I just want to be with you. For the first time in months, I’m happy and believe that my life will be good again. I don’t want to lose that,” he said.

"And then there’s the issue with Connor. We’ve got to make sure that what we have between ourselves is lasting. He can’t afford another attachment to a woman, to be taken away later,” I added.

“Ah, Connor. That could be difficult,” realized Robbie while sipping at his coffee.

"Maybe not if he isn’t threaten and we handle it carefully. Anyway, he loves Gabrielle, she loves him, he loves Shep and ice skating. That’s a start.”

“"Well, enough. This subject of being banished from your bed at night is depressing me. It’s also made me decide on some immediate decisions,” he said seriously.

“Like what.”

"Like moving down here as soon as possible. At least I’ll be able to see you more often than only on the weekends. Are you finished eating?”

"Yes. I like that. Seeing you more often. Here, let me get the dishes."

"No, not now. There's something I would rather do," and Robbie got out of his chair, picked me up and carried me up the stairs. "There's no way, that you're doing dishes now. We're going to do only one thing and one thing well."

As I got dropped on my bed, I stopped and reflected on the linear thought process of the male's mind. If they wanted something, they went for it, again and again. I was in awe of the evolutionary development that had allowed these phenomena to take place. And, deliriously happy.

Chapter 38

"Have you spoken to James? You must tell him. It is only fair, chèrie." Mom and I strolled in her garden, while Gabrielle played fetch with Shep. I had just been to the store and bought my favorite coffee and snickerdoodles.

"No, Mom. I left a message at his office to call me as soon as he returns. I hope this isn't going to be really sticky."

"You just have to tell him the truth. After all, he really is too busy to work on a relationship. A man must spend time to court a woman he wants. James should not be too surprised to hear that you have found someone else. What does he think you're doing? Sitting around like a hausfrau waiting for him. These men, so full of themselves. Well, I must say that you are glowing. I have never seen you so pretty and happy. Must be Robbie. You know, you should cover your boxwood. Now, before it snows," commanded Ghislaine.

"I'll do that tomorrow. You use burlap, don't you, and string? Yes, Robbie is terrific. And I feel so comfortable with him. You know, I was always in awe of Leif, but I never had this level of comfort with him."

"Oh, Leif. Leif was a pompous ass. He just was so handsome that we overlooked it. I always felt something wrong with him. He was too perfect with us. He fooled us all," admitted Ghislaine, while deadheading the chrysanthemums.

"I know. He really fooled me. But it wasn't all bad. I have Gabrielle."

"Gabrielle is worth everything. Especially since Leif now has no rights to her. He doesn't, does he?" inquired Ghislaine.

"No, he reneged on all responsibilities toward her. I made sure that my lawyer had it written up in the deposition. You know, I still have this nagging fear that someday he'll show up and try to claim her," I admitted.

“I wouldn’t be surprised either. But you are far away from him, and a court battle in New Jersey would be costly to him,” calculated Ghislaine.

"I have enough money to make Leif’s life miserable. Plus I have so much dirt on him he wouldn’t dare go public with a trial. Talking about dirt, I need to start working on my compost pile.”

“Anyway, I hope that things work out with Robbie. I have always liked him, and I think he would be a good husband and father. I will keep my fingers crossed for you, ma chèrie,” Ghislaine beamed at me.

“Thanks, Mom. I’m hoping everything works out well. But for now, I am so happy. Gabrielle, Grandmère and I are going into the kitchen. Do you want to play outside a little longer?”

"Yes, Mommy,” and Gabrielle continued tossing a stick into the yard for Shep. Mom and I walked into the kitchen and stood around the sink.

“Coffee?”

"Please. It gets so cold this time of year. I hope that we are going to Florida in January. Richard says he wants to buy me a winter home in Ft. Myers,” said Ghislaine while putting water in the kettle.

“Good, now I’ll have a new place to visit,” I replied as I ignited the burner under the kettle.

“Except for keeping warm, I am not crazy about the idea. I would miss you, Gabrielle, and the girls at bridge.”

“Mom, you’ll meet new friends,” I said.

“It is not the same. Tièns, the water sounds ready. Do you have any cookies?” asked Ghislaine hopefully.

“Sure, Mom, I’ll get some.” The water was boiling and I reached in the cabinet for two mugs, and placed them on the counter. The coffee beans were already grounded from the store. I got the drip carafe, placed a filter in the top, poured in the crushed beans and drained the boiling water in to the carafe.

"Where are the cookies, Vivi?"

"In the bag to the left of you, Mom. Why don't you put some on a plate so that I don't eat the whole box. Here, the coffee is ready and I've got the mugs. Let's bring the stuff to the kitchen table."

For once, I managed not to make a series of little coffee puddles on my way to the table. Success, the mugs are on the table without spilling a drop. Mom had a cookie hanging out of her mouth while she brought over a plate of them. We sat down, and began to sip.

"Your coffee is good. Where do you get your beans?" asked Ghislaine while taking a sip of her coffee.

"I bought these at the bookstore in town. They're a splurge but worth the expense."

"You know, I can't get out of the habit of worrying about your spending habits. But I know that you are doing well. It is a mother's prerogative. So, I am very curious, have you gone to bed with Robbie?"

"Mom," I protested.

"Come on, I wasn't born yesterday. Sex is natural. Did you go to bed with him?" inquired Ghislaine.

°'Yes, I did." I surrendered to this woman. Facing an inquisition was too painful. Confession was better.

"So, was he better, as good as or worse than Leif?" Ghislaine raised an eyebrow at me while serving her another cookie.

"Mother." Christ, are we getting personal. This was not a common inquisition; this seemed to be the Grand Inquisition with my mother, Torquemada de la Frenchie.

"I want to know. I know that you once said that Leif was fabulous in bed. And Robbie. How is he?"

"It's very different. Leif was like a top rated courtesan, if they have such a thing for men. He was unbelievable, but it became skilled, mechanical, with no heart. When he was upset or mad at me, he'd punish me and we wouldn't have sex for weeks. Robbie, well, he's real. Making love with him is personal and sincere. There's much more sharing and compassion involved. It's not about who is in control. It's about giving." I hoped that ended the conversation before I started sweating.

"Good. It sounds like a healthier relationship. I think that you and Robbie would make a good couple. And his little boy is charming. His mother must have been a very nice woman." Ghislaine was deep in thought while sipping her coffee.

"From what I've heard, Anne was lovely."

"Then Robbie is looking for another strong relationship. And you need a decent one, after Leif. You know, you must have been terribly strong to have held up so well in that relationship and to have protected yourself through the divorce. Pass me the cookies. I really shouldn't eat these, they are too good," she murmured while sinking her teeth into another snickerdoodle.

"Actually, some of it is to Leif's credit. He was so worried I would take something that belonged to him or I would see the actual state of his finances, that he never investigated my net worth. Anyway, he had some preconceived notion that I couldn't handle finances, so he thought that I brought nothing to the party." I explained.

"Vivi, what was he trying to hide?" Ghislaine asked.

"I think he had a cocaine habit and he was dealing in the stuff. I found some evidence one day in the house. Maybe he didn't want me to find out about a bank account, or extra cash, or that we were possibly mortgaged to the max. I don't know. But because of it and his paranoia, I walked out of the marriage with a lot of stock options which became my nest egg."

"And how is Robbie's financial position?"

"Probably as good as mine. He sold his computer company and never has to work again in his life. But you know Robbie, he's always trying some new concept, "I said.

"I like him very much. Zut, look at the time. I had better go to work. We are having some couples over this evening to play bridge and I need to get started making a dessert. I think I'll make my charlotte." Mom started to rise from her chair.

"Save me some if there is any left over. I'll call Gabrielle so she can come in and say good-bye." I slid out of the chair, walked over to the kitchen door, turned the door knob, and poked my head out the door.

"Gabrielle," I shouted. "We are leaving. Come say au revoir." Gabrielle and Shep came flying through to the kitchen.

"Ah, ma petite. Your Grandmère must go to work in her kitchen. Give me a big bisou," and my mother leaned over to offer her cheek to Gabrielle. Gabrielle put her arms around her grandmother's neck and gave her a big smacking kiss.

"Bye-bye, Grandmère. I'm going to color Thanksgiving pictures. I'll give you one." Gabrielle promised.

"That reminds me. Are we having Thanksgiving at your house? It is only two weeks away," asked my mother while walking us to her front door.

"Yes, Tom, Lena, and the kids will be down from Connecticut. It makes sense to have it at my place. Less work for you, Mom," I said while looking for my keys.

"May I volunteer the dessert, my Charlotte Russe, and my special cranberry sauce?" asked Ghislaine as I was unlocking my car's doors and getting Shep in the back seat area.

"I'd be delighted. Also, can you make the yams in bourbon recipe? I always loved those yams."

"Yes, it has been years since I last made it. Anyway, ciao, Gabrielle, and make sure that you safely secured your seat belt."

"Bye Mom," and I started up the engine and began pulling out of her driveway in the new car.

"Bye, Grandmère." We drove off and away. In ten minutes we were at our house and parked in the driveway. Gabrielle and Shep made a beeline for the front door. I got out of the car as quickly as possible to unlock the large red front door.

"Mommy, there is a message on the answering machine," Gabrielle shouted to me.

"Thanks sweetheart. Can you please close the door?" I winced from the sound of the front door slamming.

"I'm going upstairs to color, Mommy," and I heard a pair of feet and paw sounds heading up the stairs. I walked over to the answering machine and played the message.

"Vivi, it's James. I'm back and sorry that I've missed you. Listen, I need to talk with you. How about if I drop over this evening around eight o'clock. If I don't hear from you I'll figure that we are on tonight. You have the number."

Damn it. Time to rake up the dead leaves in my life.

Chapter 39

"Mommy, can I be excused? My doll, Mary, is very sick and Shep and I are going to operate on her tonight." Gabrielle just finished her dinner and was wiggling her little fanny out of her chair.

"Why yes, Dr. Gabrielle. I hope that you're able to save her. By the way, James is dropping over here tonight." Gabrielle wrinkled up her nose. "Now, none of that. I want you to be polite and come down to say hello. Please," I requested firmly.

"All right, Mom. But I can only do it after Marie's operation. Anyway, why is he going to be here? I thought you liked Robbie?" asked Gabrielle.

"I do like Robbie very, very much. But that's no reason to be mean to James. So I want you to be nice and polite. Okay?" I asked sternly.

"I guess so," grimaced Gabrielle. "Can I go now?" I nodded.

In a half hour, James will be here. I had better start cleaning up the kitchen. I grabbed the plates, cups and flatware and tossed them into the dishwasher then put the food back in the fridge. Quickly I washed off the table. Now to go upstairs and freshen up.

What was I going to say to James? I was not very good at reciting Dear John letters. In fact, before my marriage to Leif, when I wanted to break up with a man, I'd try to make sure that they would do the breaking up. It would take a bit longer, but it was the easy way out. *Okay, let's practice in front of the mirror.*

"James, you're out." I took a strong stance and threw out my arm.

"James, I've met someone and slept with him and .... you're out." This was not progressing well.

"Hi, James, I'm Vivi's cousin and she told me to tell you that—"

"Hello James, my mother has something to tell you," I was digressing.

"James, please sit down. I'm afraid that what I have to say might upset you," sounding like I was reporting about a death. This was going nowhere. Just put on a fresh shirt and some make-up and tell him the truth. Maybe I shouldn't put on any make-up so I'd look like shit and he'd realize what an ugly woman I was and that he'd just had a narrow escape. Perhaps God had a plan or maybe He just wanted to see me sweat. *Come on Vivi, get some lipstick on. Damn, the doorbell just rang. Quick, put on the cream shirt and run down stairs. Calm down. Breathe easy. Now, open the door. Smile at James and let him in.*

"Hello, James, nice to see you back. Come in." I stepped aside so that James could enter the living room.

"Hi, Vivi. You look great," and planted a kiss on my cheek. "I'm glad that you're free tonight. I really need to talk to you," James said earnestly.

"I was just going to make a cup of coffee. Would you like some?" This would give me some time to get my act together and think of a way to bring up the "let's be friends" subject.

James looked relieved. I wonder what is on his mind. "Coffee would be great. De-caf preferably. Make mine black, please," and he sat down in one of the deep blue chairs.

"De-caf it is," and I walked into the kitchen. *Vivi, collect yourself, put the kettle on the fire, get two chipless mugs and grind up the beans. Now say something to James.*

"How was the trip? Seemed longer than most. What were you up to?" I asked politely.

"Oh, some unexpected stuff happened while I was in London and I needed to stay for two more weeks. The real estate deal is finally going through. I found a Qatar prince as one of the principle backers. Financing the development is a done deal. So now we just need to get the bids from the contractors. I can't believe how much time this project is taking. It'll be responsible for a major part of my firm's earnings, but the time involved has been costly. For example..."

Good James, just babble away while I get the coffee. All right, I've got a tray, two mugs with coffee; one with cream for me, napkins and some oatmeal cranberry cookies. Vivi, time to face the music.

"...and so I said to Charlie Adams, "How much more money do we need to complete the deal" and he said we had enough — Oh, Vivi. How nice. Let me help you with the tray," James politely rose and took the tray from my arms.

"Thank you, James." James placed the tray on the coffee table. I sat down on the red sofa. "I'm glad to hear that the project is finally going through, but you do look tired."

"Hey, in a few days, I'll be back to my normal self. It was a real difficult trip and I'm glad this part is completed. Now, I have to deal with local contractors and planning boards but that part is at least in my own back yard. London was miserable and the travel is getting to me." James straightened himself in the blue chair. "Which is why I need to talk to you," he said seriously.

Oh, good. I didn't need to talk yet about my little news flash. "What is it James?" I asked.

"Well, I've been thinking all the time about what you said to me at the beach about my kids. I've been really selfish, thinking that what my kids need is more money and not more of me. I'm doing exactly what I reproached my dad for doing. So I went to see Karen who's been living in London for the past year, to talk to her about Erin and Sean." James was looking at his feet and his ears were beginning to turn red. Cute.

This could be good. Maybe I won't have to read the "Dear John" letter to James. "And what did she say?"

“She’s in agreement and says that Erin and Sean are too much for her to handle alone. Also, she’s tired of traveling and settling down in the States has been on her mind for a while. The crux of the matter is that we’re thinking about trying to get back together again or at least be more in tune with each other for the kids’ sake. She’s going to lease a house here for a year while we work something out. The problem is that I don’t know where this is going, and I’ve made some commitments to you. I don’t want to....” I had better interrupt James before this confession went any further. After all, he was a very nice man and a very good lawyer. I could always use a friend and good legal advice.

“Before you go any further James, I need to tell you about a new arrival in my life. I think it will make this evening easier for the both of us. As you know, with all of your traveling, you haven’t been around a lot. Our relationship hasn’t progressed very far and we’ve never made any sort of commitment to each other. While you were gone this time, and old friend came back in my life and has become very important to me. So any commitments that you believed you’ve made are not holding.” James looked a little stunned but the red color was beginning to subside.

“Vivi, are you telling me that you are serious about someone?” he said incredulously.

"I’m very serious. I apologize. It happened out of the blue. This is very uncomfortable for me to talk about but I need to explain the situation to you. It’s only fair. You’ve been a good friend and there’s no reason for us to burn any bridges, especially since none have crossed.” James’ coloring was returning to normal and he was sitting more comfortably. Several cookies disappeared in his hands.

“Damn, I’m relieved, but sorry. You know, if it hadn’t been for this project, I think we would have had a chance. I think we could have made it together. Don’t you?” he said brightening up.

Vivi, don’t destroy this guy’s ego, but you’ve just escaped a life of chintz living rooms. The thought of having James naked in my bed was not at all appealing. Lucky break for me. “I believe you could be right, but in the long run if you can get back together with Karen, it’s the best thing that could happen. The best for your family and for your kids.” James grabbed several more cookies.

"Are we still friends?” James reached for his fifth cookie. He must be calming down.

“Of course we are, James.”

"I know this isn’t my business, but is the person that you’re serious with, someone I know?” asked James.

"I don’t know. He doesn’t go around with Winston’s group. He and I dated in high school. Maybe you do know him. Robbie Terhune,” I replied.

“Robbie Stein, Robbie Terhune. The name sounds familiar. Wasn’t he a really smart, tall, skinny kid? I think he was in my chemistry class.”

“That sounds like him.”

“So what is he doing?" asked James.

“His wife died two years ago and he’s been thinking of moving back to Princeton with his son. He recently sold his computer company and is doing contract programming. He’s still tall, but not so skinny anymore,” I said with a laugh.

“So, you’ve fallen for a computer geek. Vivi, I’m just joking. I should drop by and give him my card. He might need a lawyer in the area. Well, I need to be going soon. Karen’s coming down at the end of the week and I’ve a million things to attend to. I’m really sorry that we didn’t have a chance. I feel that I lost you to my business, but now I’ve a chance to regain my family.” James rose from his seat and started for the door.

“I’m happy for you, James. This is the best outcome that could happen. I hope everything works out.”

"I do too. Thank you, Vivi, for setting me straight on my kids. Let me give you a good-bye hug for everything."

After James gave me a hug and a very nice kiss on the forehead, he ran down to his car. I closed the door and took a deep breath. *Yes, it was over and nicely done, I must say. Pat on the back, my girl.* I didn't blow it. I was so proud. Another great day in the book *Vivi Grows Up*. What a relief. My euphoric state was broken by my daughter's piercing voice.

"Mommy, was that James? Is he gone?"

"Yes, pumpkin," I shouted back.

"Is he coming back? Do I have to come downstairs? I'm very busy."

"No dear, I don't think he is coming back ever. You can keep playing."

"Good. I still have more operations. My dolly is very sick. Can you bring me some medicine for her?"

"No problem, sweetie," and I headed to the kitchen to get some gummy bears. Good, there were some in the drawer. I put a handful in an empty jar, picked out a red one for myself and closed the lid.

"Okay, Gabrielle, I'm on the way with the medicine," I shouted on my way up the stairs.

"Thanks, Mom. It will save my dolly." I climbed to the top of the stairs and headed to Gabrielle's room. "Poor baby, poor baby. Medicine is coming and you'll be better. Hi, Mommy. Can I have the medicine please? Baby's so sick. We operate one more time and she'll be all better."

I handed over the jar of gummy bears to Gabrielle who opened the lid and ate three. Then she plucked a bear from the jar and stuffed it into her doll's mouth. "See, all better," as she smiled. "Thanks, Mommy. You have to leave now, we operate one more time. Then she shyly asked, "When are Robbie and Connor coming back?"

"Maybe this weekend, sweetheart. They're supposed to come down to find a house to rent. You know, Connor is in school in Boston and they can't leave until they find a place to live," I replied while cherishing the picture of my daughter, Shep and a doll wrapped up in blanket.

"They can live here. That will be nice," said Gabrielle quietly.

Sweetheart, you move even faster than your mom. "I think it is better if they live in their own house for the time being."

"Oh, I like Robbie and Connor. We have extra room. Connor can live in the room next to me and we can share Shep. Shep likes that. Okay?" decided the little commander.

Think fast, Vivi. "Honey, we'll need the room when Lena comes here for Thanksgiving."

"Oh, that's right," mumbled Gabrielle with a crestfallen face. "Maybe for Christmas," she added and her face lit up again.

I had to get out of here, away from my little schemer. Saved by the bell. The phone was ringing. "Sweetheart, Mommy has to answer the phone. You better operate soon."

"Okay, Mommy."

I ran to my bedroom and grabbed the phone off the night stand. "Hello, this is Vivi."

"Vivi, it's Robbie. How are you? I miss you. Tuesday called and said she might have found a house to rent near the lake, so we should be coming down late on Friday. I can't wait to be with you. So, anything new with you?" he asked as I was getting back my breath.

Some things were better left alone. A woman must have her secrets. "No, it's been a quiet day here. I miss you like crazy. Gabrielle is operating on her doll and wondering if Connor can move into the room next door to hers. Fast worker, eh. By the way, what plans have you made for Thanksgiving ...?”

Chapter 40

"So tell me, Babycakes, all about Robbie. It's been years since I've seen him. Is this true love?" Lena was stalking me like a tigress in my kitchen while I was trying to stuff a turkey.

"Yes," I said quietly while getting the stuffing far into the cavity of the bird. Totally gross but the end result will be delicious.

"And how long have you been with each other in the biblical sense?" questioned Lena with a lifted eyebrow.

"Oh, a little more than a month. Can you pass the salt?" I asked once the bird was stuffed.

Lena grabbed the salt on the counter and handed it to me. "And how is it?"

"What?" I replied while seasoning the skin of the turkey.

"You know. It. Sex. Sex with Robbie. How is he in bed?" demanded Lena with eyes wide open.

"Wonderful. And all I want to do when I see him, is to take off his clothes, jump into bed with him, and spend the night. Don't ask me why. I mean, he looks like a normal nice-looking man. But I can't wait to be alone with him. Which isn't often, due the children factor. We're moving cautiously since we don't know what we're doing and don't want to upset Connor. Does that look okay to you?" I finished sewing the bird closed.

"Vivi, it looks perfect. Screw the bird. I want information. How are they getting along?"

"Who?" I said while opening the oven.

"For goodness sakes, Vivi. Stay on earth while I give you the fifth degree. Connor and Gabrielle. How do they like each other?" Lena was leaning on the old fashion kitchen counter with a glass of wine in her hands.

"For two kids of disparate ages, great. They go down to the brook and play, go ice skating and play with Shep together. Connor is very patient with Gabrielle. He's a sweet boy. And Gabrielle is crazy about him and Robbie. Now the turkey is starting to roast, Mom is bringing dessert, yams, and cranberry sauce, and I baked the bread last night. We just have to work on the vegetables and soup."

"What happened to the other man? James. The guy you had a crush on in 9th grade Spanish class. God, he was ever so handsome? Did you sleep with him too?" Lena was all ears to hear about my continuing saga of *Love in Princeton*.

"We said good-bye. He went back to his wife, who by the way is a real bitch. Very thin, but very good to have around for show. A centerpiece. I'm lacking in that department. It was one of my many little traits that Leif tried to correct. Lena, I think I'll make sweet potato soup with sour cream."

"Sounds wonderful. You know, I can't see you as the country club wife. You're not disciplined enough. I can't wait to see Robbie. It's been years. When did you say they were coming today?" she asked.

"Robbie and Connor are having their Thanksgiving supper around two today at the in-laws. I expect they'll drop by around seven tonight for a light snack and dessert," I replied, pouring myself a glass of riesling from Joseph Meyer Vineyards in Alsace.

"Has your mother met Robbie?" Damn, when was Lena going to get off of this subject?

"Once," I replied, not usually known for monosyllabic answers.

"And how does she feel about him?"

"You know Mom. If he's perfect and treats me like a queen, she loves him. Actually, she's on the pro-Robbie side. She likes him a lot more than she liked Leif. Mom wants me to remarry. She says that I've been alone for too long." This could be the longest Thanksgiving ever.

"She's right. You have been. What are the kids up to?"

"Oh, they went down to the brook with Shep to look for frogs and fish. It's late in the season so they'll just come back to the house a bit muddy with red little checks."

"It's not dangerous, the creek, is it?" said a concerned Lena.

"No it's almost dry, and Shep is watching them. Do you know that dog gets up three times a night to check on Gabrielle?"

"Well, what can I do to help'? And where did Tom disappear to?" asked Lena, finally getting off of the Robbie subject.

"Oh, Tom and Richard are over at Mom's house watching the game. I expect that she'll overfeed them with treats. They won't have monster appetites for dinner. They should be back by five. Do you think we should make pearl onions or forget it? I have scalloped potatoes, peas in cream sauce, and green salad," I asked.

"I like them. But it sounds like too much food. What's for dessert?"

"Mom is making her Charlotte Russe and I have a pumpkin cheese cake that I made yesterday."

"Yum. I've been looking forward to this weekend for weeks. By the way, the guest room is gorgeous and for once, there's a good bed. Much appreciated, maybe we'll move in with you. I'm starting to hate the rental," admitted Lena.

"Why. It was lovely when I was there."

"I can't stand the wind that blows from the ocean. It's numbing. And the house is badly insulated. Our heating bill was astronomical for last month. I hate to think what January's bill will be like," she groused.

"Bummer. When can you buy?"

"Tom's business is doing well. Which reminds me, when you casually mentioned that you were seeing Robbie, he did some investigations into Robbie's old business. If ever Robbie needs investment capital, Tom would love to do business with him," Lena took another small sip of wine.

"Robbie did that well?" I answered.

"That well, and believe me after the Leif story, Tom would investigate any guy you were dating seriously," declared Lena. "Back to the housing subject, we'll probably start hunting in the spring. Tom is thinking about moving to Princeton since he can take the commuter train into the city."

"Really. That's wonderful news. I'd love having you in the same town. How do you feel about it?" I asked.

"Mixed. It would be wonderful for the kids. The schools are good and the town offers plenty of diverse activities for them. Personally, I don't know. After all, I did my best to get away from here. Coming back, I wonder why. It really is a lovely town," admitted Lena with a sigh.

"I know what you mean. Maybe it's because we weren't part of the wealthy, boarding school set."

"That could be it. And I don't want my kids to turn out like little stuffed shirts or unbearable rich snots. But you're right. It would be great being in the same town with you." Out of the corner of my eye, I saw three little kids and a dog running and skipping toward the kitchen door. "Oh no, here come the kids. Mud up to their ears. Bath time. Which reminds me, what time is it?" I asked.

"It's about two. Here they come," and the troops rolled in, one filthier than the other. The only one that was clean was Shep; the kids were little pig pens. "My, don't you look like you had fun."

"Mom, the brook is really neat. You should come. Lots of things in the water. We played Jungle Book. Gabrielle was the monkey, Alexandra was the leopard, and I was Mogli. We tried to make Shep into the tiger, but he wouldn't growl. When is dinner?" queried Tara.

"At six-thirty. And you guys need a bath. Everyone to the bathroom," commanded Lena.

"And I want you to strip down to your underwear right here. No going anywhere with those muddy shoes and clothes," I added to the command.

Little groans were heard, and the children started taking off their clothes. Lena marched them upstairs to the tub in my bathroom and turned on the bath water. I could hear the water running and little squeals emitting from above.

Time to concentrate on cooking. Funny, when I was by myself, I had the luxury of daydreaming about Robbie. With company for the long weekend, not only were my dreams interrupted, but there was little chance of us spending anytime alone. Not that I wished that Lena went back home, but I was a little bit peeved of having my routine interrupted and not having Robbie to myself.

Well, let's get the show on the road, Vivi, and start preparing the soup. I needed chicken stock, yams, and onions. I pulled out my homemade chicken stock from the fridge and emptied it in a pot. Then I reached into the dry foods bin and grabbed a large yam and two medium-size onions. Good, everyone was out of my kitchen. I had a few minutes of quiet to daydream and to slice onions. The last few weeks had been delicious.

Robbie found a house to rent, and we had been able to see each other several times each week. Sometimes we were able to be alone when Connor was in school and Gabrielle was with Loretta. Those were precious moments, moments when we could shut out the world. I missed him at night, and not being able to wake up in the morning lying next to him. I didn't know how long this could continue. I wanted to be with him all the time.

Last weekend we took the kids to Washington's Crossing for the final burst of the autumn colors. It was a beautiful warm day, probably the last. We marched Connor and Gabrielle all over the area, and after lunch, both kids collapsed and fell asleep on the picnic blanket. Then for a brief period of time, I laid down with Robbie.

Cuddled in his long arms, we fell asleep with the sun gently filtering through the remaining leaves on the trees. Luckily we awoke before the kids. Getting the fifth degree from kids was not my favorite activity.

All done. Time to clean up the kitchen, take a nap, get into a nice dress and set the table for the dinner. It was the first time that I was using the dining room. I'll have one of the guys set a fire in the fireplace. I threw the dirty dishes in the dishwasher and I was done. I removed my apron, and headed upstairs to my bedroom. First, I needed to check on the bath situation. I walked over to the giant communal tub. Big noises and squeals could be heard all the way down the hall. I pop my head in and say hi.

"Howdy. What's happening?" I asked

"Hi, Mom. We're having a bubble fight. Tara's winning. Tata Lena went to go get some more towels." There were little clumps of bubbles everywhere.

"Oh my, try to keep some water in the tub. After you get dry, I want you girls to take it easy for a couple hours. Gabrielle, you need to take a nap, and it wouldn't hurt the rest of you to do the same. I know that Lena and your daddy got you up early this morning to drive down to Princeton, so you probably are a bit tired. Tonight is going to be a late night. Okay?" Lena slid into the bathroom.

"Lena, I was just telling the girls that I want them to take a rest for this afternoon since we are going to be up late tonight," I said.

"Great idea, Vivi. Girls, I've got your towels. Time to get dried off and into your rooms for a nap."

"Lena, I'm going into my room to lie down. I'm feeling weary myself. Everything is ready in the kitchen. All that's left to do is to set the table." I wiped off the water drops on Gabrielle and helped her to get into her underclothes.

"I'm with you on this nap idea. Tom is probably asleep at your Mom's, and I'm going to get at least one hour of peace. By the way, thank you again for having us. It really is lovely being together again." Lena's two girls had slipped into their undershirts and panties.

"You know that I love having you and the family here. Okay, kids. Back to your rooms and in bed." The children scattered to their bedrooms. "Lena, I'll see you in a couple hours," I murmured while yawning. It was time to take it easy.

I strolled over to my bedroom, took off my shoes and got under the covers. I really hoped that this would be a lovely evening. I hoped that Lena's family would have a good time. I hoped that Mom and Richard would enjoy themselves. I hoped that Connor was happy. I hoped that Robbie loved me. And I drifted off to sleep.

Chapter 41

Lord, what time is it? Oh my God. Six o'clock. Get up, Vivi. Quickly, jump into the shower. That feels good. Now dry off and get dressed. Swiftly, I scanned the closet, pulled out the midnight blue velvet dress, and laid it on my bed. I rifled through my stocking drawer for a navy pair. *Eureka, found them.* Then I looked into the closet again to find my black pumps with the little satin bows. In five minutes, I was dressed. It was time to arrange my hair and put on some make-up. I dashed to the bathroom and started brushing my hair in front of the Victorian mirror. I grabbed my navy brocade wired ribbon and began twisting it in my hair. Excellent, an elegant chignon and I was ready. No, not exactly, I was missing my lips. *Oh, what was in the magic drawer that can do the trick tonight? Yes, a deep, berry lipstick.* Now it was time for my pearl choker and earrings. One passing glance in the mirror. *Oh Vivi, for a middle age broad, you don't look too bad.*

I left my bedroom and in the hallway I could hear the sounds of children awakening. Good. They will be ready in time. Downstairs I took a good look at my surroundings.

It was amazing. A little less than a year ago, I panicked and came back home with few possessions and nothing to hold me to California. Now, I had a gracious house that glowed of comfort, warmth, and happiness, and a wonderful life surrounded by friends. I guessed that I finally picked the right curtain in the Game of Life. I was a most lucky woman.

So, most lucky woman, time to get this show on the road. I walked over to the fireplace and knelt down to light the kindling. Darn, there was a knock at the door.

"Come in," I shouted. Tom opened the door, entered and scanned the living room.

"Hi, Vivi. I fell asleep at your Mom's. Man, don't you look terrific. Don't worry about the fire. I'll take care of that. Ghislaine and Richard will be here in fifteen minutes. Where's my wife?" he asked taking off his lovely camel coat and tartan scarf.

"Asleep like the rest of us. Seems that everyone was worn out. I'm going to start setting the table," I handed Tom the matches and started walking toward the dining room.

Lena popped out of the guest room wrapped in a towel with damp hair. "I woke up about five minutes ago. Give me ten and I'll be ready to pitch in."

"I think you'll need to go upstairs and help the girls," I said while clearing off the dining room table of my permanent house accounting papers.

"Good idea. What a nap. We must have all been exhausted. Well, I'm getting hungry for some turkey." Lena demonstrated an exquisite yawn and headed back to the guest room.

"Yikes, the turkey. I forgot about it," and made a beeline for the oven. I heard Tom go outside, probably to get more firewood. I opened the oven door and peered in. The turkey was golden brown and smelled the way a delicious turkey should smell. This will be a fabulous meal. Intelligently, knowing that food had a propensity to be attracted to my clothing, I donned an apron and began the final preparations. The yams were pureed in the food processor and returned to the chicken stock to stay warm, the scalloped potatoes needed ten more minutes of baking time (thank heavens for time baking), and the remaining vegetables needed only a final touch of heat. Good.

Time to set the table. I seized the two centerpieces composed of mums, oak branches and holly, and carried them to the dining room. In the great wooden Asian chest, I found a bright yellow table cloth, placed it on the table, and laid the centerpieces.

Crystal goblets purchased from numerous estate sales, antique silverware from an auction, and Herend china discovered at a flea market, were removed from their various hiding quarters in the great chest and deposited on the table. I arranged the china, tiny orange and gold flowers on a white basket weave relief background, along side of the black linen table napkins. Next came the goblets, incredibly heavy pieces of crystal, adorned in pineapple cuts. Finally the antique silver, engraved with a former owner's initials lending authenticity to the setting. I took from the chest various serving plates and bowls that needed to be filled with the bounty from the kitchen. For the piece de résistance, I added golden candles, set in massive silver holders from Spain. *Step back and take a look, Vivi. Applause, applause. An exquisite, yet joyful setting.* I hoped that the room was a harbinger of the evening to come.

I turned and walked to the living room. Tom had made a wonderful fire, with plenty of wood still on the side of the hearth. I presumed that his lack of presence in the room indicated that he was changing his attire for the evening.

"A penny for your thoughts," and I turned around. Lena, resplendid in a deep burgundy brocade dress, smiled at me.

"I was looking at the beauty of the fire, and thinking about Thanksgiving. You know, I am so lucky. Five years ago, I'd never believe this happening. To me, it's a miracle, a small one, in the scope of the world, but a miracle nevertheless. It's nice that we have at least one day a year to appreciate friends and family. And even pets," I said admiring the room.

"Vivi, don't make me all mushy. My mascara is fresh. But you're on target. We're so lucky, especially to be here together. And especially to look this good at forty," joked Lena

"Yeah, let's open some champagne and toast our ancestors. You know, for decent bone structure and good skin."

"Yes, and for good hair," added Lena.

"And for great hairdressers. Mine does a great job on the gray."

“You’re on and you’re right about opening up the bubbly. I could use a moment of vanity rejoicing,” and Lena gave me her arm as we turned and marched to the kitchen. “I’ll get the champagne, and you get the glasses,” she commanded. I reached to the highest shelf in the kitchen cabinet and pulled out two champagne flutes. Lena deftly uncorked the bubbly and poured it into the glasses.

“To us,” she toasted.

“To us, and to loved ones and life,” I added. We took a sip and Tom sauntered in looking debonair in a navy blazer. "Hey, you two little pigs. Where’s my glass?” he asked.

“Up there in the cabinet. Take pity on short little Vivi, and get one down for yourself. Got it? Now, let me pour for you, my noble hero,” said Lena.

“To two exquisite women who never seem to age. And to the pathetic husband, slaving away in order to build a plastic surgery savings account.” Tom’s grin is definitely evil.

“Oh, you cad,” shrieked Lena. “But don’t worry; I’ll get you for this one.”

"Yes, I know, tonight in the guest room. We’ll test out the bed. Keep the high heels on,” laughed Tom.

"Tom, you’re impossible,” pouted Lena.

“And you married me for that exact quality. Now why don’t we go upstairs and check on the girls. It’s been too quiet.” We put down our glasses and headed to the nether region of the upstairs bedroom. Squeals and giggles were coming from Gabrielle’s bedroom. Tom, Lean and I poked our heads in the room and stared. Amidst the clothes strewn on the ground, the hats on top of the bed and an incredible collection of undergarments and stockings jumbled in corners, stood three beautifully dressed ladies of the evening. Although the girls were wearing their best dresses, they had attacked Gabrielle’s make-up and jewelry collection with an equal passion.

Thank God they hadn't made it to the perfume bottles that she saved. The odor could ruin the whole meal.

"Looks good, doesn't it, Mommy. Like in the magazines. Alexandra knows how to put on lipstick and eye stuff. See how good she got the blue stuff on," and Gabrielle presented her cheek to me, pointing at a very vivid blue eyelid.

"Looks lovely, girls. However, may I make one suggestion?" Okay Lena, let's see if you are able to maneuver around this situation. Right now it looked like we would have dinner with three miniature circus freaks. "Tata Vivi and I aren't wearing as much make-up because of candlelight."

"Candlelight?" chimed in the three ladies.

"Candlelight. In order to capture your beauty under such lighting, all make-up must be delicate and understated," pronounced the brave mother.

"Oh, you mean we have to wash it all off?" Tara looked like she would burst into tears.

"Oh no, just a little bit. And we would need to replace the red lipstick with one of a pink color. To bring out the flesh tones," continued Lena.

"Oh yes, to bring out the flesh tones," proclaimed Alexandra.

"So why don't I help you, just to make sure that your dresses stay nice. And then I can do your hair," suggested Lena. The ladies agreed and Tom and I left the scene to work on more mundane things, such as the Thanksgiving dinner.

"Close call," I said as we walk down the stairs.

"Don't worry, it gets worse. And then they're thirteen years old," muttered Tom.

“Tom, I forbid you, on a night of thanks, to remind me of the inevitable. Now, why don’t you answer the door and help with the drinks while I step into the kitchen and finish up with the last minute details,” I said.

We each went our own way. Tom ushered Richard and my mother into the living room, dealt with their coats, my mother’s contribution to dinner and served the champagne. Five minutes later, Lena and the girls descended. Thank heavens, the ladies of Lexington Avenue had left and three little beauty pageant queens had taken their place.

“Oh, you look so lovely,” exclaimed my mother.

"See Grandmere, we have lipstick. It’s for the candlelight,” piped up Gabrielle.

“It is very lovely on you. Vivi, do you need help in the kitchen?” my mother inquired.

“No, I’m almost ready. If everyone can take their place in the dining room, I can start bringing out the food. The food exodus commenced; soup, salads, vegetables, condiments, breads, and sauces, and they were rolled out on a cart. Lena and my mother deftly unloaded the dinner onto the sideboard and the table. I returned to the kitchen, procured the turkey from the oven, undid the skewers, foils, cheesecloth and placed it on an immense china platter. I carried the turnkey out to the dining room where it received “ohs” and “ahs” from the gallery.

Once the turkey was placed on the sideboard I quietly asked, "Who will say grace for all of us on this lovely day?” Alexandra volunteered. A minute later the feast began.

This was a meal to put into the book of memories, especially due to the company. The girls were discussing their Christmas lists, which was growing exponentially. Tom and Lena were relating the highlights of living in Europe and Mom was making notes of future places to visit. Richard was in turkey heaven, for Thanksgiving was his favorite holiday, and I was glad to have everyone under the same roof for this evening.

An hour later, after we had finished our meal and had cleared the table for coffee and dessert, the door bell rang. Must be Robbie and Connor. I rose from my seat to answer the door.

"Sorry Vivi, but I'll get it. I haven't seen Robbie in years. I want to get the door." and Lena ran off to the living room. I could hear her opening the front door.

"Robbie, all grown up. Happy Thanksgiving. Hi, you must be Connor. I'm Lena, and an old friend of your Dad. How nice you look. Gabrielle has been telling me all about you. Come in," she said enthusiastically.

"Lena, boy do you look lovely. Connor, let me have your coat and I'll put it in the closet. Well, let me give you a hug. It has been a long time," said Robbie.

I could hear Lena, Connor and Robbie walking toward the dining room. I turned around to look up and my heart lurched. Robbie and Connor were dressed in blazers and ties, looking incredibly dashing and handsome. Robbie came over to give me a kiss on the check and murmured, "Happy Thanksgiving, Vivi." He turned to Tom and introduced himself and Connor. We made room at the table for the two invitees. The girls were in a flutter to have Connor sit with them.

"So Connor, how was Thanksgiving at your grandmother's house`?" began Gabrielle.

"It was good. I've already had dessert, but I can have more, can't I, Dad?" begged Connor.

"Sure, Connor. Well this is great. Tom, did you know that I use to date your wife in high school until she got bored with me. She traded me for Vivi's date," joked Robbie.

"I wouldn't be surprised. I'm just glad she didn't continue that practice," replied Tom.

"Oh, Tom, don't embarrass me," said Lena with a smile.

"It's true. Just think you could have traded me and would have ended up with Leif. Robbie, Leif and I met Lena and Vivi at the same time," teased Tom.

"Oh you. It wouldn't have happened. Leif was geographically unacceptable," retorted Lena. "Plus I don't like blond men."

"Oh, great. So you picked me out that night due to geographical preference."

"Yes, I'm a very practical woman. See how nicely it all worked out," said Lena smugly.

"Ah, Lena, once again your logic defeats me. I surrender."

Robbie's blue eyes were dancing and he looked amused. "Surrender is the best weapon when it comes down to dealing with the superior sex. Now, may I surrender myself to the desserts? By the way, I brought some after dinner libations; cognac, single malt scotch, Irish cream, and Grand Marnier. Vivi's liqueur closet has slim pickings," he explained.

"Robbie, I look forward to that scotch. Just the thing to end a great meal," voiced Richard.

"Just make sure you don't have too much, Richard or I will drive," threatened Ghislaine. Richard looked up to the ceiling and nodded his head.

Round two: Desserts. It seemed that Mom went overboard and along with the Charlotte Russe, she also made a pear custard tart and cream puffs. Amazingly, there was little left at the end of the dinner. Tom, Richard, and Robbie had at least two servings of each of the tasty treats and left the dinner table groaning. The kids, bored with us, decided to feed Shep turkey and vegetable leftovers. Afterward, they scurried downstairs to play Ghost.

The adults moved the celebration to the living room where we sat around the fire, sipped our favorite potion, and told tales of our pasts. Around ten-thirty, Mom and Richard said good-bye and Lena and Tom put their two girls to bed. We found Connor and Gabrielle asleep in their finest on her bed, with Shep between them. Lena and Tom stayed up with us until midnight, when they made their apologies and retired to bed.

Robbie looked at me and said, "I thought we'd never get some time alone."

"Me, too. But it was a lovely evening," I said in a warm and cozy glow from the evening.

"One of the best. It's amusing, how life is a circle. You know, us, seeing Lena again. All of that."

I know. What slays me is that I ran away from this option years ago, now to embrace it," I added.

"So will you sit next to me and let me hold your hand?" asked Robbie.

"How about it if we lay down on the couch together. At least for a little while," I begged nicely.

Robbie nodded his head and sat sideways on the couch, his long legs almost touching the other side. I sat down between his legs, with his arms wrapped around me.

Robbie started kissing the back of my neck, and released my hair from the wire ribbon.

"Pretty, Vivi. My pretty Vivi," he murmured as he started kissing the base of my neck. This was the icing on the cake, being loved like this on a wonderful night. I turned around and cuddled up in his arms while watching the fire crackle and burn. In an hour the fire would be out.

"Penny for your thoughts, pretty Vivi."

"I was thinking about this evening, and old friends, and being with you. I was thinking how much I love you." Damn, the words slipped out naturally.

Robbie's arms tightened around me. "Funny, I was thinking the same thing. Thinking of how much I loved you, my little Vivi," he whispered thickly as he lowered his head to bestow a kiss, a kiss that I wished would last forever, a kiss to seal our love.

Chapter 42

"Mrs. Vivi, are you going to bring the trampoline into the basement before it snows?" asked Connor with a concerned look on his face.

"I don't know. We'll have to see if the ceiling is high enough so that you don't bump your head when you jump. Can you pass me that bottle of blue ink?" I asked.

"I really like the trampoline. It's neat. Here's the bottle."

"Thanks, Connor. Maybe your daddy or Richard can help us out. Why don't we ask them? Is there anything else you'd like?" Connor had been preoccupied this morning and all through lunch. I wondered what was on his mind.

"No, no it's okay. I'm going back. Gabrielle wants to jump more. I'm going to show her how to twist."

"Remember."

"I know. Be careful. I will. We'll only do them in the center. Bye," and the little redhead worrywart left the studio to join Gabrielle outside.

An impulse purchase met with great success. While shopping one day at a giant discount store, I spied a trampoline with safety netting for a paltry sum. Richard set it up in the back yard, and the kids had been jumping on it like crazy. Maybe it could go in the basement for the winter.

Connor called me Mrs. Vivi, and Gabrielle called Robbie, Uncle Robbie. When we were thinking of how the children should address us, Connor quite correctly pointed out that I wasn't his aunt. He added that Gabrielle was too young to understand such a fine point, hence calling his dad, Uncle Robbie, would suffice.

I was working on a new painting of an angel sitting on the Golden Gate Bridge. Bizarre. It's been commissioned by one of my collectors who was probably worried about the bridge collapsing during the next earthquake. I had been delaying the start of the painting for several months and the guilt trip about my procrastination had been mounting. So this morning I decided to tackle my blank canvas and started sketching in the outline of the painting. After lunch, I'll begin painting.

Robbie had left Connor with me for the day. Since Thanksgiving, he had been working with Tom, evaluating start-up high tech firms for investors. Today, Tom and Robbie were in the city meeting several potential investors. A comfortable relationship between the two men was developing.

One of the benefits of having large windows in the studios is that I could watch the kids in the back and front yard. I took a peep out the window. Gabrielle had her hands on her hips while watching Connor twist in the air. Now, the two of them were holding hands and jumping together. They must be playing *Ring around the Rosy*.

I returned to my painting which wasn't off to a good start. The angel resembled a troll and the bridge looked like it would fall over into the bay. I worked on the piece for an hour more. There, that looked better and the bridge was no longer doomed. I'd work on the angel, once I got Gabrielle to take a short nap.

I straightened my work area and headed out the door. Winter was here. The days were dark and cold with clouds filled with promise of snow. I'd better speak with Richard or Robbie soon about the trampoline. It looked like if we couldn't move it, it would be out of commission until spring.

It was about time for Gabrielle's nap. I opened and leaned out of the window. "Gabrielle. Rest time."

"Wait, Mommy. We're jumping to songs."

"Five more minutes, and then up to your room."

"Okay, Mommy." I closed the window and returned to my misshapen angel. Am I really in the mood to paint today*? Persevere, Vivi, and stop daydreaming about Robbie and Christmas. Now, get that lump off of the angel's nose and make her hair look soft*. Thankfully the painting was coming around.

Oops, looked like Gabrielle was heading into the house. I had better go down and meet her. I left the studio, headed down the stairs, out through the garage and into the house. "Gabrielle," I called.

"I'm up in my room, Mommy," she shouted.

I ran up the stairs, and into her bedroom. "Did you have a nice time with Connor twisting?" I asked.

"Yes, can Whitney come over soon and Alexandra and Tara so we all can jump?" she replied jumping on her bed.

"That might be fun. Whitney can come over anytime. I don't know when Tara and Alexandra can come down to see you. Maybe they will be here for Christmas. By then we may be able to have the trampoline in the basement. I'll call Tata Lena and see what her plans are."

"You know, Mommy. Soon, I am too big to take a nap. Soon, I go to school with lots of kids. Alexandra says they don't take naps at school," Gabrielle informed me.

"That's true, but sometimes when we play really, really hard, we get tired."

"Yeah, I guess so. What's Connor going to do?"

"Don't worry. Maybe he can do artwork in the studio with me," I replied.

"He'll like that. Okay, Mommy. Can I've a kiss?" Gabrielle begged.

"Of course. Many kisses and I placed ten little kisses on my pumpkins face.

"Have a nice rest" I whispered as I left her room. Now to find Connor. There he was, outside sitting on a chair. Something was on that kid's mind. *Well, don't pry and maybe he'll talk.* I walked out to the back yard and called, "Connor."

"Yes, Mrs. Vivi."

"Would you like to join me in the studio? I have watercolors and paints that you could work with? I'm going to be there while Gabrielle takes her nap," I said.

"Okay. What have you been doing there?" Connor got up and joined me as we walked to the studio.

"I'm working on a picture of an angel protecting a bridge. So far, I'm afraid it's not very good. It needs a lot of work." We headed up the stairs in the garage and I opened the door to the studio. Connor stepped in.

"Can I make pictures of angels?" said Connor in a low serious voice.

"Of course you may. I even have some gold paint if you would like."

"Oh, Mrs. Vivi. That would be wonderful."

"Would you like to paint using the easel or a drawing table?" I took one of my old shirts and put it on Connor to protect his clothes.

"I'd like the drawing table, if that's okay."

"Fine. Let me get you a nice brush and lots of paints and water. Here's the paper and some pencils. Sometimes, I first draw in pencil the picture, and then I paint it. You do what is most comfortable for you. I'll tape the paper down so that it won't move. And let me adjust the seat. There. Now you're ready to start," I said while giving Connor my corner table.

Connor immediately got to work and for an hour and a half, I didn't hear a peep out of him. My painting was getting better but the angel was lacking a beatific look on her face. Actually, she was looking like she just had great sex. I wondered how that came about? Terrific, angels and fairies looking like wanton maidens. My career would be washed up. *Think beatific, Vivi. Better yet, take a break. What is Connor up to?* I walked over to his table.

“How are you doing?” I asked while bending over and watching him work.

“Good. These are nice paints and I like the gold stuff.” Connor had painted an angel flying over two people with two other people and a tan blob on the side of the paper.

“Can you tell me about your picture, Connor?” I asked.

“Well, this is me and my daddy. And over here, is Gabrielle and you and Shep. The angel is my mommy and she watches out for me and dad. But she also makes sure that you guys are okay, too,” he said.

“That’s lovely, Connor. And I see that you used the gold for your mommy’s wings.”

“Yes. Do you really think that my mommy is an angel? Grandma says so but why don’t I see her?” Connor’s face was tight and concerned.

"Connor, everyone has their own ideas about death and angels, but I think your Mommy loves you very much and is watching you all the time,” I said while watching Connor’s face tighten.

"But Mrs. Vivi. If I can’t see my mommy, I’ll forget what she looks like. And maybe Daddy has forgotten about her if he likes you too much.” Oh dear, so this was the problem. Poor kid, looked like he’d burst in tears at any moment. I took his hand and lead him to the sofa where we sat down next to each other.

“Connor, do you remember things that you did and times you spent with your mommy?” I asked.

“You mean like when she would read books to me? And when I scraped my knee at the park?” he replied.

"Yes, can you remember that really well?"

"Oh yes, Mommy had to take me to the doctor's. I really hurt it."

"Sometimes, Connor, we remember odd events very clearly. Maybe you need a picture of your mommy that helps you to remember. Do you have that kind of a picture of your mommy?"

"No, Grandma has pictures of Mommy, but some of them don't even look like her," he said sadly.

"See, your Grandmother has pictures that help her to remember your mommy, and you need to find pictures that help you to remember. You need to go through your family's picture books and pick out some that help you to remember. Do you have any at home?" I was sure that Robbie had hundreds of pictures of Anne.

"Daddy has some, but he put most of them away."

"Well, maybe you need to sit down with your daddy and go through all of the pictures. Your daddy can show you pictures that remind him about your mommy and that way you'll know more about her. You know, Connor. Your daddy will never forget your mother. He loved her very much. And he doesn't want you to ever forget her. She was a very special person to your Daddy." I put my arm around Connor and gave him a much-needed hug.

"Mmmm, I think you're right. Daddy talks to me about Mommy sometimes. Would Grandma show me pictures too? I know that it can make her sad. I don't want Grandma to be sad."

I don't think so but I tell you what."

"What?"

"Why don't I talk to your Daddy and he can speak to your grandparents. I'm sure that your grandfather has some stories and pictures of his own that he would like to share with you. And you know, I have another idea," I added.

"What is it, Mrs. Vivi?"

"Sometimes photographs don't help us to remember because they are so small. They're nice as reminders but you might need something better."

"Like what?" Connor's face was less tense. I hoped that this would help him work out his mother's death.

"Oh, like a video of people talking about your mommy. Your daddy could point out pictures and tell the story about him with your mommy, and your grandparents could take out their pictures of your Mommy and tell what she was like when she was a little girl. Then you could watch your mommy on TV whenever you want," I answered him.

"Could you talk to Daddy to do something like that? That would be great, Mrs. Vivi. Thank you. You know, you're okay. I think my mommy would have liked you very much. I'm glad she watches over you and Gabrielle," and Connor gave me a big hug.

"Talking about that, why don't we mount your lovely picture now, like a real artist? I think I have a frame that would fit," and I started rummaging around in my cardboard boxes of supplies that I had not yet unpacked. I found a simple wood frame and brought it over to my framing table. Connor was very excited at the thought of his artwork being framed.

"Yes, let's do it, now, "said Connor. I walked over to the dry mount press and turned it on.

"Connor, the press will take a little while to heat up, so let's go see if Gabrielle is awake and we can all work together in the studio."

"Okay, I'll go see, and you wait here for us." Connor dashed out the door, looking a lot less burden by the weight of his thoughts. I returned to my sexy angel, and decided to try again tomorrow. Time to clean up the brushes. Five minutes later both kids are back. Connor was holding Gabrielle's hand and they were both breathless.

"Mommy, Connor wants to show me his angel picture so I can see his mommy," said Gabrielle cheerfully.

Connor and Gabrielle walked over to the drawing table and Gabrielle climbed up on to the drafting chair.

"Oh, Connor. That's so nice. Your mommy looks so pretty with the gold."

"Okay, Gabrielle and Connor. I'm going to dry mount the picture, then place a mat around it, and place it in a wood frame. But first, Connor, you'll need to sign your artwork." Gabrielle got off of the drafting seat, Connor took her place, I handed him a black marker, and he signed his name.

"Oh, Connor, just like a real artist," cooed Gabrielle. Carefully I dry-mounted his picture to a piece of art board, put a pre-cut mat around it, and slipped it into a frame with glass. Connor and Gabrielle gave their signs of approval.

"Well, I need to get working on dinner, so let's close up here and take the picture in the house," I declared while my audience nodded. We turned off all the equipment, downed the lights and left the studio. As we entered the house by way of the kitchen, I turned to Connor and said, "It was a pleasure working with you today. You can come to the studio any time you'd like." Connor beamed a smile that I hadn't seen in several days. "Now why don't you kids help me snap the green beans so we can get dinner on the way."

Connor and Gabrielle opened the refrigerator and took out the bag of string beans from the vegetable bin. We sat down at the table and started preparing the food to be cook. I looked down at Connor while he struggled with an end of a green bean. Not a care, not a concern showed up on his face. Gabrielle spent most of her time eating her mistakes since she couldn't get the beans to snap. It was just as it should be with children. Their biggest worry was how to get that damn bean to snap. And that their world was secured by moms and dads, by angels and grandparents that love, shelter, and cherish their wonderful souls.

Chapter 43

Princeton was gray, cold, and very quiet. The first snow of the winter was coming down and it was beginning to stick on the roads and sidewalks. By nightfall, the roads would be slick and dangerous. My street had the appearance of a whitewash job gone haywire. I could use a dose of California at this moment.

Like most fortunate souls at this moment, we were all inside the house. I was in the living room watching the fire, while Gabrielle, Robbie, and Connor had taken over my studio for the video project. I believed I would be in exile for two more weeks. So now I had a good excuse not to work on the painting until after New Year's Day.

A car pulled up on our street and parks. I was too lazy to walk over to the window and see who it was. No company expected today. I wanted to take a break from the Christmas decorations. I had been hanging garlands around the staircase and the fireplace and I needed a break. The tree had been up for a week and the children were waiting to adorn it tonight. My next project was to string popcorn and cranberries.

The video suggestion went over well. Anne's parents and Robbie had been super-enthusiastic about creating a tape about Anne's life. Robbie had turned it in to an art project for Connor, who learned how to operate a camcorder. Connor set up the taping sessions with his dad and grandparents and had several hours of footage.

They were in the editing phase and Gabrielle was their willing audience. No one except the chosen three were allowed to see the tapes until the editing and sound work was completed. I guessed sometime after Christmas we would have an opening night.

Connor's personality had changed drastically since he started working on his project. He was much less withdrawn, and had become a fun and lighthearted little boy. Robbie had also changed by being less protective of his son. By reviewing his past and good times with Anne, he had completed his mourning period. So it had been well worth the sacrifice of one studio. Plus I could avoid the bridge angel painting for a while longer.

The clock chimed. It was two o'clock, time for tea. I got out of my chair and took a few steps toward the kitchen. Someone was at the door. Funny, I was not expecting anyone. *Oh well, don't let them stand outside on a day like today.* I walked over to the front door and opened it.

My world had just collapsed. Leif. It's Leif. What should I do or....

"Hello, Vivi. I'm sorry for the surprise, but I didn't know how to approach you. May I come in?" I stepped back and Leif walked into the living room. He unbuttoned his black cashmere coat, folded it over the edge of the leather sofa and walked over to the center of the living room.

"This is beautiful, really beautiful. The colors are wonderful, especially on a day like today. You must have hated the house in San Francisco with all the white walls." His voice was still low and melodious. I dumbly nodded my head.

"Well, like I said, I'm sorry to surprise you like this, but I knew that if I tried to call you, you'd just hang up. Not that I blame you," he said ruefully.

All right, Vivi. The nightmare from hell has just materialized in your living room. Stay cool. Be pleasant. Maybe he'll go away. Forever.

"Would you like to sit down? I was going to make a cup of tea. Would you like some?" I asked icily.

"Yes, please. I'm freezing from this weather." Leif sat down in one of the blue chairs. "I didn't know you played the piano."

"I'm not very good, never was. But I like having a piano in the room." I paced into the kitchen, hopefully to catch my breath. Damn, damn, damn. Last person I wished to see. *Bastard.*

Now Vivi, boil some water, get the teapot, and prepare the tray. I wondered if he could see how I was shaking. Maybe it was not that bad. After all, I wasn't swooning over his looks anymore. *Do not tell him anything. Do not mention Gabrielle's name. Do not volunteer information. Let him do the talking. Okay, now that everything is made, go out and face him.*

I walked back into the living room, carrying the tea tray. Calmly, I placed the tray on the coffee table, poured two cups, handed one cup to Leif, and took a seat on the other blue chair. I reached over to the coffee table, secured my teacup, and sat back in the chair.

"So what's this about, Leif?" *Don't show any emotion, Vivi.*

"I don't know where to start. I know that I haven't seen you in about five years and I need some closure in my life. I need to make some apologies to people and restitution," Leif said slowly while pouring himself a cup.

"Restitution?" I asked.

"Yeah, about seven months ago, I turned myself into a clinic for substance abuse. I almost lost my business and the house," admitted Leif.

"Cocaine?"

"Yes, how did you know?"

"There was some paraphernalia in the garage. It looked like stuff to cut up cocaine. Like something a dealer would have," I answered.

"Well, I'm not proud of it, but I did have an ugly habit before I even met you. It caused for some personality changes that probably help destroy our marriage. My mother died recently. Lung cancer. She was a committed smoker. Anyway, I went through a lot of therapy at the clinic and afterward. One of the subjects that constantly came up in conversation was about you and Gabrielle..."

I interrupted him. "How do you know about Gabrielle? Or find out where we live?" *Stay cool, Vivi. Stay cool.*

"I hired a private search firm to find your address and a little about Gabrielle. You know, like date of birth, sex. The address they were able to trace through a credit search. I swear, Vivi, that was it. I didn't hire some greasy guy in a trench coat to follow you," he implored.

"Go on. I am furious that you had me tracked down. You have no right to walk back into my life. You signed away those rights, Leif."

"I know, I know. Anyway, I'm here to apologize for being such a bastard and I want you to know that for whatever it's worth, I've willed everything I own, in case of my death, to Gabrielle."

"And..." I interjected.

"There is no "and" about it. Gabrielle may be the only child I'll ever have. Plus she deserves a more caring father. I know that I've no rights, that I signed them off, but I would like to start a dialogue with Gabrielle. I am begging with you, Vivi. I won't do anything stupid, like send her presents or money. I would just like her to know about me. This is probably useless. I even had a top lawyer review the divorce papers, who said no judge would give me five minutes with papers and a track record of negligence like mine," he said ruefully.

Damn, damn, damn. The bastard, albeit her dad, waltzed back in my life and expected me to turn over my daughter to him. Was the exodus from California for nothing? I felt betrayed and destroyed by the events of the past. What about Gabrielle? Wasn't she going to be confused with this man waltzing into her life? *Wait a second, Vivi. Maybe later in life, Gabrielle may reject you for turning her dad away.* And Gabrielle was sharp, far sharper than her naive mother. It was time to blast Leif between the eyes. He had it coming.

"You're a real son of a bitch, Leif. You and your mother wanted me to abort a child and now you're sorry. You're sorry, that's a laugh. You were such a paranoid bastard at the divorce, afraid I would take something of yours. You didn't even know what was valuable. And you now think that I am going to give her back to you. You've got a lot of nerve. I hoped never to see you again, to leave us alone. I'd say that I despised you. And what use are you to Gabrielle? I don't even know how she'll act with you."

"She's never asked about me?" asked Leif.

"Not really. She once asked me if I was married. And she does know about parts of my life that did include you, but she has never asked about you in particular. It is a non-subject around here."

"Could I see her, Vivi? Please. I beg of you. Please."

"No way. I..."

Before I could say another word, Gabrielle, Connor, and Shep came running in to the room from the kitchen outside door. "Mom, can we have something to eat? Can I have this cookie? Mommy, are you okay. I heard shouting", asked Gabrielle. She turned to Leif, looked at him in the eye and said "I'm Gabrielle, Vivi's daughter. This is my dog Shep and my best guy friend, Connor. Who are you?" Leif looked at me and didn't speak.

"Gabrielle, this is your birth father, Leif Bergstrom. Leif, this is Gabrielle." The two solemnly shook hands.

"I've never seen you before, have I?" Gabrielle looked up at Leif.

"No, that's correct. You haven't."

"So why are you here now? Mommy doesn't need you. We like it here."

Connor quietly slipped out of the room. Everything was out of my control. I was frozen in my seat, unable to move, petrified by the turn of events.

"I am here to say I'm sorry. I haven't been a nice person. I haven't been a father in any way to you, and it's time that I fix those things."

"Oh. I don't need a father. I have my mommy and other people. I have my Grandmère. I don't need you," said Gabrielle nonchalantly.

"Gabrielle," Leif interjected. "I would like to know if I can talk to you from time to time."

"About what?"

Leif continued the conversation. "About how you're doing. About how you spent the day. Just little things. On the phone."

"I don't know. I have to talk to Mommy. Can I go now? I got work to do." She grabbed a handful of cookies and headed out to the kitchen. At the doorway, she turned around and thought for several seconds while starring at Leif. "Good -bye," she said and headed back out the kitchen door.

"Well?" I asked.

"Well, she's beautiful. I really thank you. I'm sorry for upsetting you today, but there was no other way that I could think of contacting you. Even if she never talks to me, at least I saw her. And you, Vivi. You've done well. You look wonderful, but then you always did. And this house is splendid. How did you do it?" inquired Leif politely.

"Remember the stock options that you signed off at the divorce."

"Oh yes, what was it? A couple hundred," said Leif.

"No. More like six thousand." Leif took a big gulp of tea and stared at me. "Anyway they were worth enough to allow me to seriously play the stock market."

"You know Vivi, I would have never figured you to have a financial head," he said stunned by the news.

"Leif, I don't think you figured much about me."

"You're right. I just thought that you were a sweet, beautiful, graphic designer that would make a good wife. Are you doing graphics?" he asked.

"No, at present, I'm an illustrator. I didn't want to be a single working parent for Gabrielle." Suddenly, the kitchen door opened again, and several seconds later Robbie appeared in the living room. He looked wonderful to me at this moment.

"Vivi, Connor and Gabrielle just told me that you have a guest. Is there anything I can do," asked Robbie.

"Thank you, Robbie. Leif, this is Robbie Terhune. Robbie, this is my ex-husband, Leif Bergstrom." The two men cautiously eyed each other, and then shook hands. "Robbie, Leif was just about to leave. I'll be with you in a moment." Robbie quietly took a step back. I grabbed Leif's coat and walked him to the door.

At the doorway, while putting on his coat, Leif looked at me and says quietly, "Thank you Vivi. Can I call Gabrielle up on Christmas morning and wish her a merry Christmas?"

"I think that would be a nice gesture," I answered.

"He's very much in love with you, isn't he," said Leif quietly.

"Who?"

"Robbie. And you're very much in love with him."

"Yes, very much."

"Lucky man, really lucky man. Thank you again Vivi," he said hoarsely and disappeared into the blinding white afternoon. I shut the door, took a deep breath, and whispered "Thank heavens that's over." I turned around and looked at Robbie.

"Sit down, Vivi. You're trembling." Robbie held out his hand and led me to the couch. We both sat down and Robbie wrapped me in his arms.

“Don’t worry, sweetheart. It will all work out. You’ll see. These things will work out for the best. Plus, he’s terrified. I could hear you shouting at him from the outside of the house,” said Robbie in a calming tone.

“He’s terrified. I’m terrified. My world dissolved in front of me. So many things I worked for. I thought we were protected from him,” I said while tears came down my cheeks.

"You are, Vivi. And you have all of us here to make sure he keeps his distance. I won’t let anything happen to you or Gabrielle,” promised Robbie.

“Oh, Robbie. I’m lucky you came back into my life. What would I do without you?”

“Oh, you’d be fine, dating all the good looking men in this town. And talking about good looking, my ego has just had a large knock.”

"Whatever for, Robbie?”

“Leif. Your ex. That is probably one of the best-looking men that I’ve ever encountered. I must look like dog meat in comparison,” said Robbie as he kissed my head.

“Robbie Terhune. You funny man, there was only one handsome adult male in this room and it wasn’t Leif,” I replied.

“Oh, Vivi. Thank heavens that love makes you blind.”

“No, Robbie. It doesn’t make you blind. It helps you to see.” Robbie smiled at me.

“You just know how to soothe the worried brow of balding, middle age men. I hope that I can do the same for you. Don’t worry. Everything will be fine. Come into the hallway, my beloved, so that I may kiss you under the mistletoe,” and Robbie pulled me up to my feet.

Somehow, I got the impression that dinner would be a little late this evening.

Chapter 44

"Get up, Mommy. Get up. Santa Claus came. Lots of presents to open. Mom, open your eyes. There's snow. A real Christmas. Come on, Mommy." Gabrielle was jumping on top of me and singing out her demands. I opened my poor, little, exhausted eyes and groaned. What time was it? I glanced at the clock. Nine o'clock. Yes, I had better get up. This kid was about to burst with Christmas excitement.

"Okay. Mommy's getting up. Mommy is first taking a shower, a very hot shower."

"No, Mommy. Do that later. Come down and open presents first."

"I know. Why don't you go downstairs and work on your Christmas stocking, while I shower and grab my coffee," I bleated.

"Okay, Mommy. Here's a Christmas kiss," and Gabrielle buried her head in my neck. I was a blessed but tired woman. She scampered off to the living room and I hopped out of bed and ran into the bathroom. Got the shower going nice and hot and jumped in.

I was beginning to come alive. Yesterday was fairly intense. We went skating with Robbie and Connor on the lake, had dinner at my mother's house, and got to stay up late assembling a doll house for my little pumpkin. To summarize; I fell, ate and worked too much. Hopefully today would pass with little exertion on my part.

It was time to dry off. I looked down at my legs and noticed the nice bruises on my thigh. I got a beauty on my left leg that should turn to a lovely color of motley brown and blue by tonight. Really sexy. Now it was time to dress, and take care of any ravages incurred to my face, which from a quick glance, were numerous.

There. That's the best I can do. Now to get my coffee and join the little jumping bean. I went down the stairs to the living room.

"Okay, Mom. I've emptied my stockings. Can I open my presents, now?" shouted Gabrielle full of Christmas cheer.

"Yes, in a minute. I'm just going to get a cup of coffee. Be back in a second."

Who ever invented timers on the coffee machine was an inspired genius. I swiftly filled my cup and returned to the area of conspicuous capital consumption. For forty-five minutes, Gabrielle was squealing and screaming about the wonders of her presents. The doll house was a major hit. The dolls and puppets were big hits. The books, art supplies and miniature easel were big hits. And there were clothes, new collars for Shep, dress-up clothes, and toys. It was endless. She loved it all.

If someone didn't know what day it was, and was trying to enter our house, they would have thought that I had an enormous aviary, with all the squawking from Gabrielle. And that I must love paper to have had so much in the living room. We were inundated with paper; metallics and brocades, red and green and gold, ribbon of all sorts and of course boxes scattered all over the room. I needed to clean this stuff up especially before the wave of guests. They would all be here: Lena and her family, Robbie and Connor, Robbie's parents - Jenny and David, and Bill and Betty. The house would be a zoo shortly. *Damn, it's the doorbell.*

"Gabrielle, can you answer the door, honey?" Gabrielle danced to the front door, unlocked the deadbolt, and opened the door. Mom and Richard came tramping in, with boots, winter coats, hats, gloves and cheery red faces.

"Joyeux Noël. Quel temps. You'll need to have your walkway cleaned, Vivi. It is very slippery," my mother declared.

"Grandmère, Papi. Merry Christmas. See my presents. See my presents. Come. Come," demanded my little sergeant.

"Joyeux Noël, poupée," as my mother leaned over and kissed Gabrielle.

"Merry Christmas," roared Richard. "Ho, ho, ho. Don't I get a kiss, too."

"Here, Papi," squealed Gabrielle as Richard bent down to get his kiss. "Now come see. See everything Santa bought me." Gabrielle danced around while tossing ribbons and bows in the air.

"Zut, Vivi. Quel désastre. Don't worry. Richard, make a fire so we can start burning the paper. I'll get a big plastic bag for the rest."Thank heavens for Mom to the rescue. I'm saved from being buried alive by Christmas wrappings.

Ten minutes later there was a semblance of tidiness in the room. Richard and Mom helped themselves to some coffee and we exchanged gifts while sitting down in the living room. Gabrielle's level of excitement was still at a high; Mom gave her a living room set for her dollhouse. Now she was working on Richard's gift. It was a family for the dollhouse, complete with parents, two kids, a baby and a dog.

"Oh, thank you, Grandmère. Thank you, Papi. This is a wonderful Christmas. How did you know Santa Claus was giving me a doll house?" asked a wide-eyed Gabrielle.

"We saw him a couple of days ago and asked him. He said because your doll house took up so much room, he didn't have space in the sled for any furniture or people, so that maybe we could give them to you," Richard related with a twinkle in his eye.

"Oh, Santa Claus knows everything, doesn't he'?" said Gabrielle in an awe-struck voice.

"Of course, poupée. Now open up the rest of your presents. Vivi, these are for you." Mom passed me several smaller, weighty boxes. I opened them. Delightful. Mom had given me antique silver serving pieces; a ladle, salad fork and spoon, several large spoons, and dessert knives. On the other hand, Mom and Richard were quite happy with the cellular phone Gabrielle and I bought them.

"See, Richard. If we are in the car and late for an appointment, we can call. This will be wonderful if we have to drive to Florida. Oh, and what is this envelope? Mon dieu. Vivi, you shouldn't have. Look Richard, we are booked for a Caribbean cruise." Mom's mouth stopped moving for a few seconds. I wished that I had this moment on video.

There were more presents for all of us: framed photographs of Gabrielle and myself for the grandparents, a painting of Richard and my mother for their mantelpiece. Mom started to cry when she saw the painting, and some new electric wood tools for Richard. Gabrielle got more clothes, more books, and more toys. Once again we over-compensated for all the years when money was tight.

"Thank you. Thank you for a marvelous Christmas morning. Now let's clean up and get the food ready. Gabrielle, to your room. Grandmère is going to help you take your bath," commanded my mother. Everyone got kisses and hugs, and Gabrielle raced up the stairs.

"I'll take care of the paper mess and the walkway, Vivi," Richard kindly volunteered and I headed off to the kitchen to prepare the food. The trifle was made last night, and I needed to put all the cold cuts on serving trays. One tray for the smoked salmon and one tray for the California sushi rolls. What else? Mustard, cream cheese, sour cream, caviar, sourdough bread, French bread, pumpernickel and pumpkin bread. Champagne, beer, white wine and eggnog for the large copper tub at one corner of the dining room. Green salad with edible flowers. *And don't forget the desserts; Bouche de Noël, chocolate mousse, trifle (of course), cookies and cream puffs*. And finally, one large cutting board for the smoked Pennsylvania ham.

Shep followed my steps and looked at the food plates with hope in his eyes. I gave him the hambone which he happily gnawed for a half hour in the kitchen. Merry Christmas, you precious animal. Merry Christmas. I placed everything on the serving cart and wheeled the food over to the dining room. Now I just needed to set out the food on the sideboard and set the table.

Dark green and burgundy table cloth with gold napkins. Clear glass plates with gold rims and champagne glasses with gold dots. Golden angel centerpieces adorned with red roses, and crystal candle stick holders gripping the red candles. Out came the silverware, and I put to use the new serving pieces from Mom. I displayed the food, tossed the drinks in the tub, and put the ham at the lower end of the table. I stepped back and assessed the tableaux. *Bon Appétit magazine, watch out.*

I walked back to the living room. Gabrielle, freshly bathed, looked charming in a new outfit from her grandmother. Richard, red-faced from shoveling the snow, was adding more logs to the fire. Shep took the perfect spot in front of the fire. My mom walked over to the dining room, and reviewed the presentation, quality and quantity of food. She solemnly nodded her head, turned to me, and proudly said, "Bravo, Vivi. Bravo."

"Doorbell," screamed Gabrielle and she rushed to the front door. It was Lena and the gang. "Merry Christmas, Tata Lena and Uncle Tom. Merry Christmas Alexandra and Tara." The kids were jumping up and down.

"Boots and coats, off. Now," commanded Lena before the snow got tramped all over the carpet. Quickly Alexandra and Tara peeled off their burdensome apparel and ran off with Gabrielle to play in the corner of the living room with the doll house. Tom and Lena wandered over to the food.

"I'm starving Vivi. Lena wouldn't let me eat this morning. She rushed us out of her parents' house." Tom flashed puppy dog eyes at us.

"Don't listen to his whining, Vivi," said Lena. "He had breakfast. He just wanted to get a double hamburger, French fries, and milk shake to snack on while driving here. Forget it, lover boy."

"Tom, start eating, please. And can I have a glass of champagne while you're up?" I asked.

Richard headed to the dining room. "Ghislaine, I'm going to get a plate of food. Do you want anything?" he asked.

“A cream puff and a glass of champagne, please chèrie. Vivi, do you mind if I put on some Christmas music,” asked Ghislaine.

“Be my guest, Mom. There are some Christmas CD’s on top of the stereo. The changer can hold five of them at a time.” Tom handed me a glass of bubbly while holding on to a plate loaded with food. I looked up at Lena who raised her eyebrows and shrugged.

"You would think looking at his plate, that the food will get taken away any minute. Men,” mocked Lena while lifting her glass to her lips.

"Come on. You’d think I was sick if I didn’t eat like this, pussycat.” Tom buried his face in the food and all that escaped from his lips are little sighs of pleasure.

"Doorbell,” shouted Mom, as if we were deaf.

“I’ll get it,” and I opened the door to five adults and one little boy. Connor and his family came in the living room singing Jingle Bells. The girls hopped down from upstairs and gathered around Connor. Robbie collected everyone’s coats and hung them up in the closet. Boots and hats were removed and stored in their appropriate places.

“Merry Christmas, Vivi. Hi, Guys. Let me introduce my parents and in-laws,” Robbie announced. “Ghislaine, you probably know Betty and Bill. This is Jenny and David, my parents.

Quickly, the introductions took place. Mom, in two minutes, ascertained that there were enough couples for two bridge tables. Richard, Bill, Betty, Jenny, David, Tom and Lena were all avid players, leaving Robbie and I to fend for ourselves.

Ghislaine announced the day’s agenda. “That settles it. After the presents for the children and lunch, let’s play bridge. The kids will take care of themselves and maybe Robbie and Vivi can go take a walk. Get some fresh air.” I didn’t call my mother the Commander for nothing. Everyone happily agreed to the plan. The children returned to the living room to open the last of the presents (more squeals), and headed for the buffet.

Suddenly, the phone rang. I raced to the kitchen to answer. "Hello, Vivi speaking. Merry Christmas"

"Vivi. It's Leif. Merry Christmas. How is everything?" My heart sank.

"Fine, I have a lot of company and an awful lot of food."

"Sounds great. Listen, I called to wish Gabrielle a Merry Christmas. Is it okay if I speak with her?" he said in a hesitant voice.

"I'll see. Let me call her."

"Thanks." I walked to the living room and whispered in Gabrielle's ear. "Gabrielle, can you come to the phone. It's Leif. He wants to wish you a merry Christmas."

"I guess so," said Gabrielle sulkily and marched off to the kitchen phone. Five minutes later, she reappeared. "I told him it was okay to call me at Easter. Did I do right?"

"Who called you, Gabrielle?" my mother asked with a concerned look.

"Leif called. I talked about the doll house and all the toys I got and that we are having a party now," replied Gabrielle.

"O Mon Dieu. Vivi, is this true?" Mom was a-flutter and Lena leaned over to catch the conversation.

"Yes, to my shock, he showed up at my doorstep last week. I didn't want to upset you with the news. I still haven't recovered," I admitted.

"And what happened."

"Nothing much. He apologized for his behavior and for neglecting Gabrielle. He has written her in his will and he'd like to start-up a dialogue with her. He's allowed to call or write. He knows he can't get any custody rights," I said quietly.

"And how does he look? He was such a handsome man."

"I think that he is still as handsome. I don't know. Maybe not. His mother died and he's been in therapy. Anyway, I don't find him attractive."

"Grandmere, he's shiny. I guess he's okay, but shiny," interjected Gabrielle. "Can I take a sip of your drink, Mommy?" I nodded. Gabrielle took a sip of my champagne and made a face. "The bubbles got in my nose. I don't like that."

Mom continued her train of thought. "Well, I hope you know what you are doing. I would have never let him in the house."

"I don't know if I did the right thing. Gabrielle showed up while we were talking so it was out of my control. I don't want Gabrielle to reproach me for not letting her know her birth father. And the more people that love her, the better," I explained.

"Tu as raison. You're right. Still, I wished the earth would eat him up and he'd disappear," conceded my mother as she returned to eating her lunch.

Forty-five minutes later, after a large meal and from sampling all seven desserts, we groaned from the ecstasy of our full stomachs. The children excused themselves to jump on the trampoline in the basement. Richard and Tom went up to the attic to retrieve the folding tables. The rest of us straightened up the living room. Mom rifled through her purse to find the playing cards. Jenny hand-printed bridge tallies and Bill started shuffling the cards. I looked over at Robbie and smiled. He got up from his chair, leaned over to me and murmured, "Let's get out of here."

"Mom, Robbie and I are going for a walk to help digest lunch." I rose from my seat and lumbered toward the entrance closet.

"We'll be back in an hour or so," interjected Robbie while assisting me with my jacket. He took his own parka out from the closet and got prepared to assail the snowy weather. I slipped into my fleece lined boots and pulled my gloves out of the pockets of my coat.

“Don’t rush,” said Lena while opening the folding chairs. "We’ll probably be playing for a couple hours and the children are no hassle.” The eight-some sat down and wave us off.

"Come, little Vivi, I want to show you something,” whispered Robbie while opening the front door. And out into the white, powdery kingdom, my faithful and handsome knight whisked me away to an unknown destiny.

Chapter 45

"Robbie, where are we going?" Slowly, due to the icy conditions of the roads, we were taking a strange route to nowhere.

"You'll see. Just wait. It's a surprise." I looked at Robbie's face and could not read what was going on in his mind. Okay, I'll chill out, as Connor would say. Slowly, we crept past the park and crossed Nassau Street. Except for a few children playing in the snow, not a car was on the road. Suddenly, we passed Battle Road.

"Oh, Robbie, the Institute. We're going to the Institute."

"Shhh. Someone might hear you. We have to be quiet," whispered my knight with a broad smile upon his face. Silently the car pulled into the Institute of Advanced Study. Robbie found a parking space, deadened the engine, slipped out of the driver's seat and walked over to my side to help me out.

"We're here. Come," he commanded as he held out his hand for me.

In the white wonderland of the landscape, a day of soft flat light, we crossed though the open arches of the building and cautiously stepped down from the terrace.

Not a sound could be heard except for the shuffling of our boots through the snow and the beating of my heart. Robbie didn't say a word but took me down past the library, down toward the pond, down to the groove of large trees, trees that today could not cast a shadow. Trees that when we were young, lent their special magic to a night of wonder.

Suddenly, Robbie stopped and turned around to me. "See, I remember. I remember that night as if it was yesterday." He reached into his immense red parka, pulled out a bottle of champagne and two glasses.

He smiled and his blue eyes lit up, full of mischief. “You know, Vivi. I entertained the thought of making love with you again among these trees but the thought of taking off my clothes and rolling in the snow somehow has lost its appeal. But I thought we could still enjoy the champagne and the company of each other.” Robbie popped the cork off the bottle and poured the champagne into each glass.

"Here, Vivi. This one is for you.” I clasped the stem of my glass. “Cheers,” he said and we clink our glasses together.

“Cheers to what, Robbie?” I asked.

"Cheers to friends. To Christmas. To family. To love. To a gift.”

"What gift, Robbie?” I was confused about this conversation. What was he talking about?

Then Robbie smiled and shyly said, “To a gift you gave me long ago. To a gift I’m giving you.” He slowly reached down in his right-hand pocket and pulled out a small box, a ring box, nicely wrapped with a tiny bow. "Open it, Vivi. Open it,” he whispered.

Each second was crystallized in my mind. I slowly untied the ribbon and unwrapped the box.

“Open it, Vivi,” the voice echoed in my mind.

I unclasped the hinge on the box and slowly pried the box open. A flash of light escaped. A beautiful ring. A ring with diamonds bouncing the light, like the snow crystals on the ground. I had never seen anything so exquisite, so dazzling. I looked up at Robbie.

"That was the most wonderful gift in the world. A gift that meant you loved and trusted me. We should take up where we left off on that summer night. Our lives should continue together. What I’m trying to ask you here, on this piece of ground that once brought us together is will you marry me? Will you, Vivi?” he said hoarsely.

Calmly, I took the ring out of the box and placed it on my left ring finger. I looked up at this wonderful person, and once again, the face of a fallen angel materialized.

“Robbie,” I whispered hoarsely, “with this ring, I thee wed. Then the tall man leaned over and kissed me, a kiss of body and soul, a kiss that would carry through for the rest of our lives.

Suddenly Robbie grabbed me, lifted me up in the air, laughing, and then placed me back on the ground. ‘°Oh, I love you, little Vivi. Come on. We need to drink up and go tell the kids.” He waited a second and continued, “And grandparents, and friends.”

"You know, Robbie Terhune. Sometimes you really surprise me.”

“How, precious pip-squeak. Tell me how.”

“Oh, all of this. I’m really floored.”

“I knew that after your rotten marriage, it would take a major effort on my part to push some of your buttons so you’d accept my proposal. I counted on pure sentiment to get the better of you.”

I surrendered to my computer genius. “Well, it did. It really worked.”

“I hoped as much. This place does mean a lot to me and I want very much to marry you. The sooner the better. How about next month?” Robbie held my hand as we headed back toward the car.

“No way. I once robbed my mother out of her fantasy of having an outdoor wedding at her house. I can’t do it the second time and live. Forget it. It will probably have to happen no sooner than late May,” I said adamantly.

“Vivi, may I point out that in no way am I spending lonely nights by myself until May, to satisfy Ghislaine’s dream.”

“Dearest, perhaps when we make the announcement to the gang at the house, they can figure out our dilemma. After all, between my mother,

Gabrielle, and Connor's active scheming brains, I'm quite sure that they'll reach an agreement," I said mischievously.

"What do you mean, Vivi?"

°°Well, months ago, Gabrielle asked me to get her a daddy for Christmas. We can't disappoint her by getting one in May, now can we?" I replied.

"No, you're right. And Connor said that it would be nice if I married you. So let's leave it up to the professionals?" said Robbie laughing.

"Exactly my idea. Now Robbie, can I have one more kiss on the steps of the Institute so that I can be as tall as you." For the entire world to see, at least my small world, Robbie gently took me in his arms for our last embrace at the step entrance to the Institute in the crisp wintry air. Like a soft loving blanket, the snow descended faster and faster, to erase our presence and to drop its camouflage where earth, trees and sky disappeared. When we pulled apart from our embrace, we too, were covered with snow flakes.

"Thank you, Robbie. Thank you for my gift," I whispered. "Now let's go home."

We silently returned to the car and slipped into our seats. And as in the past, not to disturb the magic of the spell, we quietly exited the Institute, through the velvety downfall, to recommence where we left off in our lives, so many years ago.

-The End-